Belly of The Beast

Forrest J. Fegert

Acknowledgements

I would like to express my gratitude to the people who assisted me through the publication of this book; to those who have been helpful and supportive, talked things over, read, offered comments, and encouraged me to follow through on my vision to honor the B-17 crews. In particular, I would like to thank Ford Fegert, Elaine Hameister, Bob and Sue Wilson, Butch Abraham, Jennifer Elliott, Lisa Hahn, Mark Prevot, John Selloriquez, Dr. Greg Davis, and Dr. Bob Leitz.

Note to Readers

We all laughed when my Uncle William "OX" Abraham accidently arrived a week early in Shreveport for his bomber group reunion. I never forgot that visit. He was treated like a hero because he volunteered beyond his required twenty-five missions until all his crew reached the lifesaving number. His crew of ten was still alive that summer of 1989. They rallied around Uncle William like he was responsible for their safe return home.

I learned that week that my uncle did not like to speak of the war. I asked him about missions—what happened thirty thousand feet over Germany? After all those years, I can still see the blank, glazed look on his face. His blue eyes stared against the white walls of my living room, focusing on the past. I never asked him about the war again. The world was not at war anymore, but for him, the grief of what happened over Germany remained.

No one can ever convey on paper the true horror the B-17 crews experienced. That was written high over Germany with their blood and loss of life. Every time a German fighter zigzagged through the formation, firing their 20 mm cannons, another page was added to their story of great valor.

I have no stories from my uncle, only the memories of that distant look on his face. This is a book of historical fiction that I wrote to honor him and bring recognition to the brave crews of the B-17.

When I was ten years old, my Uncle William "Ox" Abraham gave my mother his Distinguished Flying Cross Medal. He didn't say much; just handed it to her in a way that said the medal meant nothing compared to the men he left behind. They were his heroes. He laughed and said he was on borrowed time. His time ran out a few years after his visit. He is now with the crews that never made it home. There is some solace for me in that.

My appreciation for the bravery of the B-17 airmen grew as I researched and wrote the book. The B-17 crews took off for the heavens only to find hell over Germany. We can never forget the overwhelming odds they faced with fearlessness. I hope their story of courage and gallantry lives on through all generations.

This novel is dedicated to William "Ox" Abraham, ball turret gunner on B-17 during World War II, and his 4th Bomb Squadron of the 34th Bombardment Group.

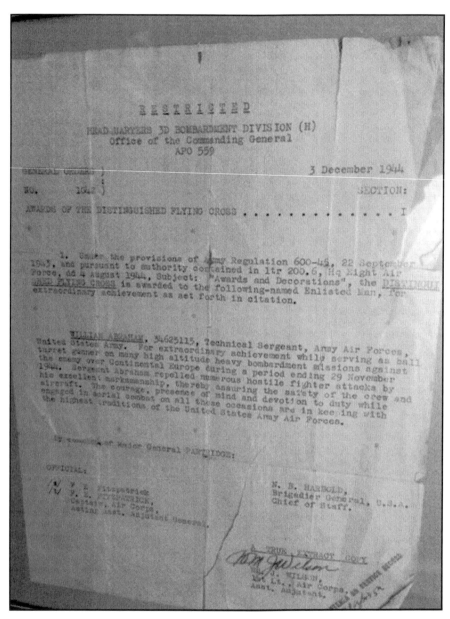

Copy of Ox Abraham's Distinguished Flying Cross Medal that was awarded in 1944 for his extraordinary achievement while serving as a ball turret gunner.

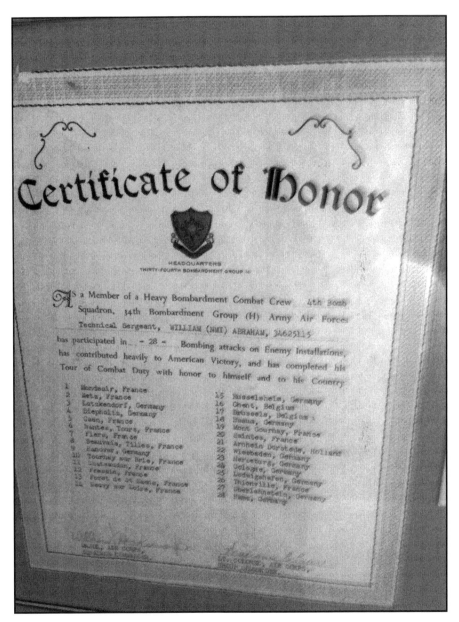

Certificate of Honor listing missions flown by Ox Abraham over Europe.

Prologue

This is a story of extraordinary valor. It's the story of young men volunteering of their own free will to experience the ultimate terror and horror on earth, volunteering to live the most frightening, unimaginable role ever created by man. It's the story of trauma so significant that many of their nervous systems were flooded with fear to the point of uncontrolled shivers and paralyzing panic. It's the story of young men becoming dismayed with humanity and understanding fully the evils it can bring upon the world. But they faced the enemy with courage and tenacity, understanding that the odds of death were high while maintaining their determination, resolve and spirit on the battle field. They lived and died in the belly of the beast.

I

At a quarter to six the referee stepped over the second rope and leaned under the top rope as he entered the ring. The square, beige, painted cinder block walls of the gym, thirty rows of anxious fans, and the tightly wrapped ropes of the square ring surrounded me. The fastest boxer in the Mid-South Golden Glove ranks stood in front of me. If I won, I'd become the 1943 Mid-South Golden Glove Champion. With a deliberate clap from the thin, muscular referee, we walked to the middle of the ring and touched gloves.

"Come on, Ox, kick his ass!" Roy, my corner man and best friend, said.

"I'm trying! He's really fast."

"We only have two rounds left. Work to his left when he misses and come over his right shoulder and knock the shit out of him."

"He's too quick."

"Get out there and make it count."

As I got off my stool and walked toward the middle of the ring, I felt defeated. I had met my match. I had won all eight of my fights by knockouts and earned the name Ox Abraham, but I didn't think I could beat The Biloxi Kid. He didn't hit hard, but was quick enough to hit me three times for each time I hit him. He was a smart, defensive fighter and kept his chin low and buried in his chest. The Biloxi Kid fought like he knew my reputation for a heavy right hand. He moved and bobbed his head so effectively that I couldn't come close to landing a solid punch.

I moved to my left, hoping he'd miss long and expose his head. My jab was slow, especially slow compared with his, but it didn't let him get inside my reach. He wanted to get inside so I wouldn't have the leverage to land the big one. As long as I kept him at arm's length, I had hoped to hit him with a hard right hand. His punches were short and quick, allowing him to cover up before I could get a clear shot. If he made that mistake I'd be ready to lay the hammer on him. He was the best conditioned fighter I have ever faced. His legs had all their bounce left; I would never catch him flat footed.

"Ox, cut the ring off trying to go inside," Roy said.

I didn't understand that strategy, but maybe I could slow down The Biloxi Kid. I cut the ring off, putting him in the corner. I used short, choppy punches to the body. We exchanged punches with no real damage. Imagining I was fighting him in a small closet, I raised my anger level and started to pound his body. While I was fighting in my corner, Roy was yelling orders. We were so close I couldn't get a shot at his chin. His chin would be the light switch; I just needed a shot.

He was working my stomach with short, choppy punches trying to rack up points. I kept waiting for a mistake. Then it happened. He tried to go upstairs with his left hook and missed. He was wide open and I went for the chin. I caught him with half of my power, but square. Six of my knockouts have been chin shots, and I got him good. He started to stagger, and fell against the ropes on his way to the canvas. The count started with a loud "One!" When the referee got to ten, I was the new Mid-South Golden Glove Champ.

The referee brought us to the middle of the ring and raised my hand to announce that I was the champion. The Biloxi Kid congratulated me. We talked for a moment about the fight. I told him that I would not want to fight him again. I knew he would not make the same mistake twice. I thought to myself that we could probably be friends away from the ring.

"Roy, get my gloves off."

"Great knockout; he didn't see that punch coming. You have a hell of a right hand for a guy that is only five foot eight and a hundred and forty pounds."

"I've never fought anyone that fast; he had quick hands. I'm starving. I have four dollars on me. Let's try the diner on the corner. I heard they have the best chicken fried steak in Mississippi. There is something real important I need to speak to you about."

I took my shower, changed into my jeans and flannel shirt, and we headed for the White Castle Diner. As we walked toward the corner diner I was quiet, trying to figure out Roy's reaction to my life-changing news. I'm sure the same idea had crossed his mind.

The diner had a long eating bar with two chrome strips that turned the rounded corner. The stools were secured to the floor and had thick, round seats that spun. I shuffled Roy to the end of the bar to give us a better chance for privacy. On my right, we walked past the red stools and the pretty, blond waitress; to my left, the booths were occupied with people engaging in small talk; behind me were the door and its bell. The waitress was wearing a simple, white dress that showed her shapely figure. Her stunning looks and smile distracted me for a long moment. We both ordered chicken fried steak and a cold Coca-Cola. It was hard to get our minds off the waitress, but I needed to speak to Roy.

"Roy, I did something this week I need to talk to you about."

"What is so important? I am trying to strike up a conversation with the waitress."

"I enlisted in the Army Air Corps."

"You did what!"

"I have enlisted. I need to be in Galveston on the week of my eighteenth birthday for training."

"That's only four weeks from now. Do your mom and dad know?

"Not yet."

"Your dad hates violence. He wouldn't even come watch you box. He is going to be very mad. Who is going to help him with the grocery store?"

"My sister will have to put off college until the war is over. This is more important."

"Why the Army Air Corps?"

"I like airplanes."

"You have never been in a fucking airplane."

"I like to watch them land and take off. Don't you remember the model planes I built when we were kids?"

"That is way different than getting your ass shot off at thirty thousand feet."

"That's real funny."

The food arrived and we made a couple of off-color sexual remarks about the waitress. Normally Roy would have been in his element, but he skillfully turned the subject back to me joining the war effort.

"William, you are making a big mistake! My uncle is in the army in Germany and says the American bombers are getting shot down by the hundreds. We are the only country doing the day raids. The British don't want their pilots to be slaughtered. My uncle said there will be more airmen killed than marines or sailors. You need to switch services."

"It's too late for that."

Roy was very quiet on the ride home. We both knew about neighbors and older kids from our school that were killed in the war. There was no kidding ourselves about the danger. To me, this was something every young man in America was obligated to do. I would never say that to Roy or try to talk him into enlisting. I would never want that on my conscience.

II

My mom and dad were first generation immigrants. They were penniless when they moved to America in 1920. Dad always joked that he got into the grocery business so he would always have something to eat. He had a big heart that almost caused him to go broke during the depression. He would always give groceries to desperate families. Dad saw a lot of bad things in his life and had no tolerance for any sort of violence. He got very mad when he found out I was a boxer and was disappointed when he heard that I broke the jaw of my first opponent. I have never been a bully, but loved to wrestle and box.

I tried to gather the courage to tell my family about volunteering to fight in the war. My mom and dad were simple, hard-working immigrants who expected their son to stay home and help with the family business. My plan was to tell them after church when we all sat down for dinner. I couldn't wait too long. I didn't want them to hear it from anyone else.

Church was over and we all sat down to stuffed bell peppers, rolled cabbage, and iced tea.

"I need to speak with everyone in the family about something important."

"What is it?" Dad asked.

"I have enlisted in the Army Air Corps." There was silence; my mom, dad, and sister looked stunned.

"Why the Army Air Corps? Larry Nasser was in the store last week and was distraught about his son, who wrote him to say that he has accepted death and there is no way he is coming home. They are losing a fourth of the planes every mission. You need to move to another branch of the military," Dad pleaded.

"I can't do that; I will be heading to Galveston for training the week of my birthday."

"You are my only son. I need you here to help with the store; it will be yours someday."

"Dad, I will help," my sister Elaine said.

"No, you are going to college next year."

"Dad, this is something I have to do. This country we love is at war and I need to do my part. Soon as the war is over I will be back home to help with the store."

It's funny how you appreciate your family and friends when you face never seeing them again. I looked around the table, trying to etch this moment in my mind. This would be the mental snap shot I'd take with me to Europe.

My dad was a short, good-looking man with strong forearms and hands; he said it was from working his butcher knife. He had a square jaw with high cheek bones. My mom was slightly overweight but was still beautiful. She had a humble, nurturing look about her. My sister Elaine was the prettiest girl at my school. She has that exotic, Mediterranean look with long, jet-black hair, olive complexion and blue eyes. I only had three more Sunday dinners before I left. I understood the dangers of war; I realized that this might be one of the last times I ever sat at this table.

I thought about the seniors that picked on my sister at school and how I had to set them straight. Who would be there for her next time? I thought about simple things Dad needed me to help with at work. Last week I helped him empty a dump truck full of watermelons, and worked the cash register while he stayed busy helping in the butcher shop. It was important for me to spend the next three weeks with my family and friends. I helped my dad finish our painting project at the store and helped him wherever possible. I took my sister fishing. She had been asking me to take her to Caddo Lake to go fishing for bream. We went fishing almost every day when we were younger. We used to fill our wagon with gar fish and walk through the poor areas of town giving them away. Maybe we could do that again before I leave. That would make her happy.

III

Five days passed.

It was Friday night; I was looking forward to a relaxing day of tight line fishing with five of my best friends. We drifted across Caddo Lake and let our lines drag behind our small boat, hoping a catfish would hit the bait. We had a full moon and plenty of beer. Charley, the star quarter back, brought up the subject of my enlistment first.

"William, where will you be stationed after Galveston?"

"Somewhere in Great Britain."

"Do you know how long you will be based there?"

"There are forty two bomber groups stationed throughout Great Britain. I think I will be with the 92nd Bomb Group stationed at Podington, England."

"I think I had a bite," Roy said. Roy was just trying to change the subject. He didn't like to think about the war.

"What are you going to be training for?" Christopher, the most studious of my friends, asked.

"Due to my build, they want me to be a Ball Turret Gunner."

"That would be scary as shit," Bert, the ladies' man at school, answered.

"I'm not going to lie, I am a little scared."

"How long will you be in Galveston?" Charley asked.

"I'm not sure; I will be on several practice missions out West. A lot of bomb runs are made near Winnett, Montana. They are in the process of requisitioning more remote acreage in west Texas, so I may stay in Galveston."

"Can we come see you and fish on the beach?" Charley responded.

"I hope they give me time for that."

"I heard there are a lot of good-looking girls in Galveston," Bert said.

"Bert, you stay away from my sister while I'm gone."

"Your sister would never date any of your friends; she thinks of us as friends only."

"I saw your sister talking to the navy recruiter at school. Is she thinking about enlisting?"

"She better not!"

The fish started biting and I was glad. I didn't want to answer any more questions. We caught twelve catfish, two white perch, and a slight beer buzz. We loaded the boat into the back of Bert's pickup truck and headed for home.

On the way home, I thought about the best way to confront Elaine about the recruiter. Maybe I was jumping to conclusions and it was just small talk. Probably just the sailor flirting. When I got home Elaine was asleep, so this would have to wait until morning.

I woke up, splashed water on my face, and shaved, the whole time thinking about how to confront Elaine. I could hear her in the kitchen; it was time to talk.

"Elaine, Bert said he saw you speaking with the navy recruiter at school."

"What about it."

"You are not thinking about enlisting?"

"Maybe."

"You can't do that! Mom and Dad need you here."

"You didn't ask anyone! Maybe I want the adventure of traveling overseas. Do you think I want to spend the rest of the war working in a factory or welding in a shipyard on the gulf coast?"

"Dad needs you here at the store."

"That would even be worse."

"Don't say that about the store!"

"Why are you leaving, then?"

I decided to let the subject drop. The last thing I wanted to do was fight with my sister before I left town. I would pay the navy recruiter a visit on Monday.

Saturday afternoons were real busy at the store. I helped Dad; working the cash register while he manned the butcher shop. Many of our customers were poor and had to buy their meats in a very selective way. Mr. Washington always asked for two slices of bologna, three slices of hog head cheese and crackers. He would leave the store, sit on the corner, and sing the blues. He was really good. One of those people that never got discovered or appreciated. I wish I'd had the money and time to help Mr. Washington. He had old shoes with holes on the side and bottoms, but tremendous talent. He was one person that I was glad to go fight for.

I worked hard in the store, but I could tell by Dad's mood that he was resentful. He was a simple man and didn't understand why I needed to fight in the war.

Monday morning I walked up to the high school, trying to remain calm. I graduated in May, but was still welcome. I walked past the principal's office on the right, and down the long tiled hall. My old math class was to the left, the school library on my right, and far behind me were the front double doors and steps to the school. I could see the outline of the recruiter's head and shoulders through the frosted glass door. I walked in without knocking. I wanted to stay cordial, but had to get right to the point.

"Are you trying to talk Elaine Abraham into enlisting in the Navy?"

"She came to see me."

"She is not joining. If you talk to her again, I will come down here and kick your ass!"

I turned around and walked out of his office. I was angry and had to leave before I did something stupid. I walked briskly down the hall for the door. One of the girls standing in the hall said, "Hi, Ox." I didn't even acknowledge her or even look in her direction. I was mad and headed straight for the front door. I was disappointed in myself because I let my emotions take over. If I ever let my emotions take over in the boxing ring I would get killed.

That afternoon, Elaine confronted me.

"You son of a bitch! How could you embarrass me like that?"

"Elaine, calm down. I've never heard you use that kind of word before. Talk lower; Mom is in the other room."

"You didn't care what I thought when you joined the Army Air Corps!"

"Elaine, don't do this."

"It's too late! I joined the Nurse's Corps as an aide and will be trained to be a nurse. I will be working on a hospital ship stationed in the Mediterranean."

I had made the biggest mistake of my life. I should have never got involved. If something happened to her, it would all be on me.

Dad sadly put his face in his hands and sat quietly while Elaine told him the news. I couldn't tell if he was crying, but I knew what he was thinking. He was wondering how a war thousands of miles away could completely change the dynamics of his family. How could he have immigrated halfway around the world to avoid violence only to have it find him in Shreveport, Louisiana. He didn't understand that I had to go fight in Europe to keep violence from spreading to America. Mom openly cried when Elaine told them the news of her enlistment. Mom cherished the time she spent with her best friend and daughter. They spent every Sunday afternoon preparing the family dinner. They would spend hours planning Elaine's wedding even though she has never had a steady boyfriend. Mom always talked about helping her with the baby when she started a family. I could see in my mother's face the hurt of those dreams being delayed or lost forever. No person knew how long this war would go on, or if we could even win.

Five minutes passed. Dad stood up, and walked past without saying a word or making eye contact. Mom walked into the kitchen and started cleaning at a fast pace. She was rattling pots and pans, and noisily dropping dishes in the sink. She was upset and disappointed, but could not find a better way to vent. I wasn't sure what I should say or do, so I gave Elaine a big hug and went for a walk.

Charley and Bert met with me over a game of pool. They wanted to discuss something with me in the absence of Roy. That was very unusual; we would never purposely exclude a friend. I met them at Whitey's Pool Hall, located on the corner of Common Street and Line Avenue. We got our rack of balls and three cold beers from Mr. White and headed for table 6. Charley broke first and I got solids. Bert was busy flirting with the Johnson girl. Everyone in the pool hall knew he had no chance at taking her on a date. Charley wanted to wait for Bert to complete his romantic encounter before having our discussion. The beer went down easy and the pool room had a relaxing feel.

Bert walked back to our table with a defeated look. We told him he had no shot at the Johnson girl, but he had to find out for himself. I lit my cigarette and sat on the edge of pool table 6 and asked what they needed to talk to me about.

"Willie, we decided to enlist in the Marines. We ship out in four weeks," Charley said.

"Did you tell Roy?"

"No, that is why we wanted to meet here. You know how he is about the war. When Christopher leaves for West Point, Roy will be the only one left in town from our group."

"Nobody asked for this war, but we must do what is right for America," I said.

"If Roy doesn't wake up and enlist, he will be drafted and have no control of where he goes," Bert said.

"That is a choice Roy must make," I said.

Bert talked about how the Marines have the best-looking dress uniform of any service. He thought it would be a big hit with the ladies. Bert had a one track mind and was probably thinking about that angle when he joined. We all lit up a Chesterfield and drank another cold beer.

"Willie, the recruiter, said we will be the invasion force for the Pacific Island Campaign," Charley said.

"Maybe we will run into some good looking Tahitian girls with long, flowing, dark hair and big breasts," Bert said with a smile.

"The only thing you will run into is to a lot of pissed off Japs that will fight to the death protecting some crappy island," Charley said, laughing.

Upon hearing that news, Bert lit up another Chesterfield. Bert had a charismatic way about him. He would never use his fingers to take a cigarette from the pack. He would shake the pack one time, then two or three cigarettes would extend out in perfect order; he would take the longest one from the pack with his mouth. With one hand he would take his Zippo from his left pocket with one smooth motion, light his cigarette and snap the lid of his Zippo shut. He was a tall, good-looking guy, but a horrible athlete. He always had his eyes on my sister, but he would never be more than a friend to Elaine.

I could see Charley making a great Marine. He was a real leader on the football field. He knew every player's role and commanded us like a field officer in the military. He was so athletic he would breeze through boot camp. Nobody at school could beat him in chin ups or the rope climb. Charley O' Brian had light brown hair with a stern, Irish look. If he led his troops like he did his players, he would be a general someday.

As I looked across the pool table at Charley and Bert, I wondered if our paths would ever intersect back in Shreveport. We were going all over the world, putting our lives on the line in a war that might last for years. I wondered if any of us would survive the war. I thought about Roy and how he didn't want to let go of high school friendships. Roy was a little clingy, but understood the importance of friendships. Would Roy be able to cope with everyone leaving to fight in the war? Bert made one more failing try on the Johnson girl and we left Whitey's for home.

Two weeks passed. Elaine and I finally got to go fishing. We decided to fish on the banks of the Red River. The river was full of thirty-pound catfish. We used our cast nets to fill our bucket with bait fish. The fishing was great; we caught six large catfish, four bass and no gars. We both knew we weren't there for the fishing. We were there to bond and think back about the happy times we had together. I was so glad for this day. We had one last thing to do on our fishing trip. We walked our wagon through the poor part of town and gave our fish away. I knew the perils I'd face; that made this time with Elaine very gratifying.

IV

As the bus began to roll out of the station, I thought about the unknown path I was about to travel. Ahead on the left was my high school, on the right my dad's store, and behind me Mom, Dad, and Elaine were all waving goodbye as they cried. War and death were far in front of me. Every foot this bus traveled brought me closer to Europe and further from my past. I stared out the window, reflecting back on my childhood. I had a renewed appreciation for my family, friends and hometown. Looking out at the passing rows of cotton, and thinking about my family and friends put me in a sad trance. The air base and B-17s were now only three hours ahead.

The bus made its third stop to pick up recruits in Lufkin, Texas. The vacant seat next to me was finally occupied by a tall Texan. I spent the first ten miles with my shoulder against the bus, gazing out the window.

He spoke first. "Are you going to Galveston for training?"

"Yes, Ninety-Fifth Bomber Group."

I learned that his name was Chase May, and we had a lot in common. He liked to hunt and fish and only had a sister and no brother. We were going to be group mates; but with his height I was sure he would be a waist gunner or radio man. We spent the rest of our trip talking about our families and fishing. We both subconsciously avoided war talk, knowing what we would face. I liked Chase's easy-going demeanor and wit. The fellow in the row behind us said we were one mile from the base.

I must admit the gate was very impressive with the MP's standing guard in their crisp uniforms. We cleared the gate and that's when I got my first glimpse of a B-17. To see it was so stirring that it had an emotional effect on me. Everyone on the bus became speechless and stared out the window in awe. All our heads turned in unison as we passed the great bomber. How could a plane that large get off the ground? If it did fly, how could it ever get shot down? There were .50 caliber machine guns pointing out in every direction.

The bus rolled to a squeaky stop. All the recruits stood up to exit the bus. I was a little embarrassed; all the other recruits were carrying their belongings in duffel bags and I had my clothes in grocery bags from Dad's store. We exited to a welcome from our drill sergeant. When I stepped off the bus what I noticed most was the activity. I could hear plane engines revving at full throttle from inside the hangars. Groups of recruits were marching in order, others throwing the baseball in the grassy area between the temporary barracks. Several planes were circling the base like distant bees.

Then I saw it; the most glorious, powerful, and mesmerizing sight I have ever seen. Through an opening between the enormous hangars, I saw a B-17 taxiing for takeoff. I notice that there was no gunner in the ball turret and both .50 caliber machine guns were facing the rear of the plane. Seeing a B-17 in motion was stunning and beyond my greatest expectations. The ground shook and the air compressed as it passed. All our eyes were so fixated on the great bomber that none of us took notice of the drill sergeant. That was our first mistake as a recruiting class.

"What in the hell are you worthless pricks looking at? Line up in a row, NOW!" the Drill Sergeant commanded.

I sure knew I wasn't at home anymore. My recruiter told me that boot camp would only last four weeks; they wanted us trained soon as possible.

"Look at this loser. Isn't it cute? He has his uniforms in a little grocery bag!" the Drill Sergeant said.

"It's my underwear. We didn't get our uniforms yet."

The other recruits tried not to laugh. That was my first big mistake as an airman. I couldn't believe what I had just said. The drill sergeant's face turned red. He was a couple inches shorter than me with a powerful build. I knew I was going to pay the price for what I said. He walked up to me. He positioned himself against my chest with his mouth almost touching the side of my face. Then he started yelling louder than I thought humanly possible.

"You stupid piece of shit! Do you think this war is a fucking joke? If you ever, I mean ever, piss on my leg again I will beat your ass!" Then he walked up and down the line of recruits, making them pay for laughing at my stupid comment.

Sergeant Delatte was crude and seemingly hateful, but there must have been some logic to his method. As the days passed we grew to respect each other. I was by far the best athlete in physical training. I set a record time on the overhead ladder and almost set a record in pull-ups. Sergeant Delatte had me lead the morning run. I started to understand the sergeant's logic and the need for boot camp. Not only were we all getting in better shape, we were bonding as a unit.

Sergeant Delatte said that General LeMay wanted to meet me in his office at 1900 hours sharp. Wow, what could this be about? I replayed the last week in my mind, trying to think of anything I could have done of any significance. We had played a practical joke on John Burgess. While he was sleeping, Craig Price and I put shaving cream on John's hand so when he wiped his face it got all over him. He woke up mad, with shaving cream all over his face. That was really funny, and everyone in the barracks laughed. But if that was the reason, why didn't they ask for Craig?

At 1900 hundred hours central standard time, the general greeted me at the door with a smile.

"Hello, I am General Curtis LeMay; would you like to sit down?

"Thanks, sir. I will stand."

"I heard you are the Southern United States Golden Glove Champ."

"That's right. I fought under the name Ox Abraham."

"Would you be interested in fighting on the Army Air Corps' boxing team?"

"Can I think about it?"

"We will give you ten seconds!" Sergeant Delatte said in a way that didn't leave me an option.

"I'll fight on the team."

"George Patton has a hell of a boxing team, and I want to beat that son of a bitch this year. George was in the 1912 Olympics and thinks he is the best damn sportsman in the military," General LeMay said.

"I'll do my best to help you, sir."

"Did you knock out The Biloxi Kid?" the general asked.

"Yes, but he has the fastest hands I have ever seen."

"He enlisted in the army. He is training at Fort Polk with the 304th Tank Brigade."

"Patton said he knocked out his best heavyweight."

General LeMay leaned back on his chair, put his feet on his metal desk, and lit up a big cigar. "Ox, you are my ace in the hole, my secret weapon," he said. He seemed real happy, as if he just pulled a fast one on his friend and archrival George Patton. The general shook my hand one more time and I departed his company to return to my barracks.

I didn't think I could defeat The Biloxi Kid again. He would not leave himself open to my power. His speed and stamina would wear me down next time. Fort Polk was in south Louisiana and only two hours from Galveston, so I was sure we would have to fight soon. I was in the best shape of my life, so maybe I could find a way to match his stamina.

V

Before any flight suits were issued or a single shot was made from the Browning .50 caliber machine gun, we had to have classroom training to define our roles as a gunners. The gunners belonged in one of two distinct categories: the turret gunners and the flexible gunners. The turret gunners required different mental and physical qualities. The ball turret gunner had to stay calm and not panic even in a closed, confining, and stressful environment. He had to have the ability to stay oriented and maintain a sense of timing as he swung the ball turret three hundred and sixty degrees in a horizontal, circular motion, and up and down in a vertical movement. The ball turret gunner had to have touch and a keen understanding of the principles of motion and its effects on ballistics. When the war started, the physical requirement for a ball turret gunner was five foot four inches or less. Due to the addition of twenty thousand planes, the requirement was changed to five foot nine inches. Most of all, the turret gunner had to possess the courage to be locked in a ball-shaped coffin with no parachute.

All gunners were trained in the classroom using diagrams and airplane models showing the coverage area of each gun. Before our first training flight, we were required to be totally familiar with all aspects of the Browning machine gun. The procedure stated that all machine guns were to be cleaned no later than the day they were fired. That meant complete disassembly, cleaned thoroughly with gasoline, dried, and wiped down with an oily rag. Under no circumstances was a gun allowed to go without cleaning. We learned that the guns got so hot the pores of the metal opened and absorbed moisture. Rust would begin to form immediately. The machine guns had to be coated with oil for seven days after shooting. A gunner's worst nightmare was a jammed gun, so we were given extensive training on how to clear all jams. Once we started shooting live rounds, we were taught how to harmonize the sights with the gun. The instructor told us on our first training flight we would concentrate on turret operation; fixing our sights on other planes and ground objects with no ammo. After the first week of gunner school, I became very familiar with the Browning machine gun and could not wait to fire my first shot.

Many crew members cross-trained in case of an emergency. Procedures dictated that three crew members other than the five gunners were required to train as gunners. Due to my mechanical background, I was assigned to cross-train as flight engineer. Some of the training took place in the classroom, but most of it was aboard the flying fortress. My instructor told the class we would be responsible for checking engine operation and fuel consumption, operating all equipment, and having basic knowledge of the roles of bombardier and radio operator. This seemed so overwhelming. He also said we would be required to work with the bombardier, and to understand how to cock, lock and load the bomb rack. I was given a long list of duties even though I had never been in a B-17 or shot a machine gun.

Once we finished our week of classroom theory and gun maintenance, it was time to gear up for flight. We were all sent to the distribution center for our flight suits. The center was a large hangar that was converted to a warehouse and supply depot. There seemed to be hundreds of tables full of flight gear, everything from goggles to parachutes. We were given one pair of medium weight wool socks, electrically heated shoes, and fleece lined boots. To keep our legs warm, we received winter underwear and electric trousers. For extremely cold flights, we were given full-body, woolen underwear. For our chests, they gave us a leather bomber jacket, a flight shirt, and an electric jacket. To survive extreme cold, they supplied us with a full-body, electric suit. Our instructor told us at thirty thousand feet it would be sixty degrees below zero, or worse. For our heads we were given hoods, face and neck protectors, and a scarf. Hands would be protected by silk-lined gloves; the instructor said all planes would be equipped with four hand muffs. I wasn't sure what those were, but was afraid to ask. We were given goggles and then sent to the parachute instruction and distribution area.

Even though I wouldn't be wearing one in the ball turret, we were told several times how the parachute would save our lives. The instructor said the harness must be on at all times when in immediate danger. He noted the only exception is the belly gunner. I jokingly told the radio man standing next to me that I would never volunteer for anything ever again. We spent two more full days learning about our flight gear.

VI

This was the day I had been waiting for; my first flight. They told us to wear standard boots, pants, and our leather bomber jackets. That morning at breakfast we noticed a flight crew was in from Germany. All the recruits were staring at their decorated bomber jackets. They had a bomb on their jackets that represented every bombing mission. There was a big patch on the back of their bomber jackets of scantily dressed women. The patch on their backs duplicated their plane's nose art. Their plane was *Lady Stardust* and they were from the 44th Bomb Group known as the Flying Eight Balls. They knew we were rookies. There was no patch on our brown leather bomber jackets. The waist gunner to my left said they completed their twenty-five missions and were allowed to return to the states and be instructors. The tail gunner to my right said they were the lucky ones; his brother told him the odds of surviving twenty-five missions are one in three. I looked back at their table and they had all lit up the cigarettes and seemed relieved to be home. They would not look our way or even acknowledge our presence. I was very impressed with their jackets and demeanor and hoped to speak with them about the war.

The large recruiting class of gunners formed in groups outside the mess hall. The instructors walked us across the grassy area adjacent to Hangar 5. We passed through the back opening of the hangar. As we walked inside, we observed maintenance crews hard at work. We passed through the large opening in the front of the hanger. We looked out to see a row of B-17 planes being prepared for flight.

The instructors took our entire class of ninety-seven recruits to walk toward the closest B-17. They used this opportunity to explain features of the plane. The highest ranking instructor started out by telling us that each B-17 had a crew of ten: a pilot, co-pilot, navigator, bombardier, flight engineer, radio operator, belly gunner, left waist gunner, right waist gunner and tail gunner. He emphasized that we didn't have the luxury to specialize. Many of us would perform dual roles. The flight engineer manned the top turret, while the bombardier manned the chin guns. My dual role was to be back up to the flight engineer. The most specialized position on the B-17 was the belly ball turret gunner. The lead instructor discussed take off speed, air speed, bomb load capacity, flight ceiling, and many other features of the heavy bomber. Then he had us form a large circle around the plane. He lifted his megaphone to his mouth and began to instruct.

"The most important thing a gunner must do is find his target as soon as possible. You may only see a cannon flash or a reflection of the sun off the enemy's canopy. Sometimes it is just a glimpse through the clouds. All crew members need to be notified immediately of the enemy fighter's position. You will use the hour hands of a clock as a quick reference point. For example, the right wing is three o'clock, the front of the plane twelve o'clock, the left wing nine o'clock, and the tail position is six o'clock. There is a high, level, and low position for all points on the clock. If a fighter plane is approaching from below the plane off the right wing, he is three o'clock low. If a fighter plane is six o'clock level, he is approaching from the rear at the same altitude. Those positions must be communicated to the crew immediately. By doing this we may get more than one gun sight on the approaching fighter, or hit it as it passes the first gun position. If a plane approaches from twelve o'clock high, he will pass under the plane and the belly gunner will be waiting to blast his ass."

We broke up into groups of ten. I was with all the belly gunners, and at five foot eight, I was the tallest. We entered the plane through the back door. We were shown several features of the plane. To the rear of the plane were an electrical generator and the tail gun position. The belly turret was located just aft of the wing. In front of me were the bomb racks, bomb bay doors, radio operator, navigator, and the two pilots.

I saw two pilots approaching the front of the plane. The athletic way they entered the front of the plane was impressive. They reached up and grabbed a bar inside the small opening. In one swift move, they pulled their legs up head high and entered the plane feet first.

We were not allowed to experience getting into the ball turret until we were airborne. This was going to be my first flight, and I really didn't know what to expect. I could hear the pilots going through the detailed checklist. I knew it was only a matter of minutes before they turned the massive propellers. One by one, the four engines made a groan, coughed out some smoke, and began to spin. I could feel the power and energy throughout the plane. I looked out the waist gunner's position and noticed one of the crew members from *Lady Stardust* walking toward our plane. The pilots waited for him. He entered the plane through the back door and we instantly began to taxi out to the runway.

We rolled out to the far end of the runway and turned into the wind. The pilots revved the motors to a high pitch. The plane vibrated as the throttle was increased; then we began to roll down the runway. The plane reached a speed of one hundred miles per hour and we gently lifted off the ground. We gained altitude and began to circle the base at a large radius.

The crew member from the *Lady Stardust* was a belly gunner named Ford. He was onboard to give us instructions. The noise level of the plane was high, but we all did our best to listen. I was nervous, but enjoying my first flight.

I was picked first to attempt to enter the ball turret. The gun barrels were rotated downward, straight toward the ground to expose the small hatch. I looked inside the turret and was surprised at the small and cramped space. There was no chair, just a heel rest for my feet. My back had to rest against the ball turret. I entered feet first. I found the heel rest by feel. My feet were placed awkwardly above the gun barrels. I had to fold myself into a fetal position. When the guns swung level with the plane, my hips were on the bottom of the turret and my back against the rear wall. My legs were held in midair by two heel rests on the front wall. I looked through my legs with my eyes at the same level as the pair of Browning .50 caliber machine guns. The machine guns extended through the entire turret. The handles were located on either side and above my head. The handles controlled the turret and fired the guns. The instructor rotated the turret to aim straight downward so I could exit the ball. I had new respect for my instructor. I was only in the ball turret for minutes and began to feel anxious and trapped. I learned that this would take more mental strength than I had ever imagined. We all got our turn in the ball turret, and then we landed.

It was early evening, and the base was quiet. Most of the airmen were outside, relaxing and enjoying the weather. There were the usual baseball players. Two groups were playing horse shoes. Most were just in groups talking and smoking cigarettes.

I noticed the crew from the *Lucky Lady* was outside listening to Glenn Miller. The recruits were afraid to approach them, but since I spent the day with their belly gunner, I approached them. I greeted Ford and introduced myself to their crew commander. He was a tall man with movie star looks. He greeted me with a smile. I asked him what it was like to fly in a B- 17 over Germany. He instantly changed his smile to a look of anger. He pointed his hard finger in my chest, poking me with every word.

"Don't ever fucking ask a B-17 crew member about the war!"

Normally, I would have taken a swing at someone who talked to me like that, but I felt really bad for asking that question and hitting a sensitive nerve. His reaction scared me. What in the hell was I about to face over Germany?

VII

I retreated back to my barracks to read my new letter from Elaine. She wrote me every week. I hoped she would continue when she left for the Nursing Corps. She says Mom and Dad missed me, but were doing fine. Dad was real busy with work and had hired Mr. Washington to help stock the shelves. Bert's mom was in the store last week and told Dad that Charley and Bert finished basic training. They would be deployed to the Pacific theater to fight the Japanese. Roy missed everyone and was drinking a lot. One of the Johnson girls was pregnant. No one had heard from Christopher since he left for West Point. For the first time, I began to feel home sick. I was glad we were going to start flying every day to take my mind off home.

Just as I was finishing my letter, Sergeant Delatte and Colonel Young walked into the barracks. Everyone got nervous and stood at attention. They came straight for my bunk.

"Patton has finished his Sicily campaign and is on his way back to Fort Polk to monitor the war games. He wants to set a fight up between you and The Biloxi Kid," Colonel Young said.

I realized that, if I played my cards right, I could use my leverage to visit Shreveport.

"I want to fight him at Barksdale Air Field in Shreveport. I need my corner man Roy with me to have any chance."

The colonel looked puzzled by my request, but said he could make it happen. He said that the date was not set yet. They were working on co-ordinating with General Patton and General LeMay. They both wanted to attend. He said he would get back with me soon.

I was in good shape, but did not have anyone to spar with. The word got around the base that I was a Golden Glove Champ. I had a couple of exhibition fights with a couple of tough guys. They were no test for me. I knocked them out in the first round. I needed to make sure the colonel set the date before Elaine left for the navy.

VIII

Four days passed.

My seventh training flight had arrived. Each of us was required to spend two hours in turret sighting air and ground targets. We would be evaluated and graded immediately. The longest I had previously been in the turret was twenty minutes. I became nauseous and unsettled. Steering the turret ball with machine gun handles above my head did not feel natural. I had trouble following my targets. That disappointed my instructors and myself. I had hoped to do better that day.

It was my turn to drop down into the ball turret. I aimed the barrel straight down, opened the hatch, and slowly lowered myself down. I was in the fetal position with my knees against my chest. It was an unwritten rule that the ball turret had to constantly be moving when under attack. The instructor told me to keep rotating and scan the sky. If I saw the enemy fighters first, I needed to relay its position to the crew.

I rotated three hundred and sixty degrees, looking out the fifteen inch, circular, Plexiglas window. We had a squadron of fighters fly in from a nearby base to simulate an enemy attack.

"Bogie twelve o'clock high!" the instructor yelled. I rotated to face the front of the plane. I waited for the fighter to dive under the plane. He passed under me at a high speed, and I got my sight on him for a split second. The instructor yelled at me to start scanning, and rotate in all directions.

I yelled, "Bogie two o'clock low!" I tried, but could not get my sight on him.

The instructor yelled, "Five o'clock low!"

I swung around toward the rear of the plane and got my sight on him, but couldn't follow.

The instructor yelled, "Abraham you need to do better than that, or your ass will be shot off."

"Twelve o'clock level!" I yelled. I over rotated, but got my sight back on him.

The instructor yelled to me, "Abraham, protect your pilots at all cost. If they die you die. Eight o'clock high, six o'clock low, ten o'clock level!"

This went on for an hour.

"Time!" the instructor yelled.

I rotated the gun downward and unlocked the latch to get out. I couldn't move. My legs were numb, and I had to be pulled from the ball turret. The instructor said I had improved, but needed a lot of work. He said I needed to react by instinct and not be so slow. Ford said the Germans attacked the front and bottom of the plane; they wanted to kill the pilots or hit the fuel tanks on the wings.

Three weeks passed.

"Abraham you have improved the most. Show these other guys how it's done," Ford said.

I dropped into the turret like it was second nature. I rotated in all directions. During the next two hours, I identified every enemy attack and followed all targets. I started to feel like part of the plane. I needed assistance out of the turret, but that was common. I still had a problem following ground targets on low flights, but I was getting close.

I was flattered when Ford asked me to have a beer and cigars with the crew from the *Lady Stardust*. They seemed to be nice guys but were aloof and stayed to themselves. We listened to Glenn Miller, Woody Herman, and The Andrews Sisters while we talked about my upcoming fight.

The date was set and the crew of *Lady Stardust* would be there. Much of my training class would be traveling by bus or military planes. The flight commander that protested my questioning of the war was drunk. He was starting to get very loud and obnoxious.

"Abraham," he yelled out, "you want to know what war is like? Most of my friends aren't coming home and you will probably fucking die in Germany." I retreated to my barracks to read my new letter from Elaine. I figured the flight commander was wounded mentally from the war. No bullets or flak had killed him, but he was wounded for life from images.

What had he seen that had caused this? Every day that passed got me closer to war and my fight with The Biloxi Kid.

We were beginning our high altitude training. We had to dress in our electrically-heated shoes and suits and depend on our oxygen masks. Our instructor told us many gunners had died from lack of oxygen. My oxygen tank was located above my ball turret in-between my two racks of bullets. There was no room in the ball turret for oxygen or bullets. All shells were discharged from the bottom of the turret. We were flying over the Gulf of Mexico at thirty thousand feet. The temperature in the plane was thirty degrees below zero. Today was our first day with live rounds. There was absolutely no room for a parachute or flak jacket. I got in my fetal position. The instructor told me to fire in the twelve o'clock level position. The noise of the machine guns was much more than I expected. I instantly became disoriented and started to suffer for the first time from claustrophobia. I broke out into a cold sweat and began to have a panic attack. Ford helped me out of the ball turret and told me to calm down. He was not mad or disappointed in me. That made me think he could relate to my panic attack. Maybe he had the same problem. I calmed down and did much better my next try.

The time had arrived to make bombing runs over the seventeen practice ranges scattered over the United States. Ford was a very good instructor due to his experience as a belly gunner on *Lady Stardust*. If he had a fault, it was that he was brutally honest. He said we had no time to waste. Losses were high, and the Army Air Corps needed replacement crews.

Our first long-range bombing mission was an eight hour flight over Oklahoma and back. My turret time was scheduled for three hours. We were going to carry sixteen three hundred pound iron bombs. We would travel our maximum range of two thousand five hundred miles at a speed of two hundred and seventy-five miles per hour.

Our twelve plane squadron took off at thirty second intervals. The first off would climb to three thousand feet and circle back over the field and start to build our three-dimensional box formation. We would stack four high in an offset, staggered diamond formation. I thought of each position as a base on a baseball field. We took second base on the bottom level. We were the tail plane in the entire formation. Ford said our position was known as "tail-end Charlie." He said the Germans loved to attack tail end Charlie first. Our squadron commander was on the lead diamond, second from the top. We would stay as close together as possible to protect the inner planes. Then we would rendezvous with other squadrons and build a three-dimensional box of three hundred bombers.

We approached our target at fourteen thousand feet. The bull's eye was a huge one thousand feet in diameter, consisting of five concentric rings spaced at one hundred feet. The individual rings were plowed at two feet wide and one foot deep and easy to see. The bomb bay doors were located directly in front of me. I loved watching the bombs leave the plane and fall for the target. They seemed to leave the plane in slow motion.

The ultimate purpose of plane and crew was accurate, effective bombing. The bombardier took absolute control and command of the plane. Sixty seconds after he yelled "Bombs away," our target was hit.

On the way back, we discussed and critiqued the operation. We got some free time during the last two hours of the flight. We picked up some Harry James music from the radio and I just stared out the waist gunner's window, admiring the beauty of the formations of B-17s against the sunset.

We made several long-range missions across the United States that involved multiple stops. We flew from Galveston to Ephrata Air Field in Spokane, Washington, with a stop at Kearney, Nebraska. Those long flights prepared us for our long trip to England. In the winter, most bomber squadrons took the long southern route, stopping to fuel at Morris Field in south Florida then to Puerto Rico, British Guiana, Brazil, across the Atlantic to Morocco, and finally England. The flights were long and tested all our mental strength. On our last flight, the temperature in the plane reached negative thirty-four degrees. They said freezing cold would be worse over Germany.

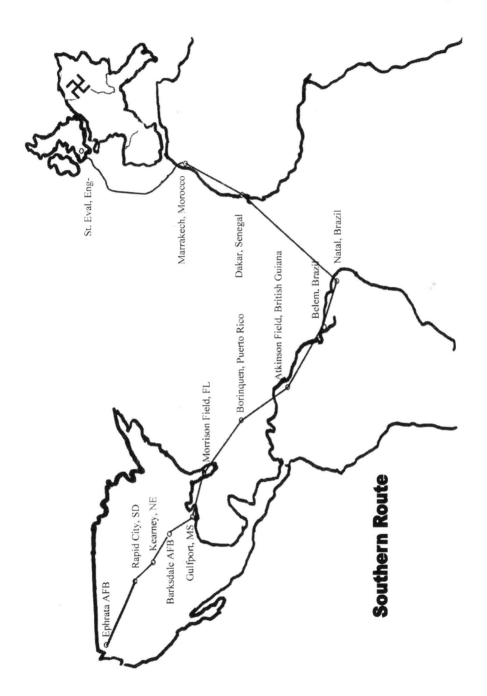

St. Eval, Eng-

Marrakech, Morocco

Dakar, Senegal

Natal, Brazil

Borinquen, Puerto Rico

Atkinson Field, British Guiana

Belem, Brazil

Morrison Field, FL

Rapid City, SD

Kearney, NE

Barksdale AFB

Gulfport, MS

Ephrata AFB

Southern Route

IX

We taxied to a stop after completing a long bombing run to New Mexico. We got to shoot live rounds at the target drones. My ears were ringing and I could hardly hear Colonel Young when he greeted our plane. He had an excited look on his face when he told me the date was set. He said both generals liked the idea of having it at Barksdale Air Field. Fort Polk and Galveston were within driving distance. Our fight was scheduled for two weeks from Saturday night. I was so glad to be going back to my home town. Barksdale was an important training base located across the river from Shreveport. Most of the crew members of Doolittle's Raiders were trained at Barksdale. They were the first to bomb Tokyo; maybe I would be on the first crew to bomb Berlin.

That night I wrote a letter to Elaine giving her the good news. I told her that after the fight I would be reassigned to the 336th Squadron to spend my last four weeks of training based in Spokane, Washington. I also told her to tell Dad I would be getting four days off and would help around the store. The letter finished by telling her how much I loved and missed them. The final thing I wrote: *P.S. I hope we get a chance to go fishing. Love, your brother William.*

I spent the last two weeks in training. I was preparing for a different kind of fight. One fight would involve bruises and maybe a knock out. The other fight would determine who lived and who died. I thought to myself; "We think we are more civilized, people than the ones before us. We are not. The gladiators fought to the death two thousand years ago. We passed through the Dark Ages, a Renaissance and a World War. We are fighting the Second World War and nothing had changed."

I worked hard on my hand speed and foot work. I couldn't match his speed, but needed to close the gap. Maybe I could catch him off guard. I doubled my time jumping rope and working on the light speed bag. The colonel told me that I had the fastest hands he had ever seen. I told him he had not seen The Biloxi Kid. The colonel liked to fancy himself a boxer, but had no talent. He tried sparring with me and took a beating. It was all I could do to not knock him out.

We flew our training squadron of twelve planes to Shreveport. The rest took buses; some drove cars. The tankers from Fort Polk were all driving in from south Louisiana. The night before the fight, the Bossier strip was full of partying tankers and airmen. I spent the night before the fight visiting with Mom, Dad and Elaine. I tried to get to bed early. I would need all my strength and speed.

I crossed the Red River that separated Shreveport from Bossier City and looked down at the people fishing. I thought to myself about how much I wished I was fishing. This fight was for the generals. I had nothing personal against The Biloxi Kid, but I would rather be on the banks of the river trying to catch a twenty pound catfish.

We pulled through the gates of the base. The MP's looked in my car and wished me good luck. I thought everyone in the military knew about our fight. To my right was the base housing, to my left the administration buildings, and in front of me were the tall control tower and a row of large airplane hangars.

The temporary boxing ring and hundreds of metal chairs were set up in Hangar 27. We used two offices as locker rooms. I changed into my white trunks and tried to stay loose. Roy taped my hands up. We were both nervous and we got the tape too tight. My circulation was cut off from my fingers. Roy cut the tape off, and we got it right the second try. I shadowboxed against the wall. Roy was impressed with my newfound speed.

"You are fast, but don't try to match punches with the Kid; he is faster," Roy said.

"I need to surprise him. When he opens the fight with a flurry or five shot combination, he will expect me to cover up."

"Keep your hands up and chin down, let him wear himself down, and we will knock him out later in the fight. You will get your ass kicked if you come out swinging."

"My chin is against my chest for hours in the ball turret; I know how to keep my damn chin down."

Roy might have been right; this fight was scheduled for six rounds, and I needed to conserve energy. Sergeant Delatte stuck his head in the door and said it was time. I was to enter the ring first. I walked through the door and down the hall. When I passed through the last open door,

I became visible to the crowd. The largest hangar on base was packed wall to wall. Everyone was standing. As soon as my fellow airmen saw me, there was a loud cheer. I walked down the long aisle receiving pats on the back and words of encouragement. I jumped on the edge of the ring and passed under the top rope, showing my energy level to the crowd. I shadowboxed for a few seconds to show off my speed and head movement. Then I heard a big cheer from the tankers in the crowd.

And there he was, standing ready to enter the arena. The Biloxi Kid looked fitter and faster than ever. He walked down the aisle to loud cheers. He jumped on the edge of the ring and passed under the top ring. He circled his square corner of the ring, showing off his speed in every direction. The crowd was impressed, but I was impressed the most. He was so fast I couldn't even see his hands.

"Did you see that speed?" Roy said.

I looked over at the two generals seated on the front row. I was most impressed with Patton. He was wearing a silver helmet with stars, a jacket with medals, pants that were puffy at the thighs, shining long boots, and a pearl-handled revolver. You could tell he was there to watch his fighter win.

The announcer introduced us by our fight names. "In the green trunks, representing the United States Army, The Biloxi Kid. In the white trunks, representing the United States Army Air Corps, Ox Abraham."

I went back to my corner, made some boxing motions, and waited for the bell. The bell rung! The Kid crossed the ring straight for me. He was a smart fighter. He didn't have my reach and would have to be aggressive to get inside. I would keep him away with my jab and step back to the left if he tried to get inside and use his speed.

He tried to put together a combination early but didn't land a punch. I became confident and became the aggressor. Roy was yelling for me to cover up and not swap punches. There were only thirty seconds left in the round and I wanted to test my speed. I moved toward The Biloxi Kid. I swung my right and missed, followed with a quick left and was long off his right ear. He moved inside my reach, hit me with a right to my left eye, and then followed with a hard left to my chin. At that moment I knew The Biloxi Kid was even faster with more power. I felt like I got hit by an iron fist. The room started to spin and get dark.

Roy yelled, "Cover up!"

The round ended. I staggered around and, in some miraculous way, sat down and landed on my stool. Roy started to sponge my face with cold water.

"What in the hell are you doing? If you try to swap punches you are going to get your ass kicked. Wait for him to make a mistake and knock the shit out of him. He doesn't have your power."

"OK."

"Now get out there and kick his ass!"

I listened to Roy this time. I kept my distance and landed a series of jabs with my left. I became more accurate with my punches as the fight went on. He tried to cut the ring off and get inside.

Four rounds passed. The crowd cheered between every round. The fight pace was fast and violent. Forty seconds left in the fight. We got in the corner directly in front of the generals and just started slugging it out. There was no more conserving energy; we both wanted the knock out. The crowd was on their feet screaming.

The flurry of punches lasted thirty seconds, an eternity for a fighter. The bell rung! The crowd cheered and screamed in a way that thanked us for the great battle. I lost the judgment and The Biloxi Kid won the rematch. Sometime you get what you need but not what you want. I wanted to win the fight, but needed to give the soldiers a great fight. The generals congratulated us both and wanted a rematch. I spoke with The Biloxi Kid and we made a pledge to have a beer together after the war.

X

I finished my last training flight in gunnery school. I was reassigned to Ephrata Air Field in Spokane, Washington. I was somewhat familiar with the base. We stopped there during our long range training missions. A third of my ball turret class was reassigned to Ephrata. Our transport plane landed on a misty, fall day. It was time to meet my crew and see my plane.

I was sent to the crew barracks first. All six enlisted crew members bunked together with four other crews. The four officers bunked together in groups of twelve. I could tell by the lack of foot lockers that I was the first to arrive. I was told the four officers in my crew had arrived and wanted to meet me. They instructed me to meet them in the mission planning room.

They were the only four in the room. The pilot was tall and lean with an educated look. He had a pencil thin mustache that suited his smile. The copilot reminded me of Charley O'Brian with his red hair and Irish looks. When the navigator offered me a Chesterfield, he shook the pack just like Bert did. They popped out in perfect order and I reached for the longest. He also had a studious, educated look. The bombardier had a serious but engaging look.

The pilot was Coleman Price. His name seemed to suit his educated look. I asked about his hometown of Boston. He had recently graduated from Harvard Law School. I was curious about his background, but he kept changing the subject back to my fight. They all seemed impressed with my boxing background. It seemed like everyone in the Army Air Corps knew about my fight.

Our copilot's name was Jordan John, from Atlanta, Georgia. He said everyone should call him JJ. He seemed fun-loving with no Irish temper. Our navigator was Sal Wilson from Paris, Texas. He graduated from Texas A&M and seemed to be from a wealthy farming family. The bombardier was Mark Martin from Southern California.

"Do you want to see our plane?" the pilot asked.

"Yes, I would love to," I said.

"It's a new plane and we just added our nose art."

She was a beautiful plane with the perfect name, *Sleepytime Gal*. The nose art was the best I had ever seen. Painted near the nose of the plane was a sexy, big-breasted blonde, yawning with both hands behind her head. She was sitting with her back arched, showing off her perfect curves.

The bomber was equipped with the new chin turret to better protect the pilots. Both Cole and JJ made comments on how glad they were to see that addition. The Germans loved to come from the twelve o'clock position and target the pilots. Mark, the bombardier, would man that gun until we began our bomb run. We toured the plane and began to bond as a crew.

A squadron of B-24 Liberators had just arrived from the Pacific. Commander Cole noticed a pilot he knew from his training class. The B-24 pilot told us the heavy bombers had more mechanical problems than the smaller planes, mainly because of weather, engine failures, loss of oil pressure, hydraulic, and electrical problems. He said the B-24 was the worst plane to belly land in the ocean because of its high wings. The bomb bay doors were not flush to the plane and would break off, causing the B-24 to come apart. He told us about a B-24 that ditched a mile from shore; five crew members survived but were eaten by sharks before reaching shore. He also said the navy was improving their search methods, but had very few success stories. The discussion made me uneasy. Our training missions would include long flights over the Pacific. We all had one more cigarette and made arrangements for drinks later that evening.

Now it was time to meet the rest of my crew. The officers returned to their barracks. I returned to my barracks. All five crew members had arrived and were busy trying to get organized.

The first one to speak was the left waist gunner. His name was Mike Gavin; he was from Marshall, Texas. He was six foot two, and had dark hair with a cowboy look. We swapped stories of our home towns, but could not find any common friends, although we both had experienced and appreciated Whitey's Pool Hall. He was familiar with my boxing background and jokingly said he wanted me on his side during any fights.

I needed to stay close to the waist gunners. I would need their help to get out of the ball turret if the plane started to go down. Once it started to roll I would not be able to get out. The pilot would give us three short beeps on the horn to prepare to bail out and one long beep to immediately exit the plane. Most ball turret gunners gave their flak jackets to the waist gunners to put on the floor so they didn't get their asses shot off. The waist gunners and the belly gunners had to work together. I had one small, four-inch window to look into the plane. If my gears got jammed, or if I lost electrical power, the waist gunner was my only hope. I would be curled into the fetal position for hours with no room to move or even scratch myself. My legs would be numb. I would be helpless.

The right waist gunner was Joel Kinder from Indiana. He was short and stocky, a former high school wrestling champion. We both lit up a smoke and discussed wrestling moves. I was a pretty good wrestler, but not in Joel's league. Joel was short enough to be a belly gunner, but way too husky. I really liked Joel and Mike; so far, so good.

The tail gunner was a blond beach boy named Kip Jones. We talked about his home town of Vero Beach, Florida and surf fishing. That was something I had always wanted to try. He said the lagoon of the inland waterway was full of snook and speckled trout. After only knowing each other for ten minutes, we made a promise to go surf fishing after the war. Kip also said he would teach me how to throw a cast net. I was impressed when he told me that he caught his own bait fish.

It was obvious our radio man was content while operating the dials to find the appropriate frequency. Greg Brinkman, a natural with the radio, was responsible for keeping our intercom system operational. That would be my only way to communicate with the crew. If the system went down I would not hear the crew yell enemy fighter positions or even know when to bail out. The chances of a belly gunner making it out of the plane were very low. But if I had sixty seconds before the plane rolled or blew, up I could get to my parachute. Greg seemed easy going but serious about his job. He would render position reports every thirty minutes and assisted the navigator to help us make our assembly point. It was complicated for over thirty squadrons from different bases to meet at the assembly point and build a three hundred plane formation. We were glad to have Greg aboard the *Sleepytime Gal.*

I could already tell that Howard Grogan, the top turret gunner, was going to be the comedian in the crew. Howard was from New York and was a practical joker. He held his hand up, stated he had something important to say, and then farted. We all laughed uncontrollably. I'm glad we had a guy like Howard to break the tension.

My crew was set. This was a crew of ten that would live or die together. We all walked over to the planning room to meet the officers. There we were, all together for the first time: left waist gunner Mike Gavin, right waist gunner Joel Kinder, and tail gunner Kip Jones. Our airplane commander and pilot, Coleman "Cole" Price, co-pilot Jordan "JJ" John, navigator Sal Wilson, bombardier Mark Martin, top turret gunner Howard Grogan, radio operator Greg Brinkman were all in the room. We all exchanged names and handshakes over a cigarette. We spent an hour trying to become familiar with each other's backgrounds and personalities. Cole seemed like a strong commander that wanted us to fight as a unit. We decided as a group to meet for dinner at 1800 hours.

After dinner, we all went to the base club for drinks. We seemed to be a strong crew that would watch each other's backs. We talked about each other's likes and hobbies, mostly small talk and pleasantries. I thought to myself that this was way more than a baseball team or fraternity. We needed to be a strong team to have any chance of surviving the war. Our performance would not determine who gets the trophy or championship. Our performance would stop a horrifying death and give us a chance to come home. If we failed, there would be no body or funeral, just death. We all got lit up on beer and whisky and decided to call it a night.

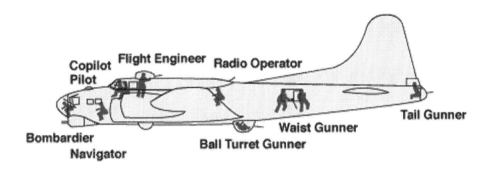

Copilot
Pilot
Flight Engineer
Radio Operator
Tail Gunner
Bombardier
Navigator
Ball Turret Gunner
Waist Gunner

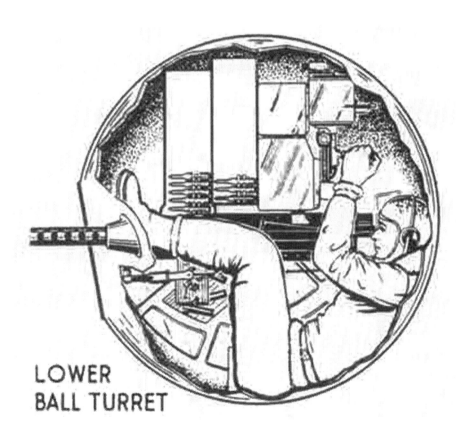

LOWER
BALL TURRET

XI

Cole called a meeting for our crew to discuss everyone's duties and brief us for our first mission. He discussed his duty to train us to fully understand the operation of the airplane: to always complete a preflight inspection of the plane and to systematically go through the pre-takeoff checklist. Cole told us about the B-17 that crashed on takeoff because the flaps were not set according to the checklist. He discussed our co-pilot JJ's duties: to maintain a complete log, to navigate day or night, to dead reckon, and to use of the radio to aid finding location and flight course. The co-pilot had to be efficient in the use of the radio in the event the radio man was injured or killed.

Cole looked at Greg and discussed his duty as a radio operator, to assist the navigator in taking fixes, maintaining a log, and understanding the role of a waist gunner. At any time a crew member could become incapacitated. Cole stressed the need for us to be familiar with each other's duties.

Cole spent the most time talking about the duties of Mark Martin, the bombardier. Our sole purpose was to find and destroy the target. Cole wanted us to rehearse how to load the bombs, fuse the bombs, and clear simple stoppages. He said nineteen airmen were killed on a base in Germany when a B-17 exploded because the bombs were armed. Mark would need to understand true airspeed, bomb ballistics, horizontal bomb trail, time of fall, ground speed, and drift. The Norden bombsight was sophisticated, but took practice to use effectively. Cole was going to make sure we trained as much as possible before leaving for England.

Sal Wilson, the navigator, would need to determine our location by referencing two or more celestial bodies. Those fixes could only have a ten mile margin of error. Instrument calibration of altimeter, compasses, airspeed indicator, astrocompass, astrograph, and drift meter were all important duties of the navigator.

The tail gunner had the duty to flash his Aldis lamp during the assembly of formations. The assembly began at seven thousand feet with a lead squadron, high squadron, and low squadron. Assembly point was very active and could involve over three hundred heavy bombers. The tail gunner had an important role in carrying out this beautiful dance. Sometimes squadron leaders would fire flares during the great assembly.

Commander Cole discussed the role of each gunner and how important it was for us to be fully trained before departure to England. In closing, Cole said for us to meet at 0600 hours at *Sleepytime Gal* for our first training mission as a crew.

"This will be a four hour flight at low altitude. She is a new plane and has less than fifty hours flying time. We will fly south down the coast and avoid any mountains. Let's have a few beers with the B 24 crews, but get to bed early," Cole said.

It was 0500 hours. We all woke up excited about our first mission together. Howard broke the ice with a couple of jokes and a well-timed fart. Howard was very crude, but likable. My mom would always say, "every time you laugh, you add a minute to your life." I hoped that was true, and that Howard would extend our lives past this war. We completed all our mundane duties, gathered our flying gear, and headed for the plane.

Sleepytime Gal was beautiful in the morning sun. She was spectacular with perfect curves. We boarded the plane from the rear door. Cole walked the outside of the plane with JJ. With preflight inspection complete, they impressively entered the plane through the front hatch. Commander Cole carried himself in a very confident way. I could not take my position until we were airborne, so I stood at the opening of the cockpit and observed Cole and JJ performing the pre-startup checklist.

Cole went down the list with a crisp clear voice. "Fuel transfer valve switch off? Check! Fuel shut off switch open? Check! Intercoolers cold? Check! Gear switch neutral? Check! Gyros? Check! Idle cut off? Check! Cowl flaps right and left locked? Check! Turbo off? Check! Throttle closed? Check! Auto pilot off? Check! Auto icers off? Check! Generator off? Check!"

"Start Engine check list," Cole said to JJ. "All clear left, right? Check! Master switch on? Check! Battery switch and inverter on? Check! Parking brake on? Check! Booster pumps-pressure on? Check! Carburetor filter open? Check! Fuel gallons per tank? Check! START ENGINES! Both magnetos on? Check! Flight indicator and vacuum pressure? Check! Radio on? Check! Crew report on intercom? Altimeter set? Check!"

Then the pilots ran up the RPMs to warm the engines. The great plane began to taxi for takeoff. I heard JJ and Cole run though the last check list at the end of the runway. Tail wheel locked? Check! Trim tabs set? Check! Gyro set? Check! Generator on? Check! Then we began to roll faster and faster until we reached one hundred miles per hour. *Sleepytime Gal* lifted off the ground with her new crew. Once airborne, and with the power reduction, cowl flaps and wheels up, we were off heading for the Pacific coast on our first mission.

We had no bombs on board, but all guns were hot. We approached the coast. The sun was behind us on this clear day. The sky was dark blue; all green colors were bright and shiny. We crossed over the bluffs and white sand and over the green-blue Pacific. There was no wind or turbulence at seven thousand feet, and we just enjoyed the flight.

Twenty miles out, we could still see the shore line. It was a crisp, clear Saturday morning. We turned south to follow the shore line to San Francisco. Commander Cole told us to take our combat positions and test our guns. Even though we didn't have a target, we could follow the tracers to get a better understanding of ballistics in motion. I aimed straight down at the ocean and fired, and then rotated to face the tail of the plane and fired a burst. Cole yelled a couple of enemy fighter positions and we all swung into action. We were low enough that we didn't need our electric suits. We all were wearing our leather bomber jackets. The flight was flawless.

When we landed, Cole said he had a surprise for the crew and wanted us to meet at 1600 hours at Hangar 3 with our leather bomber jackets.

We all arrived at the hangar promptly at 1600 hours. Cole introduced us to Sidney Loren, the painter of our plane's nose art. He painted the sexy *Sleepytime Gal* on the back of all our leather bomber jackets. We couldn't have been prouder as a crew. The next night we all wore our bomber jackets to the base club. We had a few beers, listened to some Glenn Miller, and went to bed early.

Two weeks passed. We completed fourteen missions in as many days. The hardest thing to deal with was the cold on our high altitude missions. On our last mission over the mountains to Nevada, the plane reached forty-one below zero. It was so cold it was impossible to think.

On the last mission, I came close to a claustrophobic panic attack. A horrible feeling came over me that I needed space immediately. I needed to standup, or I'd lose my senses. It was hard for me to stay in the ball turret for over thirty minutes.

We completed the five night mission over the Pacific and found our way home. Sal Wilson was a great navigator and had no problem locating our position at night. We practiced our shooting on moving targets and scored high marks.

We found out we would be taking the southern route to England with twenty-nine other B-17s. There would be our squadron of twelve, and a second squadron of eighteen planes. Our departure date was only two weeks away.

One morning Sleepytime Gal took a high-altitude, long-range training flight. The entire 95th Bomb Group was involved in this exercise. All the big brass were involved with the planning. There would be a colonel flying lead plane for each squadron. The base was humming with activity. My 336th Squadron of twelve planes and the 412th Squadron with eighteen planes were loaded with crews and beginning their pre-start checklist. One by one the engines began to roar. Just minutes earlier it was a peaceful morning. We could hear the quiet behind the birds chirping. Then, we felt and heard the power of this great beast preparing for takeoff. The ground was shaking; I could feel the pressure of compressed air from massive propellers.

The lead planes began to roll toward the end of the runway. We formed a long line of thirty planes. We took off with thirty seconds between each heavy bomber. The lead planes circled back over the base and we started to build our stacked formation at seven thousand feet. We were four levels high with a lead group offset by a second group. We looked like a huge, flying wing. The 334th and 335th Squadrons, comprised of twenty-four planes, were coming from the south to meet at an assembly point just west of the mountain range.

I could see the other squadrons approaching from the south. Because of the mountain range, we decided to assemble at nineteen thousand feet. It was already twenty-five below and we had to climb another twelve thousand feet. It was a clear, cold morning. We were stacked six levels high, with one lead group of twelve. We had a squadron of twelve planes staggered to their right one level down. To the left of the lead squadron was a group of twelve planes one level higher staggered back by only one plane length. Directly behind us was the 412th Squadron with eighteen planes. We formed a large diamond six levels high. No matter how many planes went down, we had to stay in formation. We'd have to stay disciplined during the onslaught of enemy fighters and flak. The formations were designed taking into account target size and bomb effectiveness. The box formation would protect the inner planes and would give us the best chance to make it to our target.

The formation began to climb to a cruising altitude of thirty-one thousand feet. We were making a bombing run they refer to as a "shuttle mission." We were going to bomb a target in North Dakota, land at the Rapid City Air Base in South Dakota, and then re-arm with bombs and strike a target in North Dakota on our return trip. We were practicing for shuttle runs to Russia. If the Russians could push the German Eastern Front to the west, we'd have an agreement to land on their soil, re-arm, and bomb Germany on the return trip.

We reached cruising altitude and the sight was spectacular; all the planes with their bright white vapor trails against the morning blue sky. The sun rose in front of us, and gave a clear view of the glistening white contrail stretching for miles. It showed our path in detail.

The cold began to dominate my thoughts. The electric suits were no match for sixty below zero. We had to be careful not to spit in our masks. If the oxygen line froze, I would fall asleep and die. Commander Cole said it was time to take our fighting stations. With the full electric suit, I could barely get through the hatch. Joel Kinder, the right waist gunner, had to stuff me into the ball turret. There was absolutely no room for a parachute or flak jacket. I would need assistance and at least sixty seconds to escape the ball turret.

I was extremely concerned that I would become overwhelmed with claustrophobic anxiety. I came very close on my last mission. I got to a point when I needed to stand up and be free. I would have given anything to not be confined; I felt like I was buried alive. We kept my turret moving to get my mind off the cold.

Our bomb run began, and Cole gave the order to fire all guns as he called a fictitious fighter position. We had to react without hitting another plane in formation. Three o'clock high. I could hear the right waist gunner, Joel, and the top turret gunner laying out a field of bullets. I shot a burst as if the fighter plane passed below. You learned to follow the tracers and let them guide your line of fire.

Cole yelled, "Ox, twelve o'clock below!"

That was a position that only I could align my machine guns to. I was giving him a long burst and my gun jammed.

"Ox let him have it!"

I took off my silk-lined electric glove and grabbed the side of the gun. My hand instantly attached to the gun. I could not move my hand without losing my skin. I could feel my hand turning numb from the cold. Two minutes passed and my hand lost all feeling. I decided to pull it free and all my skin was left on the gun. I put my frozen hand back in the glove. I needed both hands to fly my turret and shoot my gun. I could never make this mistake over Germany. We made a successful bomb run and headed for South Dakota.

Joel helped me out of the ball turret. I had not regained any feeling in the fingers of my right hand. My feet and left hand were numb from the cold, but there was still some feeling.

We landed at the airbase in Rapid City. I took off my glove on my right hand and had no feelings in my fingertips. Cole sent me to see the flight surgeon, Doctor Petit. He examined my hand.

"I have seen this many times in England. You have a mild case of frostbite."

"You were in England with the bomber crews?"

"Yes. Are you starting to get some feeling back in your fingers?"

"Yes, much better. Tell me about the bomber crews in England."

"Many of the airmen suffer from battle fatigue; they fight and argue over the smallest things. They deliberately pick a fight. Pilots are pushed so hard that they make mental mistakes. Some of them have battle dreams and wake up screaming."

The doctor was engaging, but brutally honest. He said many of the crews were cracking under the stress, convinced they were going to die. One of the top pilots got hysterical in the mess hall after a mission. He went absolutely berserk. Frequently, the doctors would inject hysterical airmen with sodium pentothal. Many of them were in shock and could not express themselves in their conscious state. Doctor Petit was on a team of doctors that recommended that General Curtis LeMay reevaluate daylight bombing due to the heavy losses and mental fatigue. The general was not receptive to any compromises.

After talking to Doctor Petit, I better understood the pilot of the *Lady Stardust.* He was carrying some demons from the war and I had touched a nerve. I hoped this war wouldn't change or burden me with nightmares and horrific thoughts for the rest of my life. All positions in the B-17 were stressful beyond imagination, but all flyers and Doctor Petit knew the belly gunner was the worst.

I could not wait to meet my crew mates for a cold beer and hear some music. My favorite, Glenn Miller, was on the radio. We shot pool and smoked cigarettes. We talked about baseball and music. Kip and I talked about how bad we wanted to go fishing. We knew the war was just weeks ahead but found a way to block that from our minds. We had to be in our planes by 0600 for our return bombing mission. I noticed the ground crews fueling and arming the planes as I passed. We were in our bunks by 2100 hours.

We got up at 0500 hours. The air crews shaved their faces close as possible to help with the fit of the oxygen mask. We had a big breakfast in the mess hall. After breakfast the pilots went to a short briefing about the mission. Then we all headed for our lockers and grabbed our gear. We walked as a big group toward our planes. Crew by crew, we separated as we reached our planes. *Sleepytime Gal* was near the end of the row of bombers. We boarded our planes like modern-day gladiators. All the engines started to roar. We took off against the wind into the morning sun.

The bomb run over North Dakota was uneventful, but things changed drastically as we approached eastern Washington. There was a strong head wind off the Pacific coast that created severe turbulence. The bombers were in a tight formation as we entered a group of clouds. We were bouncing hard, lifting and dropping. We would hit so hard I thought it was another bomber.

I was in the ball turret rotating and looking for the planes below. For a split second I got a glimpse of other B-17s. I was scared shitless. I didn't see how flak could shake the plane any worse. Cole said to keep looking for planes. Just when he said that, a B-17 was ten feet below me. The front of the plane was even with my ball turret. The pilot saw me and slowly backed away. He was a smart pilot; any sudden moves and he would have hit another plane.

It was cold but I broke out in a sweat. I started to doubt my mental strength. I was scared and nauseous from the turbulence and clouds. How would I handle the flak and German fighters? I was not worried about myself. Over the last six weeks I had come to terms with death. I really didn't think I would ever see my parents or Elaine again. I was not coming home from Germany. I was at peace with dying, but I did not want to let my crew down. I was the only protection for the belly of the plane. What if I froze with fear?

We landed back at our home base and I was glad to see a letter from Elaine had arrived during my absence. She started out with news of Roy being drafted into the army. Roy was my only friend that was outspoken about the war. I hoped they hadn't put him on the front lines. I honestly didn't think he could have handled the stress or dealt with the horrible things he would see. Maybe he was smarter than me; every crew member flying on a B-17 volunteered. I guess the military thought it more appropriate if young men volunteered for a suicide mission.

Elaine went on to say her nursing training was on schedule. She must not have had any news on Bert and Charley. Mom and Dad were doing fine. Mr. Washington was a big help at the store. She was grateful that the military let her train at Barksdale Air Base, allowing her a few extra weeks at home. She told me a boy she knew slightly from a different high school was killed on a B-24 Liberator. He was on a bombing mission out of Midway Island and never returned. His parents had not given up hope, but he has been missing over four weeks. She didn't want to scare me, but in closing she told me how concerned she was of my safety. She was starting to hear of all the B-17s being shot down over Germany. Some asshole at the store told her she would never see me again. What kind of jerk would say that? When I got back home, I'd kick his ass to show him I was still alive.

- PS. William, be safe. I look forward to fishing with you after the war. Love, Elaine

Elaine's letter was more than just words on a piece of paper. The war was getting closer and the subject of life and death could not be avoided. We were concerned for each other, our friends and country. I kept hearing about Hitler's secret weapons and wondered if we would even win. We were told the daylight bombing raids and heavy losses were necessary to turn the tide of the war.

XII

We had some down time over the next two weeks, and Cole encouraged us to spend time together. Cole was very smart and always had a reason for anything he said. I think he wanted us to learn each other's strengths and weaknesses. Maybe he thought we would be more effective as a team if we got closer. Most of the guys on base spent their free time engaging in sports activities or small talk over cigarettes. Other than working out in the gym for thirty minutes a day, I learned as much as I could about my crew mates. We would all probably live or die together.

I targeted Kip Jones, our tail gunner, first. We had the afternoon off and I asked Kip to go fishing. We got a couple of cane poles from the general store and walked a mile to a stream located west of the base. I was going to take the role of an interviewer, but not be obvious. I wanted to learn about my crew mates, but not come across as prying.

We sat along the banks of the slow moving stream and dropped our lines. We used a float cork with six additional feet of line, and a small hook with the worms we dug up the night before. I wanted to catch something, but not be too busy.

"Kip, what do you want to do after the war?"

"See my girlfriends, show them a good time, and drink plenty of beer."

"You have more than one girlfriend?"

"Yes, I got my blond-haired girlfriend who hangs out at the beach with me. What a body! Then I have my beer-drinking girl friend from school who knows all my friends. Then I have my neighborhood friend that comes over when my parents are not home. She is older, so we keep our relationship a secret."

"Damn, you really are a playboy. You are living a dream."

"I know; this war fucked everything up," Kip said angrily.

I really was enjoying my time with Kip. He lived that carefree-I-don't-give-a-shit lifestyle, but was a hell of a tail gunner. We talked about starting a fishing guide service. Kip thought Florida would start growing after the war. I didn't see people from up north ever moving to Florida; it was too hot in the summers. Kip thought differently and wanted me to move there after the war and start buying real estate. He saw a photo of Elaine and that was all he kept asking me about. I liked Kip, but he had a one track mind. We caught a few small bream and two catfish and walked back to the base.

Cole is one of those intellectual, New England types. He seemed always impressed and curious about my boxing skills. He asked me several times to teach him how to fight, but until now avoided the subject. I needed to spend time with Cole and this would be my best option.

"Cole we have some free time. Would you like to work out with me at the base gym? I will give you some boxing tips."

"That would be great. Let me grab my gear and we will walk together."

"Cole, what made you decide to go to Harvard Law School?"

"My dad went there and planned on me joining his law firm after college."

"Do you still want to do that?"

"I don't know, I sure like flying airplanes. I thought about being a commercial pilot after the war."

"Will your dad be disappointed?

"No, not at all. He's not like that."

We talked about our families and I learned much about Cole. He was all business, and I kept waiting for him to change the subject back to *Sleepytime Gal* and our duties.

"Cole, the most important thing to remember is to keep your chin down and gloves up. The chin is the light switch; if I hit you hard on the chin, you are going down. Keep your eyes open and try to see my punches coming. You are much taller than me so keep me away with a left jab. Don't let me inside or cut off the ring. Work to the left and keep your distance. Are you ready?"

"Yes," Cole said nervously.

Cole knew he was no match for me, but wanted to learn how to fight the hard way. We started to circle and I noticed the rest of our crew was walking into the gym with big smiles. The word spread around the base that Cole and I were about to fight. I didn't want to embarrass Cole, but I had a reputation to keep. Cole was deliberate but slow with his left jab. I could get inside anytime and knock him out, but I let him keep me at bay. I let that go on for forty seconds and decided to move inside for a couple of shots. I went downstairs with a combination to his kidneys. I could see the pain in his face so I backed off and let him get his breath as we circled to the left. Cole decided to be more aggressive and started swinging wild combinations to my head. I covered up to show him proper defense can protect you from any blow. I leaned back against the ropes and let him wail away. After twenty seconds I decided to let Cole know I was still in the ring. I hit him with a heavy right to his left cheek and he was stunned. I was worried I might have hit him too hard. He started to stagger and Howard screamed out "That's why we call him OX Abraham!"

I felt bad for Cole, but he needed some tough love. I always liked my opponents because they showed me my weaknesses and where I needed to improve. Cole dropped his hands and paid the price. He would know better next time. We sparred for five more minutes and Cole improved in that short time. We shook hands and gained a mutual respect for each other. I didn't see how we could have a better pilot or flight commander than Cole. We all decided to grab a beer and laugh about the fight. We were really bonding as a crew.

I decided to sit next to Howard Grogan, the top turret gunner. Howard was the funniest person I had ever met. We had two things in common; we were both turret gunners and loved fart humor. Howard would fart, then laugh at his own fart and get the entire crew laughing. Cole even would laugh. We had no duties, so Howard and I decided to slam down six beers each. We laughed uncontrollably and smoked a pack of Chesterfields. Howard farted so loud every one stopped talking in amazement and then we laughed so loud tears were coming to our eyes. What a night! I didn't learn much about Howard's life back in New York, but the crew was never closer.

JJ the copilot was quiet but would laugh at every joke. I thought JJ envied the way Howard was so outgoing. JJ had a great sense of humor and was fun loving, but was also a quiet observer. He loved his home city of Atlanta and would talk about it now and then. Everyone liked to talk about their home towns and what they were going to do after the war. I thought that was therapeutic and a way to deal with the possibility of no return. Cole and JJ were very vulnerable in their pilot seats. We were not allowed to bail out until the pilots gave the command. What if they died or couldn't speak? Who was going to help me out of the belly turret if the plane started to roll over?

The waist gunners, Joel Kinder and Mike Gavin, were my only hope. On missions I spent the most time with Joel and Mike. They helped me in and out of the turret and we spent time together en route. After hours in the ball turret there was no way I could get out without their help. Since I couldn't fit in my turret with my flak jacket on, I let them lay it on the floor for protection. I tried to keep them happy. Both waist gunners were extremely strong and could pull me out of the turret with one hand. Mike was a tall, strong Texan from Marshal that could have been cast in a movie as a cowboy. Joel was the one guy I wanted on my side in a fight. I knew the reputations of many wrestlers from Indiana; Joel seemed tough as nails, but a very nice person. He showed me some wrestling moves and I was extremely impressed. He wanted me to teach him how to box. I had been avoiding the issue because it could get ugly. One of us would leave the ring hurt, probably me.

Mark Martin, the bombardier from California, was the enigma of the crew. He was very purpose driven and kept to himself. If anyone hit his target, it would be Mark. He seemed so focused when he took control of the plane. Once we started our bombing run, he was all business. I didn't think German fighters or flak could break his concentration. Cole and Mark had a lot in common. Both were driven to accomplish the mission at all cost.

Sal Wilson was a sophisticated guy who loved baseball and statistics. Another airman from Paris, Texas said Sal was from one of the richest families in Texas. The governor of Texas would visit his family's ranch and there were even rumors in Paris, Texas, that President Roosevelt had Sal's parents to the White House. Sal never talked about money or acted like big me, little you. Sal was the smartest person with numbers I had ever known. He could do math in his head at an astonishing speed. He had the ability to reason through any word problem with complete accuracy. Even though Cole had graduated from Harvard Law School, Sal was the smartest person on the plane. I was glad Sal would be our navigator when we crossed the Atlantic.

I asked Sal to play pitch and catch with me so we could spend some time together. I borrowed a baseball glove from Joel and we headed for the field.

"Sal, tell me about your two sisters."

"Grace is seventeen and about to graduate from high school and Glenda is thirteen and loves to ride horses."

"I have a seventeen year old sister named Elaine who is about to become a nurse on a hospital ship."

"You showed me her picture; she is really beautiful. What are some of her hobbies?"

"She loves to fish."

"I want you and your sister to visit my ranch after the war. We have a lake full of bass and bream. Paris is only a three hour drive from Shreveport."

"That is a great idea! I promise we will visit soon as we get back."

We threw the baseball and talked for an hour. Sal had a very strong arm and stung my hand repeatedly. Joel's glove didn't have much padding and Sal was enjoying the moment. The more I showed pain the harder he threw the ball. I had a great time with Sal but I was glad when we finished. I would not pick baseball next time.

Greg Brinkman was born to be a radio operator. He was consumed by electronics and gadgets. Even though he looked like a bookworm, he could be very funny and liked practical jokes. He loved to hang around Howard and encouraged him to play practical jokes on the crew. Greg was very smart and second best in math behind Sal. He loved to smoke cigarettes and listen to Duke Ellington and Tommy Dorsey on the radio.

It was late fall and starting to get dark early. Greg and I were heading for the base club for beers and music.

We arrived at the club at 1900 hours, ordered two cold beers, and sat down together. Greg looked out of place with his skinny, studious, bookworm looks, but could party with the best. Glenn Miller's "Chattanooga Choo Choo" was playing on the old wooden phonograph. I bummed a Lucky Strike; we lit up and started to talk.

"I sure hope we get to see Glenn Miller play in England," Greg said.

"Me too."

"I think he is doing a great thing playing for the troops."

"I heard he made captain in the Army Air Corps."

"To see Glenn Miller play would be a dream come true. Ox, let's start working on that when we land in England," Greg said with complete conviction.

Greg made me think about some of the important things I wanted to happen in my life. I hoped we'd all survive war and that Greg would get to see Glenn Miller and all his dreams would come true. How many dreams were shattered because of war? Death is so final; so many things would change forever. Would I ever be able to have a family and kids? How many little boys and girls would lose their dads forever as B-17's fell from the sky? I had been in the Army Air Corps for four months and my attitude and thoughts about the war were changing.

I was glad to spend this time with Greg. I needed to get closer and better understand my radio man. We had one more beer; I lost count but the small table was covered with empty mugs and the ash tray was full with bent cigarettes. We did our share to add to the smoke filled club. We lit our last smoke for our walk back to the barracks.

XIII

Two weeks passed.

I couldn't believe this day had finally arrived. We were loading up our gear and preparing to take off. For the last week, our instructors had been instructing us on survival techniques. We spent a lot of time discussing ways to survive in the ocean. We would assemble a formation of thirty planes. Statistics said that three planes would fall behind with mechanical problems. The colonel leading our group pointed out several times that the formation never slowed down for stragglers. If you had mechanical problems or ditched in the ocean you had to survive until help arrived. That made me start thinking about what the B-24 pilot had said about the planes lost in the Pacific.

We had no bombs but the whole nine yards of ammo for each of our .50 caliber machine guns. The machine guns were all cleaned and ready for action. The two most dangerous legs of our mission were from Natal, Brazil to Dakar on the east coast of Africa, and then the final leg from Morocco in northeast Africa to St. Eval, England. The Germans occupied France and would be patrolling the coast looking for our formation. They had spies in Brazil, Dakar, and Morocco that would be informing Germany of our every move.

The last one to board *Sleepytime Gal* was Commander Cole. I was surprised to hear him say we had an important person to pick up in Atkinson Field, British Guiana. As the thirty B-17s started their engines with propellers turning, we rolled toward England. As we lifted off the ground, an empty feeling rushed over me. Would this be the last time I ever saw my country? I looked out the west waist gunner's window and got very emotional. This hurt and was different from all the training missions. I couldn't help but think of the crew of the *Lady Stardust*. I could see in their faces that war had changed them for life. What horrible things did they see that had scarred them so deeply? Would I die a horrible death, never to see my family or country again? Why couldn't the politicians and the leaders of the world be more compromising and not kill millions of young people and destroy tens of millions of families? Mark's math was right; one out of three flyers would die over Germany.

The assembly was complete and we were stacked six levels tall. Our squadron of twelve was lower, but leading the squadron of eighteen. I could see the squadron of eighteen above us trailing to the south by less than five plane lengths. Both squadrons were in the basic wing formation for our trip over the mountains. The mission called for us to cruise at nine thousand feet until we reached the mountains. As we approach the mountain range, we would need to wear our oxygen masks and electrically-heated suits. The good news was I wouldn't be required to fly in the ball turret for the crossing.

That day was the clearest day I had ever flown. Visibility was limitless and the mountains looked clear and detailed. I could see every edge on mountains on the horizon twelve peaks away. We were at thirty thousand feet so we didn't have to plot a course around any mountains. The white vapor trails followed planes for miles. I could never tire of this sight; this must have looked impressive from the ground. I wondered what the Germans thought when they saw the contrails from a formation of five hundred planes approaching from the west.

We had a tail wind and our trip to Rapid City, South Dakota, only took five hours. We topped off the fuel on the planes, grabbed a quick lunch in the mess hall located near the runway, and departed for Kearney, Nebraska. We cruised at nine thousand feet and no oxygen masks were needed.

We spent the night in a small barracks near the main hangar. The crew was tired so we had a late dinner, smoked a couple of cigarettes, and went to bed. Tomorrow would be a long flight to Gulfport, Mississippi.

We approached Gulfport from the west. We flew along the gulf coast for twenty miles. This was the prettiest shore line I had ever seen: one large wooden house after another with piers that stretched out into the Gulf of Mexico for hundreds of feet. I couldn't help but think of The Biloxi Kid as we passed over his home city at two thousand feet. The last I heard was that he was a tank commander in England preparing for the invasion. I hoped we'd get to drink that beer together after the war.

The flight took seven hours; we spent the night and rested for our trip across the Gulf of Mexico to West Palm Beach, Florida. Kip and I spoke and fantasized about fishing the gulf. Mark, Howard, Greg and

Sal played cards, Cole and JJ went over their flight plan, and Joel and Mike smoked an endless chain of cigarettes while talking about how rich they were going to get after the war.

Kip and I walked down to the beach because we heard locals were gigging flounders. It was a strange sight; twenty to thirty locals were walking in knee-deep water over a thousand feet from shore. They had flash lights on their heads and were spearing flounders. Kip and I were very jealous because it looked like a lot of fun. There was a warm, balmy breeze with a full moon. We headed back to the barracks, and off to Borinquen, Puerto Rico in the morning.

The leg to Puerto Rico was enjoyable. The plane stayed warm and no oxygen masks were required. So far, no planes had fallen behind due to mechanical reasons; maybe because all the B-17s on this trip were of the new G class with chin turrets. So far we'd beaten the odds, and I was glad.

Our next leg of the mission was to Atkinson Field, British Guiana. In our briefing, we discussed the possibility of an enemy attack. The formation would be on radio silence and I would be required to spend time in the ball turret.

We built our formation just south of Puerto Rico. The mission to British Guiana was scheduled for eight hours. Weather was a major concern on this leg. As we approached South America, our alert and awareness levels increased. The Germans were proud that they controlled much of the South Atlantic and would have loved to shoot us down. I was sure their spies let them know we were on the way.

The weather turned so bad that the Germans might not have been needed to destroy our squadron. For the first time in all my missions we had to break formation. Sal Wilson and the other navigators were working hard to make sure we didn't get blown off course. The tail gunners were busy using the light beacons to stay in contact with the separated formation. We couldn't get above or go around the tropical storm and had to ride it out. The sheets of rain were so heavy Commander Cole was afraid the engines might stall. Because of the strong wind, we dropped hard, then many small bumps, and a sudden lift to drop again. Our ground speed couldn't have been over 170 miles per hour. Cole and JJ quit any type of conversation and spent all their energy trying to keep *Sleepytime Gal* in the air. They had a very concerned look on their faces, but I had confidence in Cole. If anyone could get us through this, it would be Cole. Kip reported from his tail gunners position he had lost contact with all planes.

Thirty minutes passed. The rain subsided slightly and we hoped the worst was over. The sun should have been to our west at the three o'clock position, but the clouds had blocked out any light. We were on radio silence and could not know the fate of the others until we cleared the storm.

Finally we saw a break in the clouds. To our east, we saw three planes from our formation popping in and out of the clouds. No other signs of the thirty planes. Twenty minutes passed and we passed the storm front into clean air. The sun was where it should have been at the three o'clock level. At least we knew we were going south. Suddenly, fifteen more bombers appeared, and then all thirty. We spent the next twenty minutes getting into formation at nine thousand feet. We were nearing the coast of South America and possibly German warships. All gunners were required to man their stations until our final approach.

We landed, tired and worn out after a nine hour flight. No talk from Cole of our secret guest. I guessed we would find out in the morning. We had beef stew at the old, worn-down mess hall and headed straight for bed.

Howard kept saying our guest was going to be someone famous like Clark Gable or Jimmy Stewart. Sal said he read they both were already flying missions in Europe. It must have been somebody important because the base was on lockdown.

We finished our breakfast of eggs and ham, grabbed our gear, and headed for the plane. Our special guest boarded the plane with top secret information he was to share with the British. Rumors were he was a leading scientist in the area of physics and atomic engineering. All I knew was that he was making my plane a target. Our plane was randomly picked, and we were to stay in the middle of a box formation. A general and a colonel would be leading the two squadrons to Brazil and then across the South Atlantic. The good news was they would not let us fall behind if we had mechanical problems. Our cargo was too valuable.

Our planes were fully loaded with fuel for this leg to Natal, Brazil. Usually we would have stopped to fuel at Belem, Brazil, but there was intelligence that the Germans had fighters waiting to ambush us on our approach. We flew fifty miles west of Belem over the Amazon rain forest. Fuel was going to be an issue, but it was a risk worth taking.

We landed in Natal, Brazil from the west to avoid flying near the shore line. We landed just before dark on a warm, calm evening. No signs of the storm that had almost destroyed our plane. There was only a thin layer of clouds at a high altitude. The thin layer of rippled clouds turned purple, yellow and red with the sunset.

Immediately after we landed, Cole was called to a planning meeting. I was surprised because JJ was excluded. Cole returned to tell us our flight across the South Atlantic was going to be a night flight. That seemed like suicide. The flight was over two thousand three hundred miles. At that distance, fuel would be a huge issue. We would be at the mercy of the navigators. One mistake and we would be ditching in the Atlantic. Cole encouraged us to stay up late and sleep late in the morning. We had one day to adapt to an all-night flight.

All crews were confined to their barracks and we were not allowed to discuss our departure time with anyone stationed at the base. Armed guards patrolled the perimeter of the base with dogs and also were stationed strategically among the B-17s. We played cards and smoked Camel cigarettes until two in the morning. We all got sleepy and started talking crazy bullshit. It was like we were drunk. Cole said I was lucky he didn't kick my ass in our boxing match. Kip said he would make love to a girl from each country in Europe. Howard farted at least ten times, each louder than the next. JJ told Kip he was a virgin and was just talking a bunch of shit. The two waist gunners, Mike and Joel, were arguing over who would be the first to shoot down a German fighter. We needed this time to relax and bond. This was the first time the officers shared the barracks, and we had a great time. That was the most open and relaxed I had ever seen Cole.

Fifteen hours passed. During our mission briefing, the importance of the mission and maintaining radio silence was discussed over and over. Our mystery man had to make it to London at all costs. The tail gunners with their beacon lamps would play an important role in keeping the formation. We would be the last to take off and the assembly point was twenty miles from shore. I guess they wanted us off last to give us the best odds on fuel.

There was a beautiful full moon. It was seventy-eight degrees, with a light breeze from the west. That small tail wind could have made the difference between landing in Africa and ditching in the Atlantic. The moon worked in our favor as long as the German night fighters were not searching for us.

Five hundred miles off the coast of South America, an English-speaking ship captain asked for our location. All B-17 radio operators picked up the transmission, but strict radio silence was maintained. Then, off to the south, we noticed several search lights from German warships scanning the sky. It was an eerie feeling to see the beams of light bouncing off the clouds. That was definitely a German on the radio seeking our position. We had missed the ambush ten miles to the north.

Three hours from the coast of Africa, a message was relayed from plane to plane that *First Time Girl* was falling behind due to mechanical problems. We were still six hundred miles from the African coast and outside the range of land-based German fighters. Neither side of the war had control of Africa, so the Germans could have had fighters based in several locations near the coast.

Our guest on the plane stayed to himself and spent the entire flight staring at his mathematical notes. He was a strange bird to say the least. I didn't see how such a wormy-looking guy wearing a stupid hat could make any difference in the outcome of the war.

"We are within fighter range; everyone man their guns." Commander Cole said. Joel and Mike helped me into the ball turret and I began to scan the skies. I swung my ball turret to scan behind the plane and noticed the full moon setting in the west. It was six o'clock level and one of the most impressive sights I have ever seen. The plane behind us was perfectly aligned with the moon. The B-17's silhouette was encircled in bright white and was a sight to be seen. I could see the moonlight shining off the tail of the B-17 to our north. I kept my ball turret moving, but spotted no German night fighters.

As we approached the African coast I could see the waves breaking on the shore. The full moon was setting in the west as the sun was beginning to rise in the east. I was glad to land by daylight, but concerned that we were vulnerable.

As we got below nine hundred feet I was removed from my ball turret. We were low enough that there was no concern of an attack from below. I was glad the gears to my turret worked and I could be removed. We were running out of fuel and could not circle the field. We landed in Senegal, Africa just after sunrise. There was no news on the fate of *First Time Girl*. Commander Cole and JJ went to a debriefing of our flight. We all went to bed while the planes fueled. Our next stop was Marrakech, Morocco.

Cole and JJ returned to the barracks after their two hour meeting. "We are going to spend tonight in Senegal and tomorrow morning we'll make a run for Morocco. We will not make the usual flight up the coast. We will fly east, turn north, and cross over the Sahara Desert," Cole said.

"Why that route?" asked Sal, the navigator. The desert was always avoided due to sand storms and the fact that no side had control and there were not defined boundaries.

"There are two remote air fields in the Western Sahara Desert that can supply a fighter escort. We will fly at eight thousand feet and be escorted by six P-40 Flying Tigers. We need to stay below nine thousand feet; the P-40 will be no match for the German fighters at high altitude," Cole explained.

We only slept until noon so we wouldn't stay up all night. We spent the afternoon with the maintenance crews preparing for our trip across the desert. The incident crossing the Atlantic was disturbing and brought home the harsh reality of war. Because of strict radio silence, the search didn't start until after we landed. If the crew survived a night ditching, they would have had to spend at least twelve hours in the water. This was a mechanical issue, but over Germany there would be many planes falling behind because of fighter and flak damage. Almost all stragglers were sitting ducks and got shot down by the German fighters. I just hoped the crew of *First Time Girl* didn't experience a terrifying, spinning fall from the sky.

I didn't discuss this with anyone but I'd been having a bad dream—a dream of being trapped and helpless as *Sleepytime Gal* rolled over and began to spin. I had learned to be at peace with dying, but I was scared and horrified about how I would die. The thought of being trapped in my ball turret and falling thousands of feet had to be blocked from my mind.

Cole asked the maintenance crews several questions about the desert and what effect a sudden sand storm would have on the four engines. Sal met with several of the other navigators about our route. There was a disagreement about how far east to fly before turning to the north.

We had to pass near a small outpost to rendezvous with the first P-40 escort. After three hours they dropped off, and we picked up, a new escort of six P-40s from a supply base located in a remote area of the Sahara Desert, three hundred miles east of Morocco.

The mess hall was a converted warehouse. All the crews met for breakfast at 0500. The morning was hot and dry. The twenty nine crews finished breakfast at the same time and walked toward their parked bombers. There was very little conversation; many of us were thinking of the lost crew.

Just like clockwork our special guest was brought out to the plane just before we began to taxi. He gave us a nod good morning, but there was no conversation. It was obvious he was instructed to not communicate with anyone.

Sand from the runway began to blow across the planes as we slowly rolled in a long line toward the end of the runway. You could hear the sand hit the front windshield of *Sleepytime Gal*. This sand couldn't be good for the intake manifolds of the engines. All twenty-nine planes were in the air in less than fifteen minutes. We assembled immediately at seven thousand feet and headed east toward the Sahara and our P-40 escorts.

I was required to fly in the ball turret the entire trip. The temperature in the plane was extremely pleasant. The air was thick and warm, not thin and cold. I was cramped and stiff in the ball turret but not freezing. The Sahara Desert was beautiful in a strange way. The large sand drifts were mesmerizing. One of the P-40 Flying Tiger escort planes was just to my right, at the three o'clock low position. The plane was extremely impressive with an aggressive paint job. I was envious of the fighter pilot. He had his canopy open and seemed free as a bird. He looked very comfortable enjoying the cool breeze from his open cockpit. We made eye contact a couple of times and he gave me the thumbs up like all was OK. We were glad to have the escort. Just the week before, there were two B-24 Liberators shot down flying out of Port Lyautey in French Morocco. The entire area from North Africa across the Mediterranean was undefined, with no boundaries identifying our front line. It would have been very easy to stumble into the enemy or a trap.

Several miles to our east, almost level with the horizon, we noticed several shiny objects flickering in the sunlight. Our escort of P-40s circled to the east side of our formation to cover our flank. The shiny objects followed us for several miles. Soon we would need to turn east toward Marrakech, Morocco.

As we reached a location thirty miles south of the Mediterranean coastline, we turned to the north toward the Atlantic coast of Northern Africa. The shiny objects disappeared; the remainder of the flight was uneventful. We landed in Marrakech just before sunset.

We all learned immediately that Marrakech was a wide-open "live and let live" town. The barracks had to be the largest open room at any base. The bunks were packed in every available space with no room to spare. Between every row of bunks there were airmen playing poker, dice, and blackjack, and pitching coins. All players were circled with others trying to get in. The large converted hangar was filled with smoke, screaming, and laughter.

Kip started talking to a British airman named Elliot about the night life in Marrakech. Elliot told Kip about a couple of bars off base, but encouraged us to take our .45's. Kip immediately turned the subject to girls and asked Elliot the odds of getting laid.

"Kip, you got a better chance at getting your throat slit than getting any pussy in Morocco. Those Germans fucked everything up when they took France. The French women are the lovers in Europe," Elliot said convincingly, with his heavy British accent.

We all lit up a cigarette and discussed the war. Elliot was in his early thirties and seemed to be very worldly. I didn't want to make the same mistake I did with the pilot of *Lady Stardust* and offend him, but the war was getting closer and I had questions.

"Elliot, what is it like flying over Germany and occupied France? Is it as bad as everyone is saying?" I asked.

"Last week an American formation of three hundred B-17s bombed a factory near Brunswick, Germany, and fifty-seven planes were lost. All twelve planes in the lead squadron were shot down. The full colonel leading the mission was killed before they even started their bombing run. The area around Brunswick is full of factories and highly fortified. Germany puts their best fighter pilots there. Some Americans pilots call them the Bastards of Brunswick. Let's talk about girls and not this fucking war," Elliot said.

We noticed Cole entering the barracks after his two hour meeting. He separated our crew from all the others and gathered us in an empty office. "We are going to hold over for two days, then make a solo night flight to St. Eval, England," Cole said.

"That is suicide!" Sal, said.

"The Germans know about our passenger and have spies waiting for our bomber group to take off. They have night fighters patrolling the area around the Bay of Biscay waiting for our bomber group, but not one plane," Cole said.

"The mechanics are checking our plane for any problems. We had a drop in oil pressure in number four and they are replacing the piston rings," JJ said.

Sal would need to be on his game. The Atlantic was big and lonely at night. Sal always worked with the other navigators to get our fix and heading.

"Keep this confidential! Be ready; I will only give you an hour's notice before takeoff," Cole said.

Kip's plan to find a hot girl went out the window. We were restricted to base, no Humphrey-Bogart-Casablanca-style night club this trip. We all walked back into the barracks to vent some pressure. We all joked around, and without noticing that Howard farted so loud the groups around us all quit playing cards and looked up in amazement. With Cole's information the war seemed a lot closer. The stakes were just increased.

Two days passed and the other bombers from our group were given the orders to prepare for takeoff. It was early afternoon; it was almost like they wanted the German spies to notice them leaving. Maybe they were going to be a sacrificial lamb; I hoped not. I stood leaning against the gate and watched all the crews being driven to their planes. Jeffrey, a belly gunner I trained with in Galveston, asked for a smoke when he passed and I gave him a pack of Chesterfields and wished him luck. "Abraham, mechanical problems?" Jeffrey asked.

"Yes, we will fly to England in three days with the next squadron."

It was a humid, misty day and the noise from the bombers seemed louder than usual. It was mysterious and haunting to watch the twenty-eight bombers take off and disappear into the mist.

Two hours passed. "Prepare for takeoff! We are leaving in four hours at 1900 hours. Sal, triple check our route and understand our star reference points, we must get this one right," Cole said.

We all got very hurried and very anxious about flying solo from North Africa to England. We double and triple checked all survival gear and equipment. We plotted a course that would take us far over the Atlantic and back east toward southern England. Cole made sure the tanks were topped off. We had to fly to the western extreme to avoid the range of enemy fighters. Our cargo had to be delivered to England at all costs.

With the mundane checklist completed and propellers turning, we rolled down the empty runway. Our takeoff was purposely unannounced; no other planes, just one B-17 bound for England. We cleared the African coast and flew to a point fifty miles west of where our squadron had turned north. Our guest was more reclusive than ever; his nose was purposely down between the pages of his science books to avoid any interaction. Supposedly he was an expert on atoms.

We turned north into pitch-black nothingness—just stars and a setting, waning, crescent moon. We were at eight thousand feet and there was a noticeable change in temperature as we flew north.

"Cole! Run another calibration on compasses and airspeed indicators and make sure they align with astrograph and astrocompass. And keep an eye on that fucking drift meter," Sal said. I was standing near the entrance to the cockpit and heard the concern in their voices.

"It is hard to pick up any stars; they are fading in and out," Cole said.

"Do you see the color changing in the horizon on the setting moon? A damn cirrus cloud of ice crystals is forming above at high altitude," Sal said.

"Should we put on our oxygen masks and try to climb above it?" I asked.

"Abraham, shut the fuck up. Those ice crystals are forming above forty thousand feet," JJ said.

"Sal, what about our dead reckoning from our last ground visual reference?" Cole asked.

"Can you guarantee our ground speed, air speed, and drift have been constant since our last fix? We need a fix on two stars soon as possible; if I shout out a fix, log the time. Are all watches synchronized? One minute error could be ten miles," Sal said.

"Do you think we turned north soon enough?" Cole asked.

"That is my concern, if we are too far to the west, we need to correct now. Or we will run out of fuel."

The crew was starting to get nervous. The moon was falling behind the horizon, no stars, just our lone B-17. It was hard to tell up from down. My sense of balance left me and it was impossible for me to understand if the plane was flying level. I could see in the cockpit all gages and dials were lit and functioning.

"Cole! Hold the plane steady. The clouds are getting thin; if the North Star shows itself for just a few seconds, I will get a fix and log the time. Hold on, steady, steady, keep the damn plane steady. The clouds are thinning. There it is! I got it! I need another point of reference, hold on for another break in the clouds. Mark, clock our time and air speed.

The high altitude clouds are thin but I am seeing some faint glimpses of the stars—got it!" Sal said. "Cole, I will have our fix in two minutes, log our fix time 0123 hours and 11 seconds."

"Do we need another fix to be sure?" JJ asked.

"Yes, the plane is not a stable platform, damn it! Cole, we are ninety miles west of our plotted course. If we stay on this course we will be ditching in the North Atlantic," Sal said.

"Get another fix! It could be a bad fix from movement of the sextant bubble. Get another fix to average out any errors," Cole said.

"What in the hell do you think I am trying to do!" Sal said.

The tension in the plane was at an all-time high. We were concerned for our safety and had an important mission to complete.

"Log the time! The clouds are thinning. I got the North Star!" Sal said.

"0157 hours and 33 seconds," Cole said.

"Where the hell are we?" JJ asked.

"Damn it! My readings were right; Cole, turn two more degrees easterly. Mark, double check the math for me; help me calculate the fuel," Sal said.

Mark and Sal were the two best mathematicians in the Army Air Corps. Even if the news was bad, it would be correct.

"Cole, we need to break radio silence. If we can get a radio beacon and fly a direct course we'll make it on fumes," Sal said.

"Mark, what do you think?" Cole asked.

"Sal is right, the fuel numbers don't lie. If we lose our tail wind, we are ditching off the coast of southern England," Mark stated.

Cole broke radio silence and established our direct bearings off a radio beacon. "Look for a fire beacon on the horizon. They are lighting it just south of the runway," Cole said.

Two hours passed. Sal had us located sixty miles southeast of St. Eval, England.

"Damn, it is dark out here, pitch black," JJ said.

"Do you see the glow on the horizon?" Cole asked.

"That must be our fire beacon," JJ said.

We crossed the coast at an altitude of two thousand feet and an air speed of one hundred and fifty miles per hour. The fire beacon was straight ahead. Cole was in complete control of *Sleepytime Gal*. We crossed directly over the fire beacon at three hundred feet and landed with no time to spare.

The thought of landing in England brought mixed emotions. I was glad we made this long trip from America safely; but, England was the end of training and where reality began. The only thing between England and Germany was a wall of deadly flak and German fighters.

As we taxied to a stop, I noticed several of the bombers from my squadron. Several had light damage from battle. We entered the barracks to find out the formation was attacked by German night fighters and two planes were lost. I looked for Jeffrey.

XIV

Two days passed.

A squadron of twelve British Spitfires arrived to escort us to our home base of Horham, England. We all stared at them when they taxied to a stop. With its rounded wingtips and streamline profile, that plane had to be fast. We all knew the reputation of the Spitfire, but to see it in person made a lasting impression. The British pilots met us in the mess hall for dinner and drinks. They were all cocky, full of piss and vinegar, just like Elliot. They talked about defending London and all the air battles along the British coastline.

According to Andrew, the Spitfire command, the slow German bombers were easy to shoot down once they lost their fighter escorts of Me 109s and Fw 190s.

"Tell us what to look for; what are the characteristics of the Me 109 and Fw 190?" Cole asked.

"At low altitude, the Fouke Wolfe 190 has a higher climb, dive, and roll rate than the Spitfire or Messerschmitt 109. The big engine on the Fw 190 gives the pilot poor visibility and at 20,000 feet the Fw 190 loses some of its performance. The pilot of the Me 109 has great visibility and will fly straight at you. The 109 is the pilot killer." Andrew coldly said.

"You will not be shooting at a practice target that is slowly being dragged behind a plane." The other red-headed Spitfire pilot smirked, and lit his pipe.

"Both planes have a top speed of four hundred miles per hour and you better learn how to lead your target. I must admit though, I have a lot of respect for you Yanks. I escorted your bombers over occupied France and you would not break formation. The German fighters would kick your ass; next you would fly through a wall of flak, but never strayed from your target. I was there when you bombed the German submarine bays at Lorient, and Sainte-Nazaire." Andrew took another shot of Scotch and slammed his glass to the table.

We all started taking shots and drank more beer to help block the war from our minds. We got louder and louder. We smoked two cigarettes for every beer with a shot between. Things were getting out of control. Joel was showing off his wrestling skills by putting one of their pilots in a head lock. Greg was talking a bunch of radio and electronic bullshit that no one cared about. Mark and Sal were chasing shots with beer and bonding while they argued with three of the British pilots. Mark told the Brits that baseball was a man's sport and soccer was for girls because you couldn't use your hands. The husky Brit showed him his fist and said "Yank, I will show you what a girl is when I knock your blimey teeth in." JJ was telling everyone what a great boxer I was, to let them know not to pick a fight. The British ladies' man and Kip were trying to figure a way that they could find some girls. Kip didn't care if he lived or died, he only thought about getting laid.

"Ox, show this asshole your fist. This Brit thinks he can kick your ass," a drunken Howard said. Cole, realized things were getting out of hand and ordered us back to our barracks to sleep it off.

Everyone on my crew heard the Spitfire pilot talk about the slow, unescorted bombers getting shot down by the British fighters. No one commented, but we all were thinking the same. That would be us, but the roles would be reversed. We would be the slow bombers getting our asses shot off and dropping from the sky. The shots of Scotch did little to ease my worries.

We met in the mess hall at 0800 to discuss our flight plan to London. The British pilots were all smiles as we entered. "Good morning, mates." Even though we nearly got into a brawl, we had bonded that night.

Howard made the first wise crack at breakfast, "You Brits are lucky we left before you got your asses kicked." Everyone laughed.

After our corned beef hash and poached eggs, the Spitfire squadron leader was the first to speak. "The weather is good and visibility is ten miles. As we approach London, we need to avoid hundreds of anti-aircraft balloons. If you hit a cable, it will slice your wing off. The top brass of the British military will be at the airfield awaiting your arrival. Let's not disappoint them. I have a classified chart that shows the location of the balloons; most are eight to ten thousand feet. We cannot fly over them as we approach the city, so keep your eyes open."

"Should we stay on radio silence as we approach the balloons?" Cole asked.

"I will be on your left wing. I will signal you a thumbs up if I think it is safe to use our radios," the Spitfire pilot answered.

I couldn't understand why we needed to maintain radio silence over England. Maybe they were still concerned about spies giving our location away.

What a perfect morning. We took off at 1000 hours to an altitude of five thousand feet. The English countryside did not disappoint me; it looked just like I had imagined. I loved the old farm houses and small country roads all outlined with hedges and trees. Kip kept true to his pattern and made sexual comments about the English farm girls.

As we approached London, Cole asked me and Mark to join him and JJ in the cockpit to search for balloons. Cole covered all bases and took no chances. The Spitfires were a beautiful sight against the backdrop of London. We circled from the southwest for our approach to the airfield.

I had a pair of binoculars and was looking skyward for balloons.

"Abraham, look on the horizon at eleven o'clock low—what are those flashes and smoke?" Cole asked.

"Look at all those dots in the sky; there must be a thousand balloons," Mark said.

"We are flying into a fucking air raid!" Cole said. We looked over at the Spitfire pilot and he gave us the thumbs up to get off radio silence.

"London is being attacked. I'm going to leave five Spitfires with you and I am going upstairs to join in on the fight," Andrew announced. "Do you think spies gave our position? Could they be after us?" Cole asked.

"No, they have no fighter escort, just bombers." Andrew immediately gained airspeed and climbed with four others to join the fight. The sight of the Spitfire gaining speed and climbing straight up was spectacular and made us all proud.

"William, you and Mark stay in the cockpit and help us look for balloons. Everyone else, get in your battle stations!" Cole said. We were low enough so Cole was not concerned about a belly attack. I could see the empty airfield straight ahead. The Germans were not concerned with a military target and only wanted to kill civilians.

As we landed, the remaining five Spitfires immediately shot straight up to join the fight. They only had enough fuel for one pass at the Germans bombers. I must admit I was impressed with the British pilots' tenacity and eagerness to join the fight.

We landed and several important people approached the plane to meet our passenger. A high ranking American and a British general shook Cole's hand. They shook his hand in a way that made us feel we had just played a major role in the war. Until that moment, I hadn't realized the importance of our mission. The air raid was over as quickly as it had started.

Sleepytime Gal was fueled while we ate lunch. As we ate, we got news that the other twenty-five bombers made it safely to Horham.

"We need to depart as soon as possible if we are going to make Horham before dark." Cole said sternly.

We all finished a quick, late lunch, boarded our plane, and took to the skies. I had one more look at the London skyline as we headed north east toward the coast.

"Everyone man their guns; we have no fighter escort." Cole commanded. I was surprised at that order; we were flying alone over the English countryside at five thousand feet. I used the opportunity to practice flying my ball turret. I picked some stationary ground targets and worked on turning down to the left. My biggest problem was following a target flying from the two o'clock high position crossing under the belly on the plane to the eight o'clock low position. That motion was not natural to me and needed some work.

I hoped there would be a letter from Elaine waiting for me at Horham. In her last letter, she had no updates on Charley, Bert or Roy.

"Cole, can you call out some positions?" I asked.

"Good idea."

We practiced for thirty minutes. Two hours passed and we landed at our new base just as the sun set.

XV

I went straight to the base post office to check for mail. Happily, I found a thick envelope from Elaine. The letter updated me on Elaine's extensive nursing training and her concern she might get too emotionally attached to patients that were near death. The time she spent training in the burn ward made her think war was idiotic. She went on to say over several paragraphs that she would never understand how man could bring this upon himself. I could tell by the tone of her letter she had seen more horrible things than she was revealing in her letter. I knew Elaine, and she kept a lot inside. The only news she had on Charley and Bert was that they had been in some heavy battles in the Pacific theater and were still alive. Roy was in the Army, about to ship over to England for our invasion of occupied Europe. I was shocked by Elaine's post script: *Love, Elaine P.S. Send me a photo of Kip.* How in the hell did Elaine know Kip? I knew there had to be a reason why Kip was hanging around my bunk as I read my letter from Elaine.

"Kip, how in the hell does Elaine know who you are?"

"You showed me that beautiful photo of her, so I wrote her a letter. We are going fishing together after the war." Kip said. This was a new low for even Kip.

"Stay away from my sister! You are only after one thing. Elaine is not that kind of girl!"

"You asked Sal to go fishing with you and Elaine after the war. I guess I am not good enough."

"You can go fishing with Elaine after the war," I said, laughing. We both started laughing. This was a stupid thing to argue about; we just wanted to survive this damned war.

Cole and the other pilots walked into our barracks that held thirty enlisted men from our squadron. Three of the experienced squadrons would be departing at 0600 hours on a classified mission over Germany. We were scheduled for three training missions before we joined the fight. We would take off at 1000 hours, and the mission was to learn the coastline.

"Why are we waiting so long to depart?" Joel asked.

"They will need at least two hours to build their formation of three hundred planes. Bomber groups are assembling just south east of Horham near the coast before their run to Germany. We need to stay out of their way. Our mission will be only four hours; we need to land before they return to Horham," Cole advised.

Every thirty seconds another B-17 full of bombs took off. We all stood near Hangar 4 and quietly watched the bombers depart for Germany.

We were only three missions away. We saw other bomber groups from airfields north of Horham approaching to join the circling ballet.

Kip wanted me to walk three hundred yards to visit the damaged decommissioned B-17s that were saved for parts. I was afraid of what I might see, but decided to make the sad walk to the B-17 boneyard. As we approached, I heard the cold, damp breeze whistling through the thousands of flak and bullet holes. I was surprised at the number of planes; there had to be over a hundred, each with its own story. The first plane we looked inside was littered with empty cartridge cases and dried blood. There were so many holes; I didn't know how *Twin Peaks* ever made it back to Horham.

"Kip, I don't want to see anymore. Let's get back to our barracks and prepare for our mission."

The coastline of England was spectacular from eight thousand feet. The majestic cliffs reminded me of the Northern Pacific coastline. We spotted reference points and practiced honing in on radio beacons used for assembly points. Greg had no problem directing us to the several beacons used as assembly points. We flew over radio beacon Buncher 8, down to Splasher 6, and finally Splasher 7. Those would be our assembly points as we circled and gained altitude to cross the English Channel.

We landed back at Horham at 1600 hours, well before the groups from occupied Europe returned. We quickly completed all the mundane tasks required after a mission. We all were concerned, and anxiously gathered under the airfield's observation tower. The wooden tower was over thirty feet tall with a fenced walkway circling the top floor.

After twenty minutes, we noticed the base commander and his staff walking out onto the balcony. They were all holding binoculars and looking toward the east. The first to point out the approaching bombers was Colonel Renner. They knew the losses were heavy, but hoped for the best. We learned as they approached that their mission was the rail yards in Munster, a vital junction point between Germany's northern coastal ports and the heavily industrial area of the Ruhr Valley. The area was defended by Germany's best fighter pilots.

From a mile away, we could tell many of the planes were damaged and struggling to stay in the air. Parts of wings and tails were missing, some had trails of smoke, and others could not lower their landing gear. We heard the engines sputtering; some propellers were not turning. Then the red flares started to drop from the bombers with injured crew members. The ambulance and rescue teams readied themselves. The scramble to save the injured and remove the dead was unsettling.

One day passed. Horham was famous for its club, The Red Feather. The club had murals, painted by the airmen, and was packed with B-17 crews drinking and smoking. We went there to have fun and forget the war for a while.

One of the bomber pilots was alone with his thoughts, beer, and empty shot glasses. He had strong features with a mature look and pencil-thin mustache. He was one of the older pilots with a touch of gray on his side burns. All my crew members were busy, so I decided to strike up a conversation.

"I'm William Abraham; would you like a smoke?" He reached out and took one without saying a word. He took a deep drag from the cigarette; slowly let the smoke out from his mouth and nose, and looked me straight in the eye with a condescending look.

"Kid, you don't know shit. If we don't get fighter cover in and out of Germany, we are going to lose this damn war. Do you fucking realize how bad we were slaughtered over Schweinfurt and Munster?"

"What happened over Schweinfurt?" I asked.

"They conceived an ambitious plan to fly a double strike mission deep into Germany and cripple the German aircraft industry. After several weather delays, the mission was flown on the damned anniversary of the first daylight bombing raids by the Eighth Air Force. The 4th Bombardment Wing reached target at Regensburg, Germany before we crossed the English Channel. That gave the German fighters time to refuel and arm before we reached Schweinfurt. The bomber missions had to be simultaneous to have any chance. We crossed into Germany with nine B-17 groups organized into three bomber wings. Protocol called for us to fly between twenty-three thousand and twenty-six thousand five hundred feet. Due to cloud cover, our formation had to stay under seventeen thousand feet, making us extremely vulnerable to the German fighters and flak."

"Where was your plane in the formation?"

"The worst goddamned spot! We were in the bottom of lead formation, in the tail end Charlie slot. We must have been a hell of a target against the white sky," the pilot said as he slammed down his shot glass.

"How did they attack your formation?"

"Our formation was twenty miles long as we approached the target. Our lead squadron was attacked continuously from underneath and head-on by both Me 109 and Fw 190 fighters. My plane took a .20mm round from a Me 109, and it put a hole in the fuselage a foot in diameter. The belly gunner in the lead plane took a 20mm round to the head. They couldn't reach him on the intercom, so the waist gunners opened his hatch and discovered his headless body. If you survive the fighters, you run a gauntlet through a barrage of flak. I have seen many planes get ripped to shreds or explode from a flak burst. After our bombing run, the fighters returned."

"Was the mission successful?"

"Hell no, we lost thirty-six bombers and hundreds of lives and missed most of the targets. Some of the mission planners blamed it on bomb drift and others blamed it on smoke blocking the bombardiers view. The crews on the mission know the real reason." He slurred his words to another shot of bourbon.

"What was the real reason?"

"You really are a dumb shit! We were getting annihilated forty-five minutes before we even started our bombing run. We didn't have fighter cover and those bastards were waiting for us. Our formations were loose and all crews were trying to just survive. Don't pass judgment; you have no fucking idea what is waiting for you! We will be going back to Schweinfurt soon to finish the job."

"I volunteered for this war and understand I may die," I said.

"Die, or worse," the mystery man said as he chuckled and drank more beer.

"What do you mean worse?"

Shell shocked! Blinded! A limb perfectly dissected from your body. This war can really fuck your mind up. One of those red flares yesterday was for a pilot I respect highly. He was the best pilot in the god damned Army Air Corps. He didn't have a wound on him, but after twenty-three missions got a case of frozen stick and his co-pilot had to fly the plane home. Kid, you don't know shit." And he downed another full beer and slammed it on the table.

"Is he going to be all right?"

"None of us will ever be the same. To see someone suffering from shell shock is the saddest thing in war. Their mind has a fear overload, and they may live the rest of their lives mumbling and yelling meaningless words in a state of uncontrollable terror. Joe saw the 100th bomber group get slaughtered by head-on attacks. His squadron was trailing offset one level higher to the left. They got the next wave of German fighters. It was a feeding frenzy. The plane to his right got hit head on by a German fighter plane that miscalculated his attack angle. Both planes exploded, allowing no survivors. Joe started to rub his face with his gloves, over and over, covering his eyes. The new co-pilot asked several times if he was OK with no response. He started shaking uncontrollably and mumbled hysterically. He may take years to recover, or stay in the condition for the remainder of his life."

"What happened to his last co-pilot?" I asked.

"On Joe's mission over Bremen those German bastards were relentless. His co-pilot took one to the head. The only thing visible was his lower jaw. Joe flew the remainder of the mission with his co-pilot to his right; I think that sight really fucked him up. The crew members were too busy tending to a severely injured waist gunner and could not remove the co-pilot's body from his chair until they were over the English Channel. Joe seemed to become very distant and on edge after that mission. They should have given him a break after that mission. You could tell he was at the breaking point."

"He should have been grounded."

"You never know when you may lose it. Joe flew on some of the most deadly bombing runs in the war."

I started to visualize that scene and the disfigured look of the co-pilot, and immediately tried to block that image.

"Kid, you can't be very smart if you volunteered to be belly gunner. That is the worst place to be on a B-17. You have no chance to bail out if the plane starts to roll over. If your plane gets shot down, you will die in that fucking ball turret. I am not trying to scare you, just get out soon as you can. Most of the belly gunners go down with the plane."

"What is your name?" I asked.

"Red Wright."

"Captain Wright, you don't know what in the hell you are talking about. I will make it home!"

Others heard our discussion and joined the table. Red slammed down another beer picked up the whisky bottle and poured a round of shots. He was the first to drink his shot and then slammed it to the table to let everyone know he was about to hold court. Others stood around the table. Judge Red Wright was drunk with a resentful, scowling demeanor. He was angry about the war and I was his vehicle to vent.

"Kid, you don't fucking get it! We are being sent on suicide missions. I told the commanding general that the day light missions should stop until we can fly with fighter cover. Do you know what that bastard said?"

"What!"

"'Accept the high possibility of death, don't think about going home. Thinking about going home will only add to your anxiety.' The sad thing is, that bastard is probably right."

"Red, we will survive the war and I look forward to having a drink with you back home."

Red reached across the table and helped himself to one of my Chesterfields, lit up, and looked me in the eye.

"Do you think you will go home the same person? You have not seen what I have seen. This war is going to enter your soul and change the person you are. You will be haunted by the death you see until the day you die."

"Red, you are letting the whiskey talk. You will see things differently in the morning."

"It's not that we die, it is how we die! When the German fighters appear and you see the flashes from their 20mm, you will pray to almighty

God himself. You will pray for a painless death. If you are lucky the plane will explode before the spin back to earth."

"I'm ready to die for my country."

"I have seen hundreds of my friends die horrible deaths for their country. Will you be the big hero, ready to die for your country when the plane rolls over and you see the blue sky above for the last time?" Red drank another shot of whisky and continued to rant. "What do you think it was like for those hundreds of airmen that were pinned to the walls of their planes as they violently spun out of control? What about the belly gunner from the 92nd from Podington who was trapped in the turret?

"What about him?"

"That poor bastard's turret gears locked up due to a flak hit. His crew couldn't get the landing gear down by hydraulics or manually. His turret was frozen in position with no way out. The only thing working was his oxygen. His crew struggled for three hours to get the landing gear down and repair the gears. He begged them on the intercom system to get him out. The plane was shot to hell and should have never made it back to England."

"What happened?"

"When his crew's attempts failed repeatedly, he knew the inevitable was approaching. The clock started to wind down when he was over the North Sea. His crew said he began to pray out loud as his plane crossed the cliffs of England. The crew kept working frantically to unlock the gears to the turret. The damage was so severe that they knew their attempt was in vain. When the Captain informed the crew that he could only keep the plane airborne for twenty more minutes, his waist gunners looked at the belly gunner through the small viewing hole and said he was calm. As the bomber approached the runway, the belly gunner looked down at the farmland and started talking about his childhood. His life must have been flashing in front him. He spoke to the crew about their fun times together as the plane made its final approach. The crew was silent as the plane descended below one hundred feet; they used every possible tool aboard to free the turret but failed their friend and crewmate. They battled that gear frantically until the plane skidded to a sad stop. They witnessed helplessly the death of a belly gunner."

The mood at our table changed after Red's story. We parted ways after our last beer and a cigarette. I don't know if I made a friend or enemy with Red. Either way, soon we would depart faithfully on a mission over Germany.

XVI

"Due to the heavy losses, our training has been cut short and we are going on the next mission," Cole informed us.

"When and where?" Mark asked.

"Within the next three days, we are just waiting on the weather. The assembly will be over two hours and will involve several air fields. I will not be told the target until the morning of the mission."

Several more meaningless questions were asked by the crew. Cole could not give us any specifics. The target location and details of the mission were highly confidential due to concerns about spies. The odds of spies in the Army Air Corps were low, but we spent a lot of time with the civilians in Horham. The civilians seemed loyal to England and America, but why take a chance?

Dear Sister Elaine, October 13th 1943

Elaine, I wanted to write you and tell you how much I love you, Mom, and Dad. By the time you get this letter I will have flown my first mission. I am scared, but fully understand my role in this war. Always remember that I volunteered of my own free will and always understood the risk. I have the best commander and crew in the Eighth Air Force and if anyone survives the 25 missions it will be us and Sleepytime Gal. They have cut our training missions short because they need every available plane. We have been waiting for the weather to clear and I think tomorrow will be the day. If something happens to me, I want you to tell Mom and Dad how much I love them. Think of me only in a happy way. If I do not return, I will be in a German prison camp or the arms of God Almighty. Remember our oath to each other. That is how you can honor my life. Live on with your life and be happy.

Love Always,

William

Cole came into our barracks after briefing in the mission control center. "We have a mission tomorrow; takeoff is 0700 hours. We will be told the target during our morning briefings. Wake up will be at 0330 hours. Get some rest; see you in the morning." Cole's directions were clear.

The night passed with very little sleep. At 0330 hours, Cole entered the barracks with JJ. "Everyone meet in the mess hall in thirty minutes for breakfast; your briefings are scheduled for 0445 hours."

I was the last to leave our barracks. Before walking out the door I looked back; all beds were made tightly and crisp, with green flat lockers at the foot. Would I see this room again? Would my foot looker and belongings be quickly processed to make room for my replacement?

It was difficult for any of us to eat. I could tell the experienced crews from the rookies; they were eating the scrambled eggs, potatoes and toast; some were joking. Howard and Kip nervously smoked a pack of cigarettes for breakfast. I had black coffee with my pack of Lucky Strikes. Before I left my barracks, I stared at the date on my pin-up calendar: Thursday, October 14. Would that be the date on my head stone? Would this be the day it all came to an end?

The gunner's pilots, navigators, bombardiers and radio men had separate, specialized briefings. I entered the briefing room and sat next to Jeffrey. The briefing officer did not mince words.

"The target is Schweinfurt."

The veterans in the room groaned. The briefing officer continued.

"It is important that you don't run out of ammo during an attack; the ground crews installed the tracers to change to red for the last hundred rounds. Top gunners, keep your eyes open. The Germans are using the Junker 88's, the night fighter, and Junker 87's to dive bomb the lower formations; they will be slow due to their fixed landing gear, but dangerous. The Messerschmitt 110s and 210s will stay out of the range and shoot rockets into the formation. You will lose your outbound fighter cover near Aachen and they will pick you up on the return route. Make every shot count."

After the briefings, all flyers met in the crew room adjacent to the mess hall to put on their cold weather gear and pick up escape kits.

Several crews gathered near the mess hall to catch a ride. The jeeps passed, going at moderate speeds; there were officers with their handsome, leather-billed hats to the right of the driver and several crew members dangling their legs off the side of the jeeps. Most everyone was smoking a cigarette; there was very little conversation, only a serious demeanor existed. Trucks with and without canvas tops shuttled most of the crews to the waiting bombers. Kip and I joined Jeffrey's crew on a truck with metal framing only. We were the first stop.

"Ox, I will see you for a beer at the Red Feather Club," Jeffrey said with a smile.

Kip and I said "beers on us," as we jumped off the back of the open truck.

Horham Airfield was large, with three intersecting runways going in different directions to accommodate the wind. Most of the bombers were armed at night near the eight circular areas attached to the runways. The base was in motion, the ground crew methodical and deliberate. In contrast, the morning was quiet and still; no wind, just a thin mist in the low lying areas with some moisture on top of the grass from dew. The sun was beginning to rise with a filtered, yellow cast.

Cole and the remainder of my crew arrived at the plane in separate jeeps. We all met under the wing of the great bomber as Cole touched on many important issues.

"JJ, it is important that we do not deviate from our climbing slope of three hundred feet per minute and maintain our ground speed of one hundred and fifty miles per hour. There will be three hundred planes assembling; we have to be in our designated location as we pass through the clouds. Greg, lock on those beacons and work with Sal on our location fix. Kip, make sure the trailing planes pick up your lamp as we assemble."

"Where are we in the formation?" I asked.

"Bottom squadron of the bottom group."

Our bomber group of twenty-one planes, comprised of three squadrons, would be separated by eight hundred and fifty feet from bottom plane to top plane. When we assembled with the other bomber groups, we would build the formation to four thousand feet. This was a maximum effort mission; all available bombers would be in the air, over three hundred. Planes would assemble from airfields in Podington, Thorpe Abbotts, Molesworth, Chelveston, Bury St. Edmunds, Thurleigh, Kimbolton, Ridgewell, Grafton Underwood, Polebrook, Bassingbourn, Glatton and other locations spread out over England. We needed to assemble as fast as possible. We had three thousand, one hundred gallons of fuel; our overage was figured at four hundred gallons.

"What did you find out during the weather briefing?" Mark asked Cole.

"Over the target they predict 20-40% high clouds and 20-50% middle clouds—visibility five to six miles. On the return route 50-70% low clouds as we approach the North Sea. Freeze point seven thousand feet, thirty-two degrees below zero over target at twenty-three thousand feet."

"What is our bomb load?" JJ asked Mark.

"We are delivering fourteen five hundred pound general purpose bombs. The bomb time delay is set to detonate based on the target's construction and estimated impact speed. My target point will have a large L-shaped, light-colored roof just west of a large, tall smoke stack. We will cross the city before reaching the target point. The target is located on the northwest side of the city next to the bend in the Main River. There is a bridge that crosses the Main next to my target point. If the weather holds, I will hit the target."

"Mark, double check the bomb racks. Let's all board the plane and start our preflight!" Cole commanded.

Cole's voice was always professional and serious, but this time it was more than deliberate with purpose. He went down the check list with complete conviction; he triple checked the intercom system, emphasizing the importance of communication.

I entered the rear door of the tilted bomber which sat on its tail wheel. Walking in front of me, wearing his cold weather suit and parachute, was Howard; behind was me Joel. To my right was the generator and Kip's tail gun position; to my left the offset waist gunner windows with .50 caliber machine guns and their nine yard belts of ammunition; past that was my ball turret topped with two belts of bullets ready to feed. Between the two belts of ammo and my white oxygen tank, I could see the backs of Cole and JJ, already in their seats, busy preparing to taxi. Greg was putting his head phones on for his first radio check; Sal was walking back and forth from the navigator's position to the cockpit discussing last minute details with Cole and JJ.

We were all scared but alert with adrenaline, on edge but focused. I wondered if my emotions were similar to those of the gladiators of ancient Rome. How could they be any different? A fight to the death; that was what we had in common. I was going to kill a German fighter pilot before he killed me; a person I could have laughed and share a beer with in a different time and place.

I moved to the front of the plane to see the long line of bombers slowly waiting for their turn to take off. Every thirty seconds was the schedule; all planes had to be airborne to start climbing to the assembly point soon as possible. The mission deep into Germany had to begin in less than two and a half hours to meet our fuel window. Bombers had to be in formation at twenty-five thousand feet before we crossed the English coast. Our turn came for takeoff. Cole turned *Sleepytime Gal* to the left to face the open runway. As the plane in front of us lifted off the ground, Cole gave our bomber full throttle and our flying fortress, heavy with bombs and ten scared crew members, began to gain speed. Due to the weight, we vibrated and shook more than before; the motors were unusually loud pulling us down the runway, but finally we lifted off the ground to begin our climb.

The assembly point was just south of Horham, which meant that that our climb had a tighter circular pattern than the other squadrons.

"Everyone double check all oxygen connections; keep your eyes on the oxygen lines and connections over Germany. Make sure no leaks get near a fire. We just crossed eight thousand feet; prepare to go on oxygen," Cole ordered.

As we circled, Joel and I could see the eight squadrons, with over one hundred planes, approaching from the north. I moved to the left waist gunner's window and Mike Gavin pointed out the high squadrons moving through the clouds to our southwest.

"Ten Thousand feet—oxygen masks on," Cole commanded.

I could hear General Kemper and Colonel LaSalle on the radio.

"Lead squadron, tighten your formation."

"All squadron leaders maintain climb slope and ground speed entering the clouds"

"Lower squadrons, close in and hold position."

Kip was in the tail of the plane using his Aldis lamp to help build our four thousand foot high, twenty mile long formation.

Forty minutes passed. I could hear the pitch of the motors change as our plane leveled out at twenty-three thousand feet. I looked out both waist gunner windows and saw bombers for miles, lined up horizontally, vertically and offset in a perfect order. Some white puffy clouds passed as the formation moved to the east.

"Crossing over the English coastline," Cole announced.

I noticed Jeffrey's plane *Show Girl* was in the tail end Charlie position, flying directly behind us at the six o'clock level. Our paths intersected in Galveston; at sixteen we were carefree; suddenly at eighteen we were scared and facing a horrible death, both of us belly gunners, just a hundred feet apart at twenty three thousand feet.

"Approaching the coast; all gunners man your stations," Cole commanded.

I rotated the gun barrel toward the ground to expose my hatch. Mike and Joel helped lower me in to the ball. I only carried my relief tube, leaving my flak jacket on the floor and my parachute wedged against the wall and Greg's radio gear. I made Joel and Mike aware of that fact in the event I needed their help to retrieve my parachute for a quick exit.

The weather was cold and clear, and our vapor trails were long and bright white against the blue sky. Our position no longer a secret, the German fighter pilots were scrambling for the kill.

To my left, the Netherlands; to my right, the coastline of France; below me, the cold, gray, choppy waters of the North Sea; behind me, America and the life I missed; in front of me, three hundred German fighters and a wall of flak.

"We are approaching the coast of Belgium; the flak officer gave us a route to avoid the shore battery. We may encounter naval fire. Sal, what is our first reference point?" Cole asked calmly.

"The railroad tracks that run east to west from the coast and should be visible to our right; the port city of Amsterdam should be barely visible to our north."

"What is our ETA over target?"

"1430 hours"

"What is our ETA for the IP point?"

"1350 hours. We will hold our assigned heading until we reach the IP point, the turn for our bombing run will be forty-five degrees true. The low bomb group will turn toward the target first."

"We are crossing the coastline of Belgium," Cole announced.

I closed my eyes for a moment. I had a clear picture of Mom, Dad, and Elaine. I could see their faces. I opened my eyes to block the thought of going home out of my mind.

"Four German fighters, two o'clock high!" JJ shouted.

"They are attacking the top squadron. Where is our damn fighter escort?" Howard said from his top turret.

"Did you see that closing speed of those fighters? They came out of nowhere. Every one keep your eyes open," Cole said with concern.

"They are making another pass on the third element on the top squadron. Son of a bitch, he is right on their ass." Joel said from the right waist gunner's position.

The fight was two thousand feet above me and out of my view.

"They are getting hammered. Where are the P-47s?" Cole asked.

"Smoke is coming from the number three engine of the last plane!" Howard yelled.

"Christ, did you see that? Get out! Oh shit they are going down. Bail out! Get out of that damn plane. Did you see that! The whole right wing came off the plane!" Joel shouted in a panic.

"Calm down. Look for parachutes," Cole ordered.

"Here they come at them again. They are going after the pilots," JJ said.

I was scanning for the B-17. The burning bomber came into my view as it passed below the formation. The plane with one wing was in a flat, counterclockwise spin, leaving a spiraling trail of smoke. Not one parachute was in sight.

"A second bomber is hit and slowly falling behind the formation, trailing a lot of smoke. Those bastards are making another pass to finish it off," Howard said.

"They are going down!" Joel yelled.

The second falling bomber came into my view. "I have seven parachutes! Wait, two more crew members leaving the plane. I have nine chutes!" I yelled.

One of the crew members didn't make it off that bomber. I knew he was the belly gunner. Before German fighters could make another pass, our P-47 Thunderbolts joined the fight. The dog fight between the swift fighters took place below me, just south of our element.

"Ox, keep an eye on those fighters. They might break free and make a pass at the bottom of our formation," Cole calmly said.

"The German fighters are making a run for it," I said.

"Did the P-47s stay with the formation?"

"Yes."

"They are climbing back above the formation," Howard said.

I noticed Jeffrey's ball turret followed the falling bombers. I wondered what thoughts went through his mind. What in hell did those belly gunners experience? Was the belly gunner the tenth man in the second falling bomber? That was what we both were thinking.

I was becoming very uncomfortable and needed to get out and stretch my legs before I had a claustrophobic anxiety attack. I needed to calm down and get my mental strength back.

"We are twenty minutes from crossing the Rhine River into Germany," Sal said.

"We are going to lose our fighter cover near Aachen; that is only ten minutes after we cross into Germany," Cole reminded us.

"I see the Rhine," JJ said.

"Where?" Cole asked.

"Just short of the horizon, look you can see the sun reflecting off the water where the river turns."

"I got it, I see it now. Are the fighters still with us"?

I could hear Howard's turret turning. "They are above us at six o'clock high," Howard said.

"Let me know when they turn back," Cole ordered.

I was thinking about what Red said that night at the Red Feather Club. I know he is in the squadron above us, scared about what is going to happen when our fighters turn back.

"We are crossing the Rhine into Germany," Cole announced.

"Do you think they will roll out the welcome mat for us?" Howard said, joking.

"Maybe a German Fraulein will pay us a visit," Kip said.

"Maybe they will send up a big-breasted blonde to serve us beer," Howard answered.

"Keep the intercom open and cut the shit," Cole ordered.

"One hour and twenty minutes to IP point," Sal announced.

"Our fighters are turning back!" Mike Gavin said from his left waist gunner position.

Ten minutes passed.

Mark manned the chin turret and was determined to protect Cole and JJ from the Messerschmitt 109s. All three thousand crewmen aboard the B-17s were searching the skies for German fighters. It was just a matter of time.

"Cole, what count does intelligence give for the German fighters?" Mark asked.

"They said the Germans will have three hundred fighters available to protect Schweinfurt, and many will refuel during our bomb run and trail us back to our fighter cover. Due to our bombing raids, they have moved fighters from the Russian and African fronts to protect Germany. Some of those crazy bastards may even follow us into the flak."

"What did the flak officer say in his briefing?

"They have added gun batteries to defend the plant. Flak will be extremely heavy during your bomb run. How long do you need control of the plane?"

"The bomb run is scheduled for six minutes."

"I need to give you the plane for six minutes? Why so long?" Commander Cole asked.

"They don't want us to miss this time. I have reference points I need to hit as we move toward the target."

"German fighters two o'clock high!" Howard shouted.

"Ox, watch our belly," Cole said.

There were only six B-17s to my left, two hundred ninety bombers to my right and above me, and no bombers below me. We were scanning all positions but concentrating mostly on the twelve o'clock low to nine o'clock low. Behind me was Jeffrey in *Show Girl*; they were in the tail end Charlie position, so they had better watch their back side.

"Ox, look at the deck eleven o'clock low. Do you see that?" Cole asked.

"It's got to be fighters moving that fast."

"It looks like they are trying to circle around behind us."

"They are at least three miles to our north. I will keep an eye on them."

Howard opened up with both .50 caliber machine guns as the first wave of German fighter passed far overhead, out of realistic range. The sound was poignant, the first defensive shots fired from *Sleepytime Gal*.

"The fighters are climbing and circling around behind us," I said.

"How many?" Cole asked with distress.

"Twelve."

"Kip, be ready."

"Six 109's twelve o'clock level!" JJ shouted with fear and anxiety.

"Mark, do you have them?" Cole asked.

"Yes, they are coming right at us!" Mark said with trepidation.

"Two dive bombers three o'clock high breaking through the formation, heading straight for us!" Howard shouted.

"The fighters are closing in behind us!" Kip informed.

In a long, terrifying moment, twelve of our .50 caliber machine guns were firing at the same time. *Sleepytime Gal* was vibrating and shaking from our guns as we trembled with fear. I saw a small piece of *Show Girls*'s wing come off as the trailing Fw 190s made their pass. As the German fighter crossed our paths we let them have it, but no hits.

"Forty minutes to our IP point," Sal announced.

"Three bombers going down. One bomber smoking and falling behind. Those bastards are circling around to finish them off!" Joe hollered with fright.

"Cole, stay on heading two ninety-nine until IP point," Sal called out.

"Four 109s one o'clock high!" Howard shouted.

When I heard Howard and the waist gunners open fire, I would flame their asses as they passed under the plane. The most effective way to use a machine gun was to lay out a field of fire and hope the German fighter passed through. The fighters were too fast to lead.

Howard and Joel opened fire with their .50 caliber machine guns, and I opened fire with a long burst at a point just under the right wing. The second fighter passed front to end through my concentrated grouping of bullets. I could see the tracer bullets tearing off the yellow tail of the

Me 109. I quickly turned my turret to the left to follow; the fighter pilot lost control as the nose of the plane turned upward. The plane tumbled, then slowly rolled over into an inverted flat spin. The plane fell for what seemed like thirty seconds, and finally I saw the pilot appear from under the plane and open his parachute. I was glad to see him survive.

"Great shot, Abraham!" Mike yelled.

"Two fighters, twelve o'clock level, coming straight at us!" Mark shouted out.

"They are going after the bomber to our right!" JJ yelled as Mark and Howard opened fire.

Pieces and smoke were trailing behind several bombers. Bombers kept falling from the sky. The air battle was going badly, everywhere. The great B-17s were being humbled as they folded over and fell through the formations. With the sun shining through the smoke, everything still seemed cold and dark. My oxygen had the taste of disaster. I swung my turret three hundred and sixty degrees and saw the German fighters stalking us from every direction. From above, from below, to my right, and to the left, the attack continued. A bomber fell from above, through the formation, and almost hit us. I saw the face of the belly gunner as the plane passed.

"Four Fw's, seven o'clock low, coming up behind us!" I shouted.

I saw the two fighters pass after their frontal attack on the bomber to our right. They flew by so fast I didn't have a shot.

"I think they got the pilot of the bomber on my side. Look, he is leaning over; they shot his window out," Joel said.

137

The four fighters started to close in from the rear. They concentrated their fire on tail end Charlie. I could not get a shot off because they were perfectly aligned with Jeffrey's plane. I could see pieces of the motor cowl and tail section of the *Show Girl* fly off as the 20mm cannon fire hit its mark. I got one burst off as the four German fighters passed below me. I could see one of my rounds hit the canopy of the third German fighter.

"Tail end Charlie's number three engine is on fire," Kip shouted.

I took my eye off passing fighters and spun my turret to the rear to check on Jeffrey's plane.

"What happened! Where in the hell is *Show Girl?*" I screamed out.

"The plane exploded! One minute they were there, then they were gone, the plane fucking exploded! No one got out!" Kip yelled.

I saw many of the bombers explode from engine fires.

"Another bomber is going down from the middle formation," JJ said.

"Here they come again. Six fighters, twelve o'clock level. They are coming straight at us!" Howard shouted.

I could hear Howard and Mark giving them all nine yards from dual .50 caliber machine guns. The plane to our right started to slowly fall behind and I noticed both pilots leaning over. The entire front windshield was gone.

"The pilots can't give the order to bail out—no one is leaving the plane!" I yelled. The right wing dipped and dug into the air causing the plane to roll over. I could see the belly gunner as the plane showed its bottom. Then a violent fast spin followed the first slow spin as the great bomber fell to earth. The spin back to earth was fast; no parachutes were seen.

"Ten minutes to IP point," Sal said calmly.

Twenty more German fighters joined the attack. For the first time they were penetrating the box formation in large numbers. As I swung my turret to the rear of my plane, I could see two bombers diving nose first with a slow spin. The pilots must have been shot; I could see no damage or smoke. Airmen started exiting both planes; they seemed to fall at the same speed as the bomber. They must have purposely delayed the opening of their parachutes. Either they were avoiding contact with the German fighters or searching for breathable air. It was an eerie sight to see them falling with the massive bombers. I would never forget that sight.

"The fighters are breaking off the attack!" JJ said.

"German bombers equipped with rockets have been following our formation. Intelligence said they will have either a time or proximity fuse," Cole said.

"Here they come. Look at that, can you believe how fast they are? They are exploding in the middle of the upper formation. Son of a bitch, those rockets are fast," Kip said from his tail gunner position.

The rockets caused no damage; I could see the German fighter circling below the formation, waiting to attack. Normally they would circle above the formation to gain a height advantage. The plan must have been to attack us from below as soon as the rocket assault was over. My ball turret was stuffy and confining but I was too scared to open my hatch or even think about looking away. The Germans had come with four squadrons of fighters, twelve per group. They would like to take us down soon as possible. It was midafternoon, cold and clear, the metal on the plane cold and dry.

I rubbed my face with my right glove as I put my left hand behind my head on the trigger of the left machine gun. Then I put my right hand behind my head on my right machine gun handle. I steered the ball downward to survey the circling fighters.

"Three minutes to IP point," Sal announced. There was no changing course or evasive action; we were trained to be steadfast and never turn back. "Cole, turn north forty-five degrees true on my mark," Sal commanded as navigator.

"Ox, be ready. When the lower group turns, the fighters below will attack," Cole said.

"Turn on my mark. Five, four, three, two, one—turn on new heading for final bomb run." Sal ordered. The lower wing of twenty-one planes turned toward Schweinfurt. Each level of the formation would turn every ninety seconds. This would narrow the formation and concentrate the bomb's force on the target. We would pass over the target twenty minutes before the last plane. The German citizens would endure twenty minutes of nonstop bombs.

The fighters seemed to dive low, as to gain speed. They were right below me going in the opposite direction. The first three fighters rolled to the left and began to climb straight for me. It was as if they had picked my plane to destroy. German fighters were five thousand feet below me and closing fast.

"Three fighters at six o'clock low heading straight at me!" I informed the crew. Twenty seconds passed. "Mark, they are going to pass right in front of the plane," I said.

I was waiting to torch their asses when they passed in the front of the plane. "Come on, you fuckers," I whispered to myself. The German fighters had yellow spirals painted on the nose of the propellers that spun impressively as they approached. The sun was also shining on their yellow wing tips and the black and yellow checkered tail section.

They shot first. I could see flashes, and then I let them have it. I laid out a long, loud burst from both barrels. Immediately the first fighter caught on fire and fell back. The second fighter opened fire at point blank range, tearing through the back of the plane. The fighters did not break off early and did just what I predicted; they passed within a hundred feet of our plane and Mark opened fire. The second fighter burst into flames and spun out of control.

I knew we were hit, and I was scared for my crew.

"Sound off! Is everyone all right!" Cole commanded.

Everyone checked in but Kip.

Then we heard Kip's voice. "Four fighters six o'clock level."

I was never so glad to hear about German fighters. We opened fire as they passed below us.

"We got hit with several rounds just in front of the generator. I don't see any damage to our electrical, hydraulic or oxygen systems, but we have significant structural damage and could lose the tail section if we get a strong shock wave from flak burst or get hit with more rounds in the area of the fuselage," Sal reported.

"Four more bombers are going down, and three are falling behind the formation with engine problems," JJ informed us. We had lost over twenty bombers and had not even started our six minute bomb run.

"Twenty minutes to bomb run," Mark said.

"Holy shit! Look at that," JJ said. I spun my turret to the front of the plane and saw a black wall of flak. For the first time, I totally accepted death. There was no way we could survive this bomb run. There was absolutely no way I would live. This would be my last day on earth.

"The fighters are returning to base to refuel and will be waiting for us on the other side of the flak," Cole said. Mark and Sal took this time to review the bomb run and verify our exact position.

You could hear the explosions of the flak over the loud noise of our engines. The shock waves delivered violent jolts. I could hear the plane get showered with small, fast-moving pieces of metal. Dark balls of black smoke from the flak burst past beneath me

I could see flashes from the large, German guns twenty thousand feet below.

"Ox, your flak jacket saved our asses," Joel said. I could see several holes on the bottom of the plane from flak. I felt a cool sensation on my back; no pain, just a cold spot in the middle of my back. The flak intensified. I saw four more bombers fall under the formation, spinning out of control. The first plane to pass my view had no left wing and was spinning faster than I thought possible. Hopefully the violent spin caused the crew to pass out and live through the horrifying, three minute fall. The second plane fell nose-first, making a slow turn to the left while it gained tremendous speed. The third plane was upside down in a flat spin. I could see the tail was missing, and two of the engines were on fire. The fourth plane passed directly under me. The front of the plane was gone. The cockpit was sheared off. I could see inside the plane as it fell away tail first.

"Cole, thirty seconds to bomb run," Mark said.

"We are approaching the city."

"The target will be on the north side of the Main River next to a train bridge. A large, L-shaped building with a large smoke stack."

The bomb bay doors opened. The plane was being pushed, shoved and jerked in several directions. How would Mark be able to keep his head on the eye piece to the bomb site?

"Cole, I am taking control of the plane!" Mark said. Three more bombers went down. The count must have been over forty planes; four hundred volunteers lost. I understood why we were rushed us into service. This week, we got slaughtered over Regensburg, Munster, and now Schweinfurt.

Two more bombers go down.

"We hit all our approach marks. Thirty seconds to the target. Jesus Christ, keep the plane steady," Mark said to himself out loud.

"I see the target through the flak!" Cole shouted.

"I got it coming into view on my bomb sight. Steady, steady—I got it—bombs away!" Mark said.

I saw the large, five hundred pound bombs slip away past the bomb bay doors. I forgot about the flak and followed the bombs all the way down. The sky was filled with thousands of bombs. The first hit just south of the target; then, like machine gun fire, the bombs hit the target in rapid successions. Quiet flashes of yellow and red were followed by smoke.

Cole took the plane back from Mark, and the remaining bombers turned back to the west toward the North Atlantic. We had a specific return route and a rendezvous point with our fighter cover.

"Mark, give us a damage report," Cole ordered.

"We have several small holes in the floor just aft of the waist gunners. One large hole was eight inches in diameter above the generator."

"The controls are vibrating. What about outside?"

"There is a piece of the tail wing missing. Three foot long and one foot deep."

Then a loud flak burst just left of the plane. The plane jumped to the right with a jarring jolt. I could hear the flak rip through the metal skin of the fuselage.

"Joel got hit!" Mike said.

"How is he?" Cole asked.

"Multiple wounds to his thigh, right knee and right arm."

"How bad is he?"

"He is conscious—I think they are superficial."

"Everyone, back on your guns! Here come the fighters! Sal, man Joel's waist gun. Greg, get on the radio and check the status of our fighter escort."

"They are just taking off; they got delayed due to weather," Greg said.

"You got to be shitting me!"

"No, the front got to the British Isles earlier than forecasted."

"Oh shit! Look at all those bastards," Howard said.

Thirty-five minutes passed. Sixteen more bombers fell from the sky; one hundred and sixty more souls either fell to their deaths or landed in a prisoner of war camp. The German assault was over three hours. The formation looked hurt and wounded. Many of the planes had their propellers feathered and not turning. I could see the setting sun shining through the holes in the plane next to me. Many of the planes had portions of their wings and tails missing. Several bombers were falling back and would never make it across the North Sea.

Our fighter escort joined us over central Belgium. I could understand why Red was so adamant and agreed about the need for fighter cover. The B-17 is a formidable plane, but no match for the German fighters.

"JJ, you should see the coastline of Belgium," Sal said.

No answer.

"JJ, are you all right?" Sal asked.

"I'm sorry—what did you ask?"

"Do you see the coast?"

"Yes, I see it. What is that ball of fire coming at us through the clouds?"

"That is the sun, JJ. Are you feeling OK?" Cole asked.

"I will be fine—give me a few minutes to gather my thoughts."

"How is Joel doing?" Cole asked.

"He will need several stitches, but should be fine," Mike said.

Now that we were over the North Sea and also had fighter cover, Cole gave me permission to get out of my ball turret. I turned my machine gun barrels down, facing the North Sea, to expose my hatch to Howard and Kip. They pulled me from my ball turret. The formation was flying at nine thousand feet, therefore oxygen was not needed. My legs were numb and stiff and I could not assist Howard and Kip during my extraction. They laid me on the floor to give me time to regain my circulation and leg strength. Joel smiled and laughed at me. I knew he would be OK. Mark was attending to his wounds as I lay next to him.

Tension in the plane was gone. All four engines were running smoothly, all gauges read correctly. We were going to make it back to England. I sat up against the curved wall and took a deep breath.

One hour passed. Two bombers ditched in the dark gray North Sea. If they survived the impact, they would be rescued. Cole asked me to come up to the cockpit.

"Ox, you did a grand job protecting our belly," Cole said.

"Thanks."

The damp weather made everything dark and drab. There were no colors, only shades of gray. The North Sea was just a darker shade of gray than the sky. There was a mist in the air and the metal of the plane was cold and wet. As soon as we reached the coastline of England, the bomber groups would break formation and head for their assigned bases. I decided not to mention the large bullet hole in the windshield near JJ, and walked back to join the rest of my crew.

XVII

Eight days passed.

There were no more missions, and none were planned. Last week's losses were making the military planners revaluate daylight operations. Red was right, those assignments were suicide without fighter protection. Due to damage and lack of trained crews, squadrons had less than 30 percent of their complement available.

I was looking forward to that night's activity. The last week had been somber, and maybe our party would change everyone's spirits. The base had an understandably gloomy atmosphere; crew members methodically completed their tasks. Airmen were standing in the shadows smoking cigarettes, without any of the normal horse play or conversation. Rumors said that some of the generals' careers were in jeopardy over the high losses. After the party we had a week of leave; I think the base commander realized the crews were at a breaking point. Cole was concerned about JJ's mental state, and was glad for the time off.

Kip spent a lot of time making sure he looked the part.

"Come on, Kip, the party is about to start," Howard said.

"I heard there would be some girls from town there. I need to look my best."

"Hurry up, I need a drink!"

"Ox, do we have enough cigarettes?" Kip asked, combing his hair while staring at himself in the mirror.

"Yes, I have two packs of Chesterfields and one pack of Lucky Strikes."

"How do I look?" Kip asked.

"Who gives a shit, let's go!" Howard answered.

"Come on! I am ready to get drunk," Joel said, standing by the door with his bandaged arm in a sling.

The large, arched, roofed quiescent hut was decorated keenly and had a festive atmosphere. The Red Feather Club was always welcoming, but today more so than ever. The maintenance staff built a wooden band stand, and above that hung a banner of our bomber group number and creed. Behind that was the arched wall with all the colorful artwork painted by the aircrews. To my right, there was a crowded bar serving mixed drinks and beer.

"Kip, let's smoke a cigarette and let the line at the bar go down," I said.

"Let's stand by the door and wait for the town girls to get here."

We both stood by the door and lit up a Chesterfield. Red walked in with his crew. "Look who it is. Why don't you two pencil dicks come sit at my table later?" Red asked as he walked by.

"Who was that ass?" Kip asked.

"His name is Red. He is all right; he just likes to give new arrivals a hard time."

Four town girls strolled through the door. Three had movie star looks; the fourth was overweight with pretty features. Kip smiled at the three pretty girls and ignored the overweight member. We followed them to the bar and all ordered our favorite cocktails. Kip didn't waste any time filling his dance card; he had all four committed to a dance before the band started to play.

Jane had wavy, reddish-brown hair; it was hard to not stare at her striking good looks. Her smile was outlined with red lipstick that accented her white teeth. Her green and white polka dotted dress clung in a way that accented her curvy figure. Kip couldn't take his eyes off Jane; she seemed worldly and comfortable around men.

Sally was a petite, pretty, black-haired girl with fair skin. Not as voluptuous as Jane, but more attractive in a simple way. Bridget was overweight with a pleasing and engaging personality. Cathy didn't smile as much as her friends, and acted like a tag-along. Cathy was cute and wore her clothes well, but didn't give the impression of being fun.

The mixture of whisky, beer, cigarettes and Glen Miller music was the perfect formula for living life to the fullest. We were all young and understood that life could be cut short. Kip was slamming down beers amid jokes with Jane, Howard was laughing between dances with Bridget and Sally, and Sal was describing his wounds with the nurse named Cathy. All ash trays were full of smoldering cigarettes, some circled with red lipstick.

Kip had his arm around Jane, giving her a hug after each shot of whisky. He whispered in her ear and she replied, "I am not that kind of girl."

"Jane, if you don't sin, churches were built for nothing," Kip said, and we all laughed.

Jane and Kip looked as if they enjoyed each other's company and were bonding. They were joking around in a sexy, flirty, but fun way, always with a smile from Jane.

It was getting late and for the first time tables were empty. We hated for the night to end. Cathy was the practical person in the group and was the first girl to say it was time to go. Everyone exchanged information on how to keep in touch as we walked the girls to the door. Red yelled out for us to have a drink with him before we left. We all spoke for a moment and exchanged hugs at the door. Kip took Jane outside the door and a few steps to the right and gave her a long kiss; Jane was happy to kiss Kip and returned the energy. The girls walk off into the dark giggling, and we returned for our drink with Red.

It was obvious Red was overserved and in the mood to insult. He had two of his crew mates at the table, one to each side. They had mischievous grins; they had seen this show before. Their table was covered with empty beer mugs and shot glasses. Red was on a mission to get drunk.

"You jerkoffs have no shot at those girls. You have a better chance at getting your balls shot off over Germany," Red said as he slammed down one more shot of whiskey. Red's two crew mates laughed as they leaned back and lit up cigarettes.

"That is the girl I am going to marry," Kip said proudly.

"Kid, you don't fucking get it. We are not going home; we are walking dead men," Red said.

"We are going to make our twenty-five missions and go home."

"Kid, they tell you twenty-five missions to give you hope so you don't go crazy; they know you will never make it."

"You're a drunk and you don't know shit!"

"We lost sixty planes over Schweinfurt, and four from our bomber group. Do the math. Six hundred airmen went down and we counted less than seventy parachutes. Ox, I promise you none of those were belly gunners."

Red slammed down another shot, stood up, and staggered to the restroom.

"Your friend Red is a real ass," Howard told his crew mates.

"He is drunk, ignore his bullshit," Red's crew mate to the left said. "He deals with the war better if he doesn't think about going home and accepts death. He is drunk off his ass. Let's all go back to our barracks," Red's crew mate to the right said.

We all stood up, lit a cigarette for the walk, and waited for Red. He stumbled out of the latrine.

"I need another drink!" Red yelled.

"You want another drink; you don't need another drink," I said, and we laughed.

We walked back to our huts. Red's conversation was a mood killer, and the walk was quiet and somber.

XVIII

The next afternoon, Kip and I asked our crew members to join us trout fishing at the nearby river. All declined, saying they needed to use their energies to recover from the night before. We had no live bait; Kip bought some handmade wooden lures from a local. The walk was twenty minutes through an open, grassy field. The river was moving slowly but was clear and cool. The sun was warm on our backs, which added to the perfect day. We could see the trout slowly swimming against the current. Kip tried a long, skinny lure painted brown with a red tip. It had two hooks, one dangling from the middle and one at the tail. I tried the shorter, fat, gray-and-white lure.

Kip threw first and landed up stream halfway across the river. I didn't want to find his line, so I threw further downstream along the rivers bank.

"Got something!" Kip said as he planted the hook. The fish broke the surface and put up a fight against our light tackle. I stopped paying attention to my line and watched Kip land a beauty. While Kip spent the time to release his catch, I quickly reeled in and cast where he caught his trout.

"Got you!" I yelled. The trout took my line and swam up stream. I gave him some slack to keep from breaking the line. "This is a big one!" I shouted to Kip. I walked along the river bank to keep the line tension. I landed the huge trout near a sandy spot where the river turned to the north. We couldn't believe our eyes, big as any river catfish from home. We fished until dark.

We fished every afternoon that week. On the way back to our barracks, we were laughing and Kip told me he loved me like a brother. He caught me off guard and I didn't know what to say. My dad never told me he loved me, and I didn't know how to answer. I wanted to say I love you, but could not make the words come out. If something happened to Kip over Germany, I would regret this moment. I told him about how much fun we had together, but could not say the word "love."

XIX

After our fishing trip, more missions followed:

#2 November 3 – Target –Wilhelmshaven, port area, Flak- Weather –overcast and cold, 4/10 bombed visually, Bomb Load- 10, 500 pound incendiary, no losses in our bomber group, flak light, no damage, Results –Target hit.

#3 December 13 –Kiel, port area, Weather- light, overcast, cold , Flak-extremely heavy, Bomb load – 40, 100 pound conventional, Damage-flak hole in fuselage over drift meter, flak hole in wing between number 2 engine and fuselage, see 5 B-17s go down, three explode, no parachutes, Fighter- light against our group, heavy lower group. Results-Target hit.

#4 January 11 –Brunswick, industrial area, Weather- extremely cold and clear, formation and vapor trails 50 miles long, Bomb Load- 12, 500 pound all purpose, Flak- extremely heavy, city well defended, enemy fighter very effective. Damage – see several bombers go down, bomber to my right explodes, navigator killed on lead plane. Our plane has several 20mm holes from enemy fighters, top turret shattered gunner not hurt, bullet hole above radio man's station. Problems with electrical system made us no match for German fighters. Target hit.

XX

It turned out to be a damp and overcast morning. The air was cool, still, and humid. Hundreds of crew members from our bomber group met for breakfast at 0430 hours. I felt a little sick and nauseated during breakfast. There wasn't a lot of conversation about the mission; just small talk about baseball and girls from home. There was no goofing around; no one was in the mood for practical jokes. The officers were finished with breakfast and gathered for the mission briefing. We all knew it was going to be somewhere deep into Germany with no fighter cover.

After we ate scrambled eggs, biscuits, and ham, the gunners headed for their briefings. We all sat in rows on wooden benches. The gunnery officer walked in and immediately said we were going back to Brunswick. There were a few moans, but mostly quiet prevailed. We touched on the usual details concerning the German fighter, heard a brief statement from the flak officer, and stood up and headed for the supply station to suit up.

We dressed for severe cold; electric coats, pants, gloves and boots. Each person methodically began to dress for battle. Nobody made eye contact; all crew members seemed to be reflecting on their own thoughts about war and death.

I walked out with the crewman who had dressed to my right. I lit a cigarette. I offered one with no response. We reached the large stone path that lead to the pickup area. He had good looks, but seemed sad and defeated in appearance. His electric boots were untied and loose, his jacket low on his shoulders.

"What plane are you on?" I asked.

"*Johnny's Girl.*" He seemed very distant.

"What's your name? Where are you from?" I asked

"Joseph Regginelli, from Brooklyn"

As we walked he reached into his chest and pulled out his dog tags and a silver cross. He rubbed the cross and said, "Hosanna, Hosanna."

"What did you say?" I asked.

"`Save me, save me."

"My name is William Abraham from Shreveport. Are you OK?"

"I have a funny feeling about this mission. I will never ever understand why they send us deep into Germany without fighter cover. I don't think I'm coming home this time."

"What squadron are you in?"

"The 412th."

"I'm in the 336th; you will be above us, offset by two."

He seemed disturbed and defeated; he had a definite premonition that he was not going to survive this mission; I could see it in his face. He sensed death.

We wasted no time once we reached our planes. Cole had a short meeting under the wing to discuss bomb load, bomb run, and weather. JJ and Cole did their pre-startup checklist, and then we heard the great roar from the engines. The engines seemed louder than usual; the stress of the mission had caused my senses to be elevated. All sixty planes were creating a thunderous deafening noise. I could feel the wind in the air from the turning propellers.

We were the thirty-third plane in line for takeoff. I looked out over Cole's shoulder and saw a line of thirty bombers waiting for takeoff, the tails close to the ground and noses in the air. Some pilots were turning the tail fins back and forth, testing systems until the last moments before full throttle.

Sally Sue was pulled from the line due to high oil pressure and a vibration in engine number four. They were spared.

We slowly moved forward, waiting for our turn. Our line was on a runway parallel to the takeoff runway. We were slowly moving in the opposite direction of the planes, building speed for takeoff. The planes in front of us would make a U-turn onto the main runway, immediately build up their power with increased throttle, and slowly gain speed until their wheels lifted from the ground. The planes struggled to gain ground speed due the heavy load of bombs. Engines were at a high pitch; the noise was carried by the moisture in the air. The smoke from the exhaust had nowhere to go and swept through the line of planes. The air tasted of used fuel.

Five more planes had to go, and then it would be our turn. It was announced on the radio that five squadrons were approaching from the south to start the assembly. There was no time to waste due to the need to save fuel. We made our turn and I looked between the shoulders of JJ and Cole down the long runway. The plane in front of us seemed to struggle to gain speed. We were at maximum total takeoff weight of sixty-five thousand pounds; that included our twelve five hundred pound bombs and fuel.

Cole and JJ pushed hard against the throttle. With a loud roar, the plane wheels began their first, slow roll. The plane vibrated and the engines strained as we reached our take off speed of one hundred and five miles per hour. The sun was low against the flat horizon, filtered a dull orange by the morning mist. That afternoon the sun would be high, clear and bright; the perfect place to hide a German fighter.

Planes were converging on the assembly point from all directions and altitudes. We were the second level from the lead squadron, offset by two squadrons. Mission Commander Colonel Jacobs was in the first squadron. He turned the great formation of five hundred planes toward the North Sea and Germany. The weather was clearing just as our meteorologist predicted. The morning sun was in our faces as we moved east. The mission directed us to approach from the north just east of Hamburg.

The top of the formation approached the coast at a maximum altitude of thirty-five thousand feet; we were at thirty thousand feet, with the 412th Squadron and *Johnny's Girl* above us. We could see flashes from the shore batteries as we approached. The flak was heavy. I didn't have the premonitions of dying like Joseph Regginelli, but I was scared.

Two bombers immediately went down in the lead group. *Sleepytime Gal* shook violently as shrapnel passed through the fuselage and tail wing. I noticed two more bombers losing altitude as they passed below our left wing.

The flak stopped to give the German fighters a chance to attack before we started our bomb run. Our fighter escort turned back for England. A string of nine German fighters circled low from the east with their swords drawn. Our shield would be a wall of lead from our .50 caliber machine guns. Just like the gladiators, it was a fight to the death.

We all missed as the German fighters closed in from the three o'clock position. Cannon fire tore through our midsection creating an electrical fire.

"Get that fire out! Watch the oxygen lines!" Cole shouted out.

"Check my line! I'm not getting any oxygen!" I yelled.

"Ox, you have a hole in your line. I will try to patch it," Joel said.

"I can't breathe! Get me out of the damn turret!"

"Calm down, I almost have it."

"Hurry!"

"Don't let that fire near the oxygen!" Cole shouted on the intercom.

Howard and Kip were firing at the planes attacking from above and the rear as Mark, Joel, and Greg fought the fire. I shot as the German fighters passed below. The spinning of the turret and movements of the plane seemed to disorient me. I was slow and missed. I started to feel cold and faint.

"Ox, you should be getting oxygen! Ox, are you conscious?"

"I'm getting some oxygen, but it has a bad taste."

"You have smoke in the line," Greg answered.

"I'm starting to feel sick."

"Do not throw up or spit in your mask; throw up in the turret; it is thirty-seven below zero and will freeze. Wipe your face clean so your mask can seal."

I turned the turret to aim toward the horizon, threw up between my legs on my pants and on the turret just below the round window. If I got shot, I wondered if they would hose out my blood, guts and vomit.

"Give your oxygen line time to clear," Mark added.

I started to feel more alert, but still nauseated. I joined the fight as a German rocket plane approached from underneath the formation at a tremendous speed. It was a small plane with short wings that climbed straight up for one pass. We saw the rocket plane for the first time on our last mission and were amazed by its climb rate; it would fly through the middle of the formation, circle in front of us, and glide back to earth. The rocket plane showed new German technology and had an intimidation factor, but scored no hits.

"The formation above us is getting hit hard. JJ, watch for falling planes!" Cole commanded.

"Christ, did you see that!" JJ said.

Just as he said that, a wing, large parts, and four limp bodies from a B-17 passed below our plane.

"What plane was that? I asked.

A few seconds passed.

"That was *Johnny's Girl*" Cole answered.

That news really hurt. I would never forget the look on that gunner's face. His premonition was accurate. Maybe he'd felt the hand of God on his shoulder. If God's greatest gift is life, why do we create so much death?

The battle went on. Our bombs hit their mark. More bombers were lost. Turning back toward England, we tried to tighten the formation. Over a third of the planes were lost or fell behind. Many airmen were injured or died aboard the remaining planes.

We had reached our fighter cover over the shoreline of North Germany. Many of the smoking, damaged bombers would ditch before England. My thoughts couldn't leave the gunner who died over Brunswick. Would I know that day when it came? Why wasn't he spared like the crew from *Sally Sue*? I would never forget how brave he was. He boarded *Johnny's Girl* knowing he would never return. I could take some solace in the fact that the pain of war was over for Joseph Regginelli.

We had several more missions over Germany: Berlin, Rostock, Magdeburg, Politz, Merseburg, and other industrial areas. Losses were the highest over Berlin, Brunswick, Rostock and Kiel. Twenty to 40 percent of our bomber group was lost on each of those missions. We felt guilty surviving, but they were the lucky ones. It was all over for them.

XXI

Over the next six months, Kip spent his free time fishing with me or courting Jane. Kip was probably smart for trying to squeeze so much out of life. He was never bored or sulked; he just lived for the day. Jane and her friends were excited to see Glenn Miller; they had been to four base parties over the last six months. But nothing like this.

"Kip, you need to lay off the cologne—I can smell you from a mile away," Howard said.

"Let me have a shot of that cologne, I don't want to be at a disadvantage with the ladies," Sal said, and we laughed.

"We are going to have a lot of competition. Did you see all the chairs they are setting up in front of the stage? There will be hundreds of hard tails from other bases," Howard said.

"Yeah, but there will be a lot more girls. I heard nurses and Red Cross girls are coming from London," Mike said.

"Kip is the only one with a chance for some action; he has invested the time. You all would rather play cards and drink than court a girl from town," I said.

"Ox, you're the same way," Kip said.

"Not anymore. I'm going to ask Sally to go bike ride with me."

"I will bring Jane."

"That sounds like fun."

The stage was set up in a large, grassy area near Hangar 4. The afternoon was clear and warm. Not an England day, but a spring day in Louisiana. Twenty miles out, a squadron of P-51 mustangs was circling the base. Many officers, enlistees, civilians were gathering in groups near the rows of white chairs.

Banners were up, and the American flag was blowing in the light warm breeze. Colors were bright from the sun; the girls looked beautiful; dresses and hair shone. Kip's neck was stretched as he looked for Jane. Joel looked over my shoulder as a pretty blonde walked through his line of vision. Cole stood with us like our big, protective brother. JJ was smoking a cigarette while surveying the talent. Mike was asking about food. Mark and Greg were talking about their favorite Glen Miller song. Sal was looking down at the ground in a deep sad thought, and Howard announced he had bad gas. We all laughed.

I was proud to be standing with my crew and feel grateful we were all safe.

Kip was so much like Bert; both were good-looking and loved to flirt with the ladies. I couldn't believe he was really gone. He was killed on a beach landing; Elaine's letter was missing details, but I hoped it was fast with no pain. We all tried to bury our thoughts and block the horrible sights from our minds. A short peek back needed to be put in check; if more thoughts persisted, we used beer and whiskey to stop the pain. I would never talk about this war if I made it home.

"Ox, snap out of it. Let's go get a beer," Howard said.

"Sorry, I was thinking about a friend."

"Let's get drunk and forget this damn war."

"Good idea—let's go get a beer before the band starts."

I heard a big cheer as Captain Miller walked onto the stage. He addressed the crowd and let us know how honored he was to entertain the Army Air Corps. As he spoke, his band formed behind him. They were in rows, one higher than the next: trombones in the back, three trumpet players to their left, clarinet and saxophone players down a row, and three cute girl singers and a drummer in the front row.

We were sitting middle back, stage left. Kip had his arm around Jane in a loving way. Sally was between me and Howard. Cole and JJ found two girls from the Red Cross and sat four rows back. Mike and Greg were on the edge of their seats waiting for the first set.

We all held a drink in hand, trying to forget the war. Glenn Miller knew that his real role was to provide an escape from the stress. He was our pressure relief valve. I could see in our faces that many of us were near our breaking point.

As the music started to play, I looked over at the new silver B-17 parked just to the left of the stage. Cute girls and airmen were sitting on the wings, watching the show. Flashbacks crept into my mind of heavy bombers falling from the sky, racing back to the earth humiliated and fatally wounded. I see Red and all my friends who died sitting on those wings. The friends I made playing baseball, cards, and drinking. I see Dale from Houston who asked me to teach him how to box and I see Frankie from Memphis who died when his B-17 exploded over Brunswick. I see Jeffrey from gunnery school.

"Ox, snap out of it. Let's do shots of whiskey," Howard said.

"Give me your flask, I need one!" I said.

"Ox, give me a shot and a cigarette!" Sally asked.

"Pass that flask over here," Kip and Jane requested.

"Ox, let's dance?" Sally asked.

I was not a good dancer, but I took pleasure in the way Sally pulled me toward her. Her hug was what I needed, a necessity. The smell of perfume on her neck and the feel of her soft bosom cleared my mind of outside thoughts; I was living in the moment. I kissed her on her red moist lips; she hugged me firmly and returned the kiss. Sally had told Jane, who told Kip, who told me, how much she cared for me. I had been shy, timid, and introverted toward Sally. Now she knew my true feelings of affection. We walked back to where Jane and Kip were sitting holding hands and smiling.

The more we drank, the better the music sounded. Every motion was for that day, not tomorrow. Most girls were sporting the latest hair styles and fashions. Airmen and sexy girls flirted back and forth. Glenn Miller finished his last set and the party began to break apart.

Kip and I walked Jane and Sally to their bicycles. Several airmen departed in cars; crews came from over twenty different air fields. Some piled in jeeps and trucks that were confiscated from their bases. After the rush of people cleared, we were still standing next to Jane and Sally. We walked along with them for a mile. Plans were made for a picnic and an afternoon at the river. The girls stopped walking and straddled their bikes on the side of the country road. We gave them long kisses; we smiled at each other and parted ways.

XXII

Kip and I departed the base just after lunch and began our thirty minute walk to the village.

"Sally was on my mind all night. I love the way she kisses," I said.

"She told Jane that she wants to spend time with you. Did you notice the fond way she looks at you?" Kip said.

"No, do you feel guilty about getting close to Jane?"

"What do you mean?"

"What if we don't come back? She will be hurt."

"We talked about that and she understands the risk."

"I guess we should live like we will make twenty-five."

"Did you remember to bring cigarettes?"

"Yes."

The girls' boarding house was a white, wooden, two story house with low hedges that outlined the perimeter. The driveway to the house was made of pea gravel and the gardens had a natural, but cared for, look. The walkway to the front door was stone and also framed with low hedges. Kip met the stern, prim and proper landlord several times. This would be the first time for me, and I was slightly nervous.

"Hello Miss Calverton, we are here to pick up Jane and Sally," Kip said.

"Good afternoon Kip, introduce me to your friend."

"This is William Abraham; we are on the same bomber."

"Would you boys like to have a cup of tea before the girls come down?"

"That would be nice," I said as Kip gave me a funny look.

Miss Calverton was slow and took her time bringing the tea and small assorted pastries. Kip was a little mad that I accepted her invitation, but I figured she was lonely and would appreciate ten minutes of our time. Jane and Sally came down the wooden staircase with puzzled looks on their faces. Kip looked at me to let them know it was my fault we were having tea and delaying our trip to the river. Miss Calverton was engaging and pleasant, but somewhat prying. We said our goodbyes and left for the river.

Jane held Kip's arm with one hand and the picnic basket with the other. She seemed very happy to be in the company of Kip. She looked deep into his eyes and smiled with affection when he spoke. Jane looked attractive in her plaid skirt and white sweater with pearl buttons. Sally's yellow dress was adorable and showed off her figure. She had a casual, comfortable way about her that made me loosen up and unwind.

The slow-moving river had a grassy bank lined with trees. We found a place near a large willow tree to lay down our supplies and spread out Jane's blanket. Kip lay on his side, propped up on one elbow. He smiled with a long piece of grass in his mouth. Sally was sitting next to me; Jane was sitting against Kip with a slight lean. We all lit up a cigarette and took pleasure in a glass of wine. Talk about the war was avoided; I was surprised to hear Jane speaking of returning to the United States with Kip. Even though Kip was also nineteen, he seemed so much more experienced with women. I had never been in love or been intimate, but this seemed to come natural to Kip. I wanted that; I would hate to die before experiencing love and sex. Sally was just a friend, but I hoped for more.

The sandwiches the girls prepared were exceptional; the hard bread and unique cheeses in England were first-rate. The fruit was fresh and went well with the red wine. I know the girls did not have much money, and Kip and I were grateful.

Sally asked me to take her for a walk along the river. She stopped at the spot she enjoyed as a child. Before we turned back she gave me a long kiss that eclipsed the one from the night before.

We joined Kip and Jane for a glass of wine, cigarettes and more conversation. Sally was impressed with my boxing background. Kip brought the subject up after we finished the bottle of wine. The wind started to blow as the cold front approached, so we folded up the blanket and packed our supplies as quickly as possible. We reached the boarding house just in front of the lightning. Kip and I said our goodbyes and started our walk back to the base.

"Kip, what is it like to be sexual with a woman?" I asked.

"It is exhilarating, electrifying, and thrilling."

"Were you nervous the first time?"

"I was petrified and anxious. I was so scared and tense I had a problem performing, but she was loving and patient and helped me through."

"Is it better if you love and care for the person?"

"Yes, wait until the time is right. Make sure you feel affection and love for the girl."

"Do I have time to wait?"

"Don't be so negative; we have only eight missions left."

"It is starting to rain, let's run the last mile."

XXIII

A special briefing was announced for all crew members. The topic was a new, secret weapon created by the Germans; a fighter plane with no propellers; a jet that flies five hundred and forty miles per hour. The intelligence officer stated the jet is fully operational and would probably attack our bombers on the next mission. We would have P-51 flight cover, but the new German jet fighter would be over one hundred miles per hour faster, with a higher climb and turn speed.

In addition, the German rockets were becoming more effective. In closing, the intelligence officer said that some of the civilian militias had been shooting the captured American airmen. It was better to be captured by the German army. The gunners had a special meeting to discuss tactics.

XXIV

Greg was squatting on his heels making last minute adjustments to his radio. Howard was alone sitting under his turret. He was in a melancholy mood; that was unusual for the jovial Howard. That was a little disconcerting for me. I could always count on Howard to be positive. I leaned against the rounded fuselage and faced the window for the right waist gunner. Joel and Mike were seated side by side on the floor just below the window. Next to our plane I could see the *Cocktail Kid* floating up and down with the lift from the warm air. Then, I saw only sky. A few seconds later she would reappear. My peripheral vision was limited because of my distance from the window. I moved towards the window and stood just to the left of Joel. I saw over 200 bombers making formation while they slowly moved back and forth with the currents of the wind. The morning sun was shining against the cliffs and shoreline of England. The waves breaking on the shore were bright white. The long parallel lines they created reached the horizon to the south. The northern rail yards of Hamm, Germany were just five hours away.

The mission over Oberlahnstein changed my view on the war. Ten of my bunk mates never made it home. Their belongings were thoughtlessly processed like some necessary nuisance in order to make room for their replacements. The new replacements were the fourth group to occupy those bunks. My youthful thoughts of being invincible were gone. The war trumped all things that were good. The past few months had made me contemplate many aspects of the war. One good thing about the war, it made everyone equal. A person's family history, money, education or even past royalty didn't matter anymore. The war had shuffled the deck and we all came out the same number and with the same poor odds.

I admired Sal. He was from one of the wealthiest families in Texas, maybe in the United States. He was always humble and accommodating. He had invited the crew several times to visit his 2200 acre cattle ranch just outside Paris, Texas. Also, he had asked us to meet him and hunt at his 6000 acre hunting camp just west of Austin near the city of Spicewood. We had all agreed to meet and hunt after the war. Sal's description of his hunting camp was impressive. The 6000 square foot lodge was called "The Estancia" and sat on the high point of the property. He said the entire perimeter was high fenced to keep the coyotes out and the exotic animals in. We planned to meet after the war and hunt Addax, Axis deer, Red Deer, Aoudad sheep, hogs and antelope. He said the landscape of the camp was a combination of the native grasses, cactus, oak trees, mesquite trees and tumble weed. There was a broad slope from the lodge that ran all the way to Lake Travis. There were some hills but nothing severe. Sal was proud to say that the lodge had a rustic feel from the past. We all talked several times about the trip.

I was surprised to hear that Mark Martin was an avid hunter. I always thought of him as the beach type. He talked about all the great places to hunt in Southern California. He hunted with his late dad near the

Imperial Valley, Brawly and El Centro for big mule deer and mountain lions. Mark's eyes pooled with tears when he spoke of hunting with his dad. He would always stop before they overflowed. Sal and Mark loved hunting and bonded due their common interest.

"Ox! Snap out of it. Cole wants you and Howard to check the oxygen system before we begin our climb," Joel said.

"OK. Howard, meet me on the cat walk in the bomb bay."

On most B-17's the top turret gunner was the flight engineer. I was the most mechanically minded so Cole wanted me in that role. He instructed me to cross train Howard. Howard was goofy and mischievous but knew when to be serious. He had a problem on focusing long enough to decipher the manuals, but had a natural aptitude to trouble shoot any system. He said he had fixed items in his family's boat yard since fifth grade. He grew up near the wharves on the Brooklyn side of the East River. His dad repaired and serviced steam and diesel engines for several shipping companies that had piers on the shipping channel. Howard's dad taught him well. There wasn't a component on the plane that he couldn't disassemble and rebuild to a high standard.

"Howard, check the bomb racks, valves and relays from here to the rear of the plane. I will check with Cole and inspect the systems forward of the bomb bay." I said.

"Will do."

I moved to the front of the plane to inspect the two cheek guns and the chin turret. All oxygen connections, gauges and bombardier equipment were in working order.

"Cole, how is everything up here?" I asked.

"Number four is running a little hot."

I looked out JJ's window and saw no leaking fluid or smoke. The engine sounded in rhythm with the other three.

"Cole, I don't see anything. I will have Howard take a look from the top turret. Let me know if the gauge moves. Keep an eye on your oil pressure."

"I'll let you know if engine runs any hotter or the oil pressure changes."

"How far out are we?"

"Three hours to the coast of Germany."

"Cole, we need to make another check on our intercom system. Kip and Greg's system had problems during our last test. I think we have it worked out; but, I would feel more comfortable if we run through the test one more time."

"Let's all get in our battle stations and test our comm system and fire our guns."

"I'll let everyone know."

I moved to the bombardier position at the nose of the plane. The view from the glass bubble at the nose of the B17 was different from any other. There were no issues with my peripheral vision. I could see in all directions without having to turn the turret or my head. The entire formation of 400 hundred bombers was visible. The battle group was lined up like the great phalanxes of the ancient Greek armies. We were methodically moving towards our enemy as one unit. Our spears were our .50 caliber machine guns, our shields were our fighter cover, and our death blow would be from the thousands of bombs we were to deliver. The ancient Greek armies had their shields during battle, we would not. That was why so many B17's fell from the sky.

"Mark, everything OK up here?" I said.

"Yes."

"Soon as everyone is in position we are going to have a comm check and one short burst from our guns."

Located behind the Bombardier position was the navigator. Sal was located behind Mark but slightly in front of and below the pilot and co-pilot.

"Sal, we are going to check our intercom system soon as we are all in position. How far out are we?" I asked.

"We caught tail wind and are only two and half hours from the coast."

"What's the weather report?"

"Clear and cold. Perfect conditions for contrails at high altitude. The Germans will see us coming from a hundred miles away."

Howard was located just above and behind the pilots.

"Howard, how did everything look?"

"The auto pilot had some loose wires."

"That's it?"

"Yes."

"Get in your turret for an intercom and gun check. We have a tail wind and are only two hours from the coast. Rotate your turret several times. We had problems with the gears last mission."

I passed through the bomb bay and double checked the racks. The radio operator was posted just aft of the bomb bay. He was in the back section of the bomber with me, Joel, Mike and Kip. We had 5 crew members in front of the bomb bay and 5 in the rear section behind the bomb bay.

"Mike, my chute is tucked next to the radio station."

"Yes. You know I've got your back."

The B-17 bail out procedure called for the bombardier and navigator to exit the nose hatch. Pilots, radio operator, and top turret gunner were to exit through the bomb bay doors. The waist gunners and ball turret gunner exited through the back door. The tail gunner had his own hatch at the rear of the plane.

I knew Joel and Mike meant well, but they had no chance to reach my hatch in a nose dive. They would be weightless and unable to maneuver. If we spun, they would be pinned against the wall and need to crawl every inch of the way. Worst of all would be the inverted slow spin. The crews that survived that spin said they were disoriented and lucky to find the hatch or door. Survivors of that spin were few. I knew no ball turret gunner who had survived an inverted spin. We all knew the odds but we still talked about spending time together at home.

Mike lived in Marshall Texas, only 40 miles from Shreveport. We planned on spending a lot of time together after the war. Caddo Lake was located between the two cities and known for its large bass. He promised to show me all of his hot spots if I took him tight line fishing on Cross Lake. Mike's dad worked in the oil field and hoped Mike would go into business with him after the war. They had both dreamed of starting their own wildcat drilling company.

Joel and I had planned to go to Mardi Gras in New Orleans. He brought up New Orleans several times. With his wrestling skills and my boxing skills I thought we would be safe. Joel was always talking about hitch hiking around the country. In some ways he was the free spirit of the crew. I was lucky to have Joel and Mike as my waist gunners. Many times *Sleepytime Gal* got hit with bursts of flak and the plane lost its horizontal stability. Joel and Mike always moved towards my coffin ready to pull me out.

"Let's run our intercom test." Cole said.

Cole started with Mark and worked his way to the rear of the plane.

"Mark."

"Check."

"Sal."

"Check."

And so on. The system checked out, but still concerned me.

"Give a short burst with your guns. Mark, after you shoot the chin turret make sure you fire the cheek guns."

We had started something. All the bombers near us fired their guns at the North Sea. The ball turret gunner to my right must have been trying to impress me. He rotated in several directions with abrupt deliberate turns, and then rotated to the 90 degree down position. With both guns aiming straight down, he paused for a moment and then fired into the North Sea. He rotated back up to face me and waved. Everyone on this mission knew I won the flying cross—I guess he was out to astonish me. I hoped he had those same sharp turns when the German fighters arrived.

"Sal, where are we?" Cole asked.

"One hour before we cross the coast."

"Ox, keep an eye out for the German rocket planes. Kip, watch for any reflections."

I knew Cole said that because of our tail end Charlie position at the bottom of the formation. I had a system that I used duck hunting that allowed me to find the German fighters. I moved my eyes back and forth; not my head, just my eyes. I picked up any movement. The distance didn't even matter. The crew never questioned my shout outs.

The mission called for us to approach our target from the north. We would have no vector change at our Initial Point. Our degree of turn at

IP would be zero. We would start our bomb run by simply stringing out our formation. Hit the target and turn west for England.

"Ox, the number four engine spiked and is running hot." Cole said.

"Howard, what do you see?" I asked.

"There is oil coming from the flap ring of the cowling."

"Cole! Shut the engine down and feather the prop," I yelled.

"We are going to turn back before we reach the coast," Cole said.

We had no choice. Procedure stated that we had to return to base. We were all disappointed but relieved. We all knew it was nothing to be ashamed of. At least 20 planes needed to turn back during the last five maximum effort missions. We turned due west and stayed north of the coast. We were the lone plane, just us and our long white contrail against the blue sky.

On the long flight back, I thought about how lucky Kip and I were to have off base companions like Sally and Jane. Everyone on our crew was jealous, especially Howard. Howard was an admitted virgin like me. He was worried that he might die a virgin. My relationship with Sally was what I needed.

That night Sally kissed me and moved my thoughts from the war to romance and sex. Our time together had my hormones moving, and the war had my testosterone levels elevated. I thought about Sally often, but the daily missions and constant training had kept us apart. Also the crew had demanded much of my time at the Red Feather Club. It was hard to tell them no when we didn't know how much time we had left together. Sally was a beautiful young girl that had her own hormones to manage. I wanted to be with her, but I understood she needed a relationship with someone that could give her time and had a more optimistic future. I struggled between my lust for her and what is right. I didn't want to get her closer to me or pregnant only to be gone in a flash high over Germany.

XXV

I was eating breakfast slowly; my thoughts were on the day's mission. I was alone on the corner of the last table, next to the large open window. The sun should have been rising, but was blocked from the low fog that covers the open fields and runways. The mess hall was beginning to fill with crews about to ready for another mission over Germany.

Joel's severe case of the mumps had him confined to sickbay. We had been assigned a new waist gunner named Trevor Meeks. It was easy to get superstitious. I hoped this didn't change our luck. I was curious what my other crew mates thought of this change. Kip, Howard, and Mike were the first of my crew to arrive for breakfast.

"You got up early this morning," Kip said, looking at me.

"I didn't sleep well. I shifted side to side trying to get my covers and pillow right." I said, not wanting to divulge my frequent nightmares.

"I heard you scream out last night. Don't be ashamed; we all have nights like that," Kip reassured me.

"What do you know about our new crew member?" I asked.

"He was just released from the field hospital at Thorpe Abbotts. He was with the 404th Bomb Group, 336th Squadron, and got shot on the Brunswick mission. His plane took a lot of hits and fell behind the formation. They were with three other stragglers; they couldn't find any cloud cover. The German fighters found them just before they reached the coast. Two of the stragglers were shot down and splashed in the North Sea. Trevor's plane survived the attack and landed near the coast of Scotland. Trevor was the only injured member of his crew. His crew was assigned to a new plane and were all killed on the next mission," Mike said.

"Cole spent some time with Trevor yesterday. He said he had all his strength back and was fit to fly," Kip said.

"I guess we'll meet him at the gunners meeting," I said.

I drank my second cup of coffee as I walked to the mission briefing. My tempo was sluggish and I fell behind my crew mates. I stopped between the buildings and looked out at the B-17s through the thinning fog. The furthest planes were just becoming visible. The rows of bombers seemed to be at rest and quiet. In less than two hours the contrast would be vast. The noise and wind from the propellers would change the still, peaceful feel. Everything would be different everywhere.

We walked on this same path every mission. That day would be different. We would have a new crew member. The story about Trevor's crew made me think about two things: how much my crew meant to me and how empty Trevor must have felt. I was sure he had been looking forward to spending time with his crew mates after the war. A special bond and friendship developed between crews. Nothing could change that.

The gunners' briefing room was filling up fast with airmen. Most crews were entering as a group. I wasn't sure what Trevor looked like. I looked for a single or someone trying to contact me or Kip. Once everyone was seated, the gunnery officer and flak officer entered the room and stood in front of the large map, both holding pointers.

"Today, the target is the port city Hamburg. The naval and shore batteries will be intense. You will be approaching from the north. Your IP will be over the North Sea, approximately one hundred miles from the target. This will limit your exposure and give you a better run at the shipyards and dock area. Expect to make contact with the German fighters before you reach the shoreline. They will break off from their attack when you reach the first shore batteries. The flak will be heavy until you are thirty miles south of the target. The German fighters will refuel and return to meet you before you reconnect with your fighter escort. There is a squadron of the German's new jet fighter ME 262 stationed just west of Hamburg. If they engage the formation, make sure you adjust for their speed on your leads. The Germans have used them sparingly, but they have been very effective against our bombers. Conserve your ammunition; you'll need to fight your way into and out of the target area," the flak officer said.

The gunnery officer said, "Stay alert, and don't let the fear of battle cloud your judgment." It was funny to hear him say that; there had never been an easy bomb run over Germany. Kip was sitting to my right and said quietly in my ear, "Before our last mission, one of the pilots got hysterical before his mission briefing. They pulled him from the mission and sent him to the flak shack for rehabilitation. They say he screams out uncontrollably several times a night. This guy wants to talk to us about fear."

All the crews were leaving their assigned briefings and moving toward the supply depot to retrieve their flight suits, parachutes, goggles, and emergency gear. Crews were all clean-shaven to get a better seal on their oxygen masks.

"I want everyone to come over and meet Trevor Meeks," Cole said.

We all gathered near the door to the supply depot and introduced ourselves to Trevor. He was very thin but athletic in build. For a thin person he had wide shoulders and stood two inches taller than me. We talked about home while we headed for the jeep to take us to *Sleepytime Gal*. All ten of us found a small place to sit on the jeep. There were legs hanging off the sides in every direction. Trevor was sitting directly to my right on the back corner passenger side of the jeep.

"Are you William Abraham the boxer?" Trevor asked.

I was surprised my name was known on other bases.

"Yes"

"What's your record?"

"Thirty wins and one loss."

I was glad we were talking. I would need Trevor's help to get out of the ball turret.

The jeep came to a slow, squeaking stop.

"Let's all meet under the wing," Cole commanded.

We all circled around Cole under engine number two. Cole began to brief us. "The weather should be clear and extremely cold over the target. Temperature at twenty-seven thousand feet is estimated at fifty degrees below zero. Wind will be from the northeast at fifteen miles an hour. We will approach from the north with a slight tail wind. I want everyone on their toes when we make our ninety degree turn south at the IP. The German jet fighters have been known to travel further off shore than the Me 109s or Fw 190s. This will be a long mission, over twelve hours. We will be carrying both left and right auxiliary fuel tanks in the bomb bay. Ox, check the fuel lines and valves before we take off. Let's keep an eye on those tanks, especially during the heavy flak. Our bomb load is eight five hundred pound bombs, let's deliver them on target and then get the hell out of there."

We boarded the plane and double checked our gear. Cole and JJ went through their preflight checklist. Trevor looked around the plane with a sad, defeated stare. He briefly stopped and focused on each station. This was his first time back on a B-17. I was sure his thoughts were with his crew.

The noise and wind from the forty-seven bombers changed the quiet morning. We taxied to our assigned hardstand and waited for our turn in line. We joined the long, impressive line of bombers; we were seventeenth in line. Takeoffs were scheduled at the usual thirty second intervals. I stood in the opening between Cole and JJ. I looked down the runway at the long line of bombers waiting for their turn to face back into the wind and take off. The planes' engines were immediately put to full throttle as they turned into the wind. The planes were weighted down with bombs and extra fuel; every inch of the runway had to be used. They slowly gained speed as they rolled down the long runway.

Our takeoff slope was nearly flat as we crossed only two hundred feet in altitude over the south side of the village. Some villagers looked up waving; others just kept to their daily chores. We seemed to be lower than the steeple in the distance.

"JJ, let's bank at twenty degrees at eight hundred feet and circle back to join the others," Cole commanded.

"I see squadrons approaching from the south, approximately twenty miles out," Kip said.

"Ox, double check all systems. Make sure all lines and valves are not leaking to the Glycol heating system and anti-icing tank. Make a visual on the batteries, oxygen filler tanks, and hydraulics. This is a long trip; let's not leave anything to chance."

I was trained as the flight engineer and knew more about the mechanics of the plane than any of my crew. Cole knew I was going to check all the systems before we finished building our formation of five hundred bombers. I thought he was just burning off extra energy.

196

"Cole, the remainder of our squadron has joined us," Kip said from the tail of the plane.

"There is a bomb group of three squadrons waiting for us just off the coast," JJ notified Cole.

"We are going to stack at twenty-five thousand feet. We will be in the lead plane of our squadron, offset from the lead group by two levels. Kip, do you see any other groups approaching from the North West?" Cole asked.

"I see three groups; approximately ninety planes at our seven o'clock level position."

"What's their range?"

"Ten miles."

"The sky is clear; let's keep the formations tight," Cole requested to the other bombers.

"I got the beacon; we are good," said Greg.

"We are going to build our formation as we move north up the coast," Sal informed us.

The weather was clear and the sky was blue beyond the horizon. The sun was still low and the half moon was high above. Visibility seemed endless. The temperature was cold and getting colder. The sky was clear and deep blue; the sun was bright over the flat horizon.

"Look out at the North Sea. The next land we'll see is Germany," Cole said.

Due to the cold clear weather, the contrails from all four engines were bright white against the blue, never-ending sky. The sky was empty over the North Sea other than our great formation of five hundred bombers. Looking down, I could see the wakes of a British naval battle group below; they must have been impressed when they looked up. There couldn't be anything more impressive than a formation of five hundred B-17 bombers high above trailing long tails of white vapor. I knew the naval crews below understood the hell and carnage that awaited us. They didn't envy us, but they did respect us. They knew the overwhelming odds we faced; that's why they'd look up and stare.

As we moved north the temperature dropped noticeably; the air in the plane turned thin, cold, and dry. I took my mask off to reset it on my face. There was no air to breathe and if I tried to take a breath the cold would burn in my lungs. The rising sun stayed to our east; I knew we hadn't turned west and were well north of Germany. Our flight plan was taking us due north before we turned west toward Denmark. Our strategy was to approach Germany from the north. By not crossing over Belgium, we hoped for an element of surprise so we could cross the shoreline of northern Germany undetected. Our formation was so large it seemed impossible to not be discovered by the German Navy. Fuel would be a critical issue due to our flight plan and the length of our mission. Cole asked JJ several times for fuel readings and monitored all gauges diligently.

Three hours passed. The formation turned west approximately one hundred miles north of the northwest corner of Germany. The sun was in the eleven o'clock position level.

"Everyone man your guns. We aren't in fighter range, but let's not take any chances," Cole commanded.

I rotated my machine guns to face down at the North Sea. Trevor helped me through the hatch. I positioned myself and tested my intercom; then I rotated to face the rear of the plane. There were over two hundred bombers in my view. Our fighter escort was disappearing to the west, heading back to England.

"We'll reach IP point in twelve minutes," Sal announced.

That meant we were about to turn south for Germany.

"Everyone test their guns. Give a short burst. Conserve your ammo," Cole ordered.

I rotated three hundred and sixty degrees to get a feel for my turret. Turned down forty-five degrees and shot below the formation into the dark gray North Sea. The cold was really taking its toll this trip. We all seemed to be more controlled and preoccupied by the extreme cold than ever before. The freezing temperature was relentless. It was always on our minds.

"We are turning south and will be crossing the German coast in forty minutes," Cole announced.

I was beginning to experience anxiety and a severe case of claustrophobia. I was cold and couldn't move. My chin was against my chest and I couldn't breathe. I knew my state of mind was not good. I was worried that if I didn't get out of this confined ball I was going to have a panic attack. I felt trapped and couldn't move.

"Cole, can I get out of the turret for a moment to adjust my suit? The back of my suit is caught and pulling back on my chest and neck. It's hard for me to breathe," I asked, hoping to get out and gather my thoughts.

"Sal, check the oxygen tank above the turret, and check all connections," Cole commanded.

"Cole, the system checks out. I don't think there is a problem with the oxygen."

"Waist gunners, help Ox out of the turret and check his mask," Cole ordered.

I immediately swung my machine guns to aim down at the North Sea to expose my hatch. Cole knew I had no problem with my oxygen system. He understood that I needed just a moment to calm down. I would be fine. I just needed a few seconds to let the anxiety pass.

Trevor helped me out of my turret. He looked into my eyes and gave me a reassuring nod. My legs were numb, so I stood holding on to the waist gun and adjusted my suit with my left hand. I took some deep breaths of oxygen from my mask and began to calm down. I knew once the fight started I would be fine.

"The lead group reports several reflections moving west. They are on the horizon at the twelve o'clock position," Cole announced.

Cole didn't order me back into my turret. He knew as soon as I heard the news I would return to my battle position and be ready to fight. Mike and Trevor helped me back into my small ball.

"I see the reflections moving fast to the west. It must be the German jet fighters," JJ announced.

"They're going to get the sun to their backs and attack from the west," I said.

"Look, the reflections stopped moving. They must have turned toward us to make a head-on attack," Cole observed.

We could see the reflection from the sun off the canopies of the high speed jets. They were less than ten miles away and closing fast.

"Kip, don't fire when they pass; their separation speed will be too great. Save your ammo for when they turn back, and be ready for an attack from the rear. Waist gunners, adjust your leads for their speed," Cole ordered.

"Closing speed is over eight hundred miles per hour," JJ informed.

They were just coming into full view at the twelve o'clock level position and were closing fast. I could see them just under the nose guns. The formation tightened close as possible. We were in the lead of our squadron wing. We were located offset by four squadrons from the leading squadron. We were one of the most exposed planes for a frontal attack.

"Howard, I think they're going to pass above us. They will be too fast to shoot as they pass above. Hit them head on with a burst. Ox, stay on your toes in case they dive below us. I'll call out their position as they pass," Cole said.

I lost sight of the jet fighters as they began to fire. I could feel the plane shake as the nose gun and top turret began to fire.

"Son of a bitch; they are fast!" Howard yelled.

"Kip, where are they?" Cole asked.

"They're spreading out to circle back. Two bombers from the 404th bomber group are going down."

I thought about Trevor, I'm sure he knew them. Friends don't last long on a B-17. The crews were always being replaced. Their belongings were sent home immediately, and soon after a new airman would occupy their bunk. I replaced an airman who died, and I wondered after the mission if somebody would be replacing me. The odds were not in my favor.

"Ox, do you see them circling back?" Kip asked.

"I see seven diving low to make a run from underneath!" I answered.

"They're lining up with our squadron."

"I got them!"

"They're too low for me."

"They're making a run at our fuel tanks."

"We're approaching the coast. This will be their last pass before we reach the naval batteries and the flak," Cole observed.

"They're almost on the deck!" I informed.

"We lost nine planes on their last pass," JJ said.

"Their climb rate is incredible. Here they come."

I opened fire first. They returned fire at the plane in the tail end Charlie position. The bomber exploded in flames as it fell away from the group. I kept firing as they passed through the formation.

"They are turning back to base!" Howard announced.

That could only mean that flak was near.

"Ten minutes to the start of the bomb run," Mark announced.

The flak was immediate and intense. It was thicker than any previous barrage; we shook and jerked to the right as shrapnel tore through the bomb bay doors. The sparks and black smoke from the impact blocked my view for a moment.

Mike was on the right waist gun and said the bomber to our right took a direct flak hit and exploded. No chutes seen. A plane passed below, moving nose down to the left; smoke was coming from all engines. Their white contrail turned black. It slowly rolled over, out of view behind black smoke from hundreds of flak bursting. The white vapor trails from the hundreds of bombers were spotted with black circles from the constant flak.

We got hit again from underneath on the left side of our plane. The wind coming from the flak holes whistled through the plane. Instantly,

Sleepytime Gal filled with fumes from our fuel. I could taste it in my oxygen mask.

"The left auxiliary tanks are hit and leaking fuel!" Mark yelled.

"Help me out of the turret! I can stop the leak and siphon to the left tank," I announced.

"Trevor, help him out!"

As I rotated down to expose my hatch, another flak burst hit the plane.

"Trevor is hit!" Mike announced.

There was a gargling noise on the intercom system.

Mike pulled me out of turret. Trevor was on his back, bleeding heavily from his neck. The flak hit above his flak jacket and cut through his throat and spine. I took a moment to look. His blood was pooling as it froze on the floor.

The wind sweeping through the plane was causing the fuel to atomize; my goggles fogged from the mist of gas in the air.

"Mike, get me the portable oxygen tank, siphon hose, pump, and my tools!" I said.

"Put your chute on before you get in the bomb bay. We are starting our bomb run in thirty seconds," Mark said.

"I don't have time! One spark and the plane will explode."

"Be careful; the bombs are armed."

The bomb bay had several holes on the left side between the first and second bomb rack. The top of the left auxiliary fuel tank was blown off by the flak.

"Cole, I'm taking the plane; we are starting our seven minute bomb run. We are going to align with the east side of the inlet to the port," Mark said.

"Ox, can you fix it?" Cole asked.

"We need all the fuel to get home! I'm going to pump the three hundred gallons that are left into the wing tanks."

"Hurry! I need to open the bomb bay doors in five minutes!" Mark said.

I clipped my harness on a piece of cross metal framing adjacent to the left fuel tank.

The plane jumped violently up to the right, with a sudden drop back to the left. I was drenched in fuel. The siphon line was hard to line up with the cut line that passed through the wing stag into the left wing fuel tank. It would be risky at this temperature, but I needed to work with no gloves. I put my hose through the top of the breached fuel tank and the sending side of the pump hose into the broken fuel line to the wing tank. I plugged the large hole on top of the auxiliary tanks with my gloves and cloth. I had to limit the fumes and loss of fuel. My hands instantly turned numb in the negative fifty degree temperature. I had just enough hand movement to work the pump and maintain pressure on the sending hose.

"Ox, get out of the bomb bay! I need to open the doors!" Mark yelled.

"Open them. I will be OK!"

"Ox, get out. If we can't stop the fumes we will bail out after the bomb run!" Cole said.

Everyone was nervous about the fumes, but I knew I could stop the fumes, transfer the fuel, and save the plane.

"Open the damn doors!!" I yelled.

"Opening bomb bay doors!" Mark yelled.

I looked down as the large doors opened. As the wind rushed in, I could clearly see the inlet to the harbor, several ships, buildings, and two large factories. The wind was buffeting me against the fuselage of the plane. The view looking down was mesmerizing as the bombs slowly left the plane. The yellow tips of the green bombs gradually turned toward earth as they gained tremendous speed. They fell behind, out of view, as the bomb bay doors closed.

My hands lost all their feeling. I moved my shoulders to push my frozen hands to work the pump. No pain, just numbness. I could not fail myself or crew. The plane jerked to the right, splashing fuel on my face. I took a second and rubbed my right hand against my side. It would not open or close. The pump created a vacuum as the fuel began to siphon out of the damaged tank.

"Mike, I need your help to crimp the line shut."

"Do you want me to bring you a pair of gloves?"

"No, bring the mittens; I need to get the feeling back in my hands before the fighters return."

"I'm climbing down."

"Bring the blanket with you to plug the tank."

"The blanket is on Trevor."

"We need it to stop the fumes."

"I can't move my hands. When the fuel is transferred, take the pliers and clamp the line shut."

"Finish up fast as you can, the flak has stopped and the fighters will be here soon," Cole said.

We needed every drop of fuel. Mike and I emptied all but the very bottom of the auxiliary tank. We transferred approximately three hundred gallons of fuel to the wing tank. Mike stuffed the large hole to the damaged tank with Trevor's blanket.

"Mike, I'll need help to climb out of the bomb bay."

"I'm going to climb up to the catwalk and pull you up."

Mike pulled me free from the bomb bay just like he had several times from my turret.

I put a pair of flight gloves on and immediately got lowered into my ball turret. The German fighters never returned. We rendezvoused with our fighter escort as we crossed over western Germany. My hands were severely frost bitten. I didn't think I would have been able to protect us from an attack from below.

Mike pulled me from my turret and laid me across from Trevor. His mouth and eyes were frozen open and his face was blue. Trevor's body was at twenty seven thousand feet. His soul and spirit had left the plane for a much higher place; a place next to his crew.

XXVI

Two months passed.

It was a cold, clear, winter morning. In our mission briefing we all groaned when the planning officer announced the target was Berlin. The German army and Air Force had been pushed back from the Eastern and Western Fronts and concentrated their defenses to protect Berlin. The best German pilots had been stationed near Berlin. Cole called them the "Bastards of Berlin."

The usual routine of a wakeup call from the squadron leader, breakfast, mission briefings, and collecting all our flight gear was over. We all gathered under the wing of our beloved *Sleepytime Gal*. The sun was just clearing the horizon. The morning temperature in England was fifty-two degrees.

"Let's all stay on our toes and stay calm. Let's get through this mission and we will be going home," Cole said.

We reviewed the bomb load, weather reports, target information, IP Point and alternative landing locations in western Russia if we couldn't make it back to England.

Cole was as professional as always as he affirmed the checklist with JJ; I stood in the door to the cock pit, observing. Greg was doing a radio and intercom check, Mark and Sal were reviewing the route and bomb run, Mike and Joel were talking about home, and Kip kept to himself in the rear gunner's position, double checking his gun and Aldis lamp. We were one of over a thousand planes scheduled to attack Germany.

Our bomber group was the top lead group. Our four plane element was at the bottom right of a twenty-eight plane bomber group. The task force was broken into two clusters of over two hundred planes each. Assemblage was complete and we were over the North Sea, heading point off the coast of northern Germany before turning south toward Berlin.

Weather over target was sixty degrees below zero, cold and clear. The fuselage would be a deep freeze; if you took a glove off you would lose a finger. Cole heard on the radio that sixteen planes had turned back due to mechanical problems and three ditched in the North Sea. The North Sea looked cold and gray; I could see the tops of the waves breaking from twenty-five thousand feet.

After an hour in my ball turret, we approached the coast of northern Germany. The flak officer gave us a good route; flak was light and almost not an issue. Berlin would be different; many of the batteries had been relocating to protect the German capital.

The P-51 pilot to my lower right waved good luck as he was replaced by the second rotation of escort fighters. He peeled off downward impressively for his return trip. He headed straight down to the deck looking for a strafing target on his way home. We were scheduled for four fighter rotations during the mission.

"Everyone, keep your eyes open," Cole ordered.

"One hour to IP point," Sal announced.

"With all these vapor trails, the Germans know we are coming and will have a nice welcome party for us," Kip said.

"That works both ways; we will be able to see their fighters before they get near us," I said.

"Everyone off the intercom, and keep your eyes open," Cole ordered.

Cole seemed more uneasy and tense; not as calm as on the other missions. Cole was a great leader and I hoped we would spend time together after the war. Red always said it was bad luck to think about going home; home seemed so close now, though, we couldn't stop the thoughts. Sal spent the morning talking about going home to Paris, Texas; Mike was making plans to meet me in Shreveport; Kip was talking about bringing Jane to Florida; and Howard was back talking about starting his own business in New York.

We sent a decoy squadron to Brunswick and Kiel hoping to split the German fighters. We were coming down from a more northern direction to confuse the Luftwaffe. Only an hour from the target and I had not seen any enemy fighters.

"Here they come, look at all the vapor trails turning toward us at two o'clock high," Cole said.

The vapor trails from the German fighters were bright white against the blue sky.

"Our fighters see them; they are going after them," JJ said.

"Jesus Christ, there must be hundreds closing in from behind at our six o'clock position," Kip said

"Cole, do you see the jets low on the deck?" JJ said.

"I got them ten o'clock low coming in from the east. Look how fucking fast they are. Ox, do you have them?"

"I see them; they are starting their climb. Here they come."

"Don't let those bastards get a shot at our fuel tanks," Cole said.

"Bomber going down!" Howard yelled.

"No yelling on the intercom. Stay calm," Commander Cole ordered.

Fighters were closing in from every hour on the clock and all twelve .50 calibers were firing at once. The jets were coming straight at me from directly below. My guns were pointed vertical with my hatch and back pointing into the plane. This was a good attack angle for me; I didn't have to aim in front of the fast moving jet. The jet was impressive, camouflaged in green, brown and gray. I put him in the middle of my crosshairs and did not compensate for leading the target, gravity drop, or drift. I unloaded both barrels. I could see the tracer bullets flashing as they hit, then pieces of the jet started to fly off. I kept hitting him, over and over until he finally exploded.

"Howard is hit! Blood is dripping from his turret," Greg yelled from his radio position.

"Here they come again. There are too many. Ox, take the six o'clock low group," Kip yelled with panic.

Twelve fighters were on our tail coming directly at us. They had picked us out for the kill. Maybe this was revenge for me shooting down two of their fighters. I had already made ace with twelve confirmed kills, and hoped to get a few more of those bastards that day. Greg pulled Howard's unresponsive body from the top turret to assist Kip with the fighters approaching from the six o'clock high position. Greg was sitting in Howard's blood and flesh; those were the thoughts we needed to block from our minds; not even a peek back.

The fighters approached and started hammering our wings and tail section. Pieces of *Sleepytime Gal* were flying off both wings. Our biggest fear was an explosion. One of the German pilots looked up through his canopy at me as he passed. I missed all five fighters that slid past.

"Kip, are you OK?" I asked.

"Yes, but we are missing half our tail."

"I still have hydraulic pressure, but there is a vibration," Cole said.

"We are losing oil pressure in number two engine," JJ said with alarm.

"Turn off the engine, and then feather the prop before we have a fire," Cole ordered.

The fighters departed and the flak was heavy and accurate. Two large flak bursts directly below me, shook the plane, and tore through the wing between number three and four engine.

"Greg is hit! He is bleeding from the right shoulder and neck," Sal said.

"Can you stop the bleeding? Is he conscious?" Cole asked.

"No, he is not responding. He has a large hole in his side, and I think his neck is broken."

"We are at the point designated to start our bomb run," Mark said.

"Mark, I am going to give you the plane."

"OK."

"Damn! The autopilot won't engage; I can't give you the plane."

"Follow the other planes to the target and I will drop at my discretion."

"Will do."

"Two minutes to bomb drop."

"I am having trouble staying with the formation."

"We are losing oil pressure in engine number four," JJ announced.

"Don't shut it down; we need to stay with the formation. Let me know when we lose all pressure," Cole said.

"One minute to target," Mark said.

"There is a fuel leak between number one and two engines," I said.

"We will not be able to keep up with the formation; after the bomb drop I am turning east toward Russia," Cole said.

"Bombs away! Mark said.

"JJ, shut down engine four, feather the props on two and four engines, and turn to the east," Cole said.

"JJ," asked Cole, "we are losing air speed. Should we lower our altitude?"

"Nose down ten degrees. Let's gain airspeed and distance ourselves from Berlin and head for Russia. Level out at seven thousand feet so we can get off oxygen. Everyone keep an eye out for fighters, they will be looking for stragglers."

We leveled out at seven thousand feet.

"Oxygen masks can come off," JJ said.

"Mark, give me a status on the plane and crew," Cole asked.

"Howard and Greg are dead, the radio and generator are damaged but working, several holes in fuselage both wings, tail section severely damaged, number two and four engines down, fuel reserves low in remaining tank."

"What about ammunition?"

We all began to answer back.

Joel: "Thirty rounds."

Kip: "Only twenty rounds."

Mark: "Chin turret is empty."

Mike: "Forty rounds."

"We have a hundred rounds left in the top turret," Sal said.

"Only fifty rounds left," I said.

The weather was clear and cold; behind us was the bright sun.

"Mark, man the top turret and protect the front of the plane. Sal and Mike, get rid of any unnecessary weight; we don't have the power to climb. Dump the oxygen tanks and both machine guns from the chin turret," Cole commanded.

It was not easy for Cole to make the decision to dispose of Howard and Greg. There was a long moment of silence when they were dropped from the plane.

"There is a low mist on the horizon, we will use that for cover," Cole said.

"Two fighters at six o'clock high diving on our position!" Kip yelled.

"I see a shiny flicker in the sun. I think it's a third fighter tuning toward us at the seven o'clock level position."

"Make each shot count. Let them get close," Cole said.

I could hear the rounds from the two fighters tearing holes in the fuselage. Kip and Mark returned fire, missing as the fighters crossed over Cole and JJ.

"They are getting in front of us to make a head-on pass," JJ yelled.

I could see flashes of gun fire coming from the sun. The German fighter was well positioned and completely invisible. I opened up with both .50 caliber machine guns; I started from the top of the yellow circle and worked my way down to the bottom left. I saw flashes, then an explosion; pieces of the German fighter became visible as it fell below the sun.

"Fighter at the three o'clock level!" Joel and Mike yelled.

I could feel *Sleepytime Gal* shudder as the rounds tore through the side of the plane. I did not hear the waist gunner return the fire. Mark in the top turret put out a small burst, but missed his target. Mark and I swung our turrets to the front of the plane for the frontal attack. The two German Me 109s one mile in front of us were closing the gap at a high speed. They opened fire immediately, striking the cockpit and left wing of our bomber. We opened fire at point blank and missed our mark. Engine one trailed flame and smoke; *Sleepytime Gal* began to vibrate violently.

"Bail out! We are losing hydraulic pressure, and I don't know how long I can hold the plane steady!" Cole yelled.

I aimed my machine gun straight down to expose my hatch.

"Mike, get me out of this fucking turret!" I yelled.

No answer. The plane wing started to dip then leveled.

"Mike! Kip! Someone help me out! Get me out of this fucking place! Someone help me! I need help!"

Kip opened the hatch and pulled me out. I could feel the cold wind passing through the plane. I immediately realized the front windshield must have been shot out. The cold air was burning my lungs and my heart was racing. Mike and Joel were on the floor with fatal bullet wounds to the head. I tried to stand as Kip rushed to grab my parachute; my legs wobbled with no feeling other than the tingle of numbness. I held myself up, holding onto Mike's machine gun. Kip was slipping on the frozen blood as he handed me my parachute.

"Hurry, get your damn parachute on!"

Points on the clock didn't matter anymore. *Sleepytime Gal* would never fire another shot. We needed to get out before she lost her battle with gravity.

"Cole can't hold on much longer!" Kip said with panic.

"What about JJ?"

"JJ is dead."

"Fuck, I didn't adjust my top clip to my harness! It won't reach."

"Pull harder!"

"I'm hit and can't hold the plane much longer!" Cole yelled.

The flak returned and became more intense and the plane began to bounce violently. The plane was struggling to not roll over.

"What in the hell is taking you so damn long? I'm losing horizontal stability. We're going to roll over!" Cole yelled.

"I got it! Jump, Kip! Jump, Cole!" I said.

I jumped and looked back and saw Cole drop out of the front escape hatch. The background was a deep blue sky. *Sleepytime Gal*'s huge left wing dipped and fell from my view in seemingly slow motion. The dark green bomber seemed unhurried and proud as she slowly passed through the mist and thin, low clouds. Gravity always won in the end.

I looked to my right and found the parachutes of Kip, Sal, Mark, and Cole. They were moving to the east a few hundred feet below me and were passing just above the thin clouds. Looking down, I noticed the blood from flak wounds dripping from my boot. I looked ahead to see my crew's parachutes as they disappeared into the mist. There was something haunting about the mist with no view of the ground. I floated with the haze for a long portion of a minute.

I cleared the cloud at a lower altitude than expected. Three thousand feet below me was a farm house that was located in a clearing, to the left a dirt road that came from the forest, past the farm and a river lined with trees. Kip, Cole, Sal, and Mark were five hundred feet below me heading for the river. They were lined up in a perfect row behind Sal. Cole was last. Cole was looking back as we passed over the farm house. The goal was to land just short of the trees and find cover and bury our parachutes. Kip, Sal, and Mark landed just fifty feet short of the line of trees. They didn't run for cover and waited for Cole to land. Cole landed moments later and fell to the ground. Sal and Mark immediately grabbed Cole by the arms and pulled him to cover. It was obvious that Cole was injured by the way he fell in the field. Kip gathered his parachute and followed them into the trees. I looked back at the farm house to make sure we weren't spotted from the ground.

I looked down and realized I was overshooting the open field. The trees rushed at me, they could not be avoided. Then I felt a tremendous impact. My adrenalin was high, and the pain was blocked from my mind. My parachute got caught on the canopy of a large maple tree, suspending me fifteen feet from the ground. I looked up and twisted my body back and forth and pulled on my straps. My only option was to cut my white harness and drop to the ground. Wasting no time, I cut my right strap first causing me to swing to the left. I looked down past my boots at the ground and cut the last strap. Impact with the ground delivered a piercing blow to my left leg.

Looking straight up from my back, I could see my parachute in the canopy of trees. My parachute was visible from the farm house. My left ankle was sprained or broken. I used a stick as a walking cane and slowly moved two hundred feet up river to find the others.

Cole was bleeding from his left side just above his hip. His left foot had been severed just above the ankle. Mark cut strips of silk from his parachute to tie around Cole's lower leg in an effort to stop the bleeding. Sal was evaluating the wound to Cole's side as he administered morphine. Kip stood at the edge of the tree line holding his .45 caliber pistol.

"Ox, did you bury your chute? Cole asked me as he grimaced in pain.

"No, it's in the canopy of the tree."

"Is it visible from the farmhouse?

"Yes."

"We need to get it down. Kip, do you see any activity at the farmhouse?"

"No."

"We need to get Cole some help. Kip, check the farmhouse." Sal ordered.

"Did you stop the bleeding?" Cole asked.

"Yes," Mark answered.

"Give me something for the pain."

Kip approached the farmhouse from the east with his .45 pistol drawn. He slowly and quietly looked through each window and returned.

"The farm house is empty. Should we use it for shelter?" Kip asked.

"No, we need to move upriver and find Cole some help. We passed over a small village a few miles from here," Sal said.

"Are we going to turn Cole over to the Germans?" I asked Sal.

"Yes, that is his only chance."

The word "Germans" brought fear, but Cole was losing consciousness and seemed weak due to a loss of blood.

"Mark, you and Ox cut more strips of silk and build a stretcher; we need to get moving," Sal said.

We found suitable pieces of fallen branches. I cut notches in the limbs to help keep the silk rope in place. Mark tied the four pieces of wood together, creating a rectangle two feet by seven feet. The cross pieces were offset by six inches, leaving us a handle to carry Cole. We used silk to bridge the gap and give Cole something to lie on.

The cold river was flowing swiftly around and past the tree trunks with a swirl. Mark and Kip carried Cole as we began to walk up river. There was a light fog in the air making the rocks along the bank wet. The weather was damp and cold and dark gray. We walked for an hour and traveled approximately two miles.

"It's getting dark, and we need to find a place to camp," Mark said.

"Let's move back into the trees to camp. We are too exposed," Kip said.

We moved into the woods one hundred feet from the river. There was an open area twenty feet across.

"Should we build a fire to help keep Cole warm?" I asked.

"No! It is too risky. Cover me in leaves," Cole commanded. We were all surprised to hear him speak.

We found branches and built a low frame and covered it with leaves. This gave us cover and held our body heat. We all decided to lie side by side to keep warm and dry. The mist and dew settled on the leaves as we slept. Cole was between Mark and Sal; I was to Sal's right and Kip was next to me.

I slept well for the first hours of the night, but woke up and lay thinking of England and the time Kip and I spent with Sally and Jane. Elaine, and thoughts of spending time with her and Kip after the war, entered my mind. I was not afraid to go on; I had a lot to live for.

The next morning was warmer, but damp and cloudy. Cole regained consciousness but was not willing to eat and only took a sip of water. He was fading and needed medical help as soon as possible.

We walked three hours and four miles upriver. The current was strong and rapids formed where the river was shallow. The river was a hundred feet across with a rocky bank.

"Stop, there is a German platoon camped ahead, across the river," Kip whispered.

"How many are there?" Cole asked.

"I can see eight, maybe nine," Mark said.

"Ox, move up river and assess their numbers and weapons," Cole ordered.

I moved well inside the tree line until I was directly across from the German camp. They seemed undisciplined; they could have been deserters from the Russian Front. They had a camp fire near the bank of the river; to their right were ten rifles leaning against a large rock, and past that was an area covered with a canvas that was stretched between the trees. To the left were empty cans of rations and a German troop carrier. The river was shallow at this point, only one or two feet deep. I returned to Cole to give him my assessment.

"There are nine foot soldiers; they have rifles and side arms. They have a vehicle."

"We need to be careful," Cole said.

"Let's surrender and get Cole some help," Mark said.

"I don't trust those fuckers. Let's try to find the village," Kip said.

"We don't have time to wait; Cole needs help now!" Mark said.

"The civilian militia will be worse. We need to get Cole help now! These soldiers are our best damn choice!" Sal said.

"If they are fucking deserters they can't be trusted. If they try something, open fire and let those bastards have it," Kip said.

Cole gave us instruction. "Be smart. Kip, you move upriver above their camp and if they try something stupid, we will have them in our crossfire. Maybe you can get to one of their rifles. One of you, carry me across the river and offer to surrender."

"I will carry you across the river," Mark volunteered.

"Sal, you and Ox stay downriver. Do not cross the river; you will have an advantage if they try to cross the open river. They have rifles and more ammunition, so stay smart. No matter what happens to me and Mark, stay calm and patient, and make each bullet count. Take a position behind the log and cover yourself in leaves."

"Cole, we will see you after the war," I said.

"Let's do it," Cole commanded.

Mark picked up Cole and moved one hundred feet upriver through the trees. They reappeared along the bank just across from the German camp. Cole was standing to Mark's right trying to hold onto his right arm while balancing on one foot. Mark raised a white piece of his parachute with his left hand as a sign of surrender. We could see the unshaven leader of the Germans wave them across. Mark took Cole into his arms and carried him into the middle of the river.

"Halt!" the German leader ordered.

"What in the fuck is he up to?" Sal whispered.

"I don't like this."

All the German soldiers moved to the edge of the river and began to shout and yell. Mark was asking to surrender. Before we could act, the leader raised his rifle and shot Mark in the head. Cole fell to the cold water and tried to stand up. Sal and I opened fire, hitting two of the soldiers. They returned fire in our general direction. Cole was trying to crawl back to the bank of the river when the leader of the deserters shot him in the back. The leader and four of the German soldiers ran to cross the river. They were exposed and we emptied our clips, killing two of the Germans. We could hear Kip shooting from his position upriver. The German leader and two of his soldiers made it across and headed through the woods to outflank our position. Sal hid between some dead trees and leaves. I found a deep spot in the river along the bank to hide. All we had were our knives. The water was extremely cold but provided the best cover and escape route.

Five minutes passed and I began to shiver uncontrollably. I could hear the Germans talking and searching in Sal's direction. They were only twenty feet from me and near Sal's hiding spot. Then there were some loud shouts in German, and I could tell by their tone Sal was discovered. I pushed myself away from the bank and began to float down river. I heard two loud rifle shots. Sal must have been killed.

Everything slowed down as I pulled myself along the bank. I was cold, but alert. I heard three pistol shots from a .45 and then four rifle shots. I looked upriver to better understand where the shots came from. The shots were loud and deliberate. I kept scanning upriver to make sure enemy soldiers were not walking my way. I noticed something bobbing up and down in the current, floating toward me. The bomber jacket was too familiar. Face down, circled in blood, and carried in the fast current was Kip's lifeless body. I tried to stand to jump and retrieve Kips body, but was too slow. Kip's body hung on a tree trunk for a moment as if to say goodbye, then continued down river. I could see him moving up and down with the small waves of the river as he faded away from my view. He was a mile downstream when I saw the last glimpse of his leather bomber jacket. I could have died this day or in sixty more years, but the war had just changed my life forever. He was the brother that I always wanted.

XXVII

I received a light kick in the back; I squinted and looked up. A girl with blond hair was standing over me with a rifle. She set her rifle against the tree and offered to help me to her farmhouse.

"Can you speak English?"

"*Ja.* Let's get back to the farmhouse before you are discovered."

"My leg is broken."

"I brought my husband's crutch and I will help. Let's get moving."

She helped me stand up and propped the crutch under my left shoulder. I had my right arm over her shoulder to take weight off my left foot. We moved slowly as I scanned the open field and tree line for the soldiers who shot Kip. My .45 caliber was loaded and available. I was hoping the bastards who shot Kip and my crew would find me. I looked back at the tree line; my parachute was bright white and filled with air as it waved in the cold breeze. It would be just a matter of hours before Kip's killers found me.

The farmhouse and garden were well-kept, especially considering the war and lack of resources. The exterior walls were white stucco with a low band of stone; the windows were stained wood with dark green shutters. The shutters were faded and not as crisp as the rest of the farmhouse, and the garden was colorful with flowers. To the right of the farmhouse I saw a vegetable garden and a small barn the color of faded wood. It seemed older than the house.

The German girl walked me through the main room; I saw a fireplace to my right outlined in stone, a big table to my left, five chairs, bare walls, and a wood burning stove. The floor of the farmhouse was made of large, wood planks stained light brown. She laid me down in a small room and left me to close the shutters from the outside. The room was small, with bare walls and only my bed. She returned to my bedside.

"Can you get the syringe and small bottle from my canvas bag?" My pain was unbearable. I gave myself a shot of morphine and started a conversation to help block the hurt.

"Where is your husband?"

"My husband and father were killed in the war."

"What did your husband do in the war?

"He was a tank commander and got killed in northern Africa"

"How old are you?"

"Nineteen, what is your age? She asked with her attractive German accent.

"I am nineteen also. Do you live alone?"

"Ja, my grandfather checks on me once a week."

"What is your name?"

"Call me Berta."

"That is a pretty name. My name is William Abraham; you can call me Willie or Ox."

"I like Willie. I will call you Willie."

"Why are you helping me?"

"I hate the war."

"I am getting drowsy from my medicine; if I fall asleep, wake me if you see anyone coming toward the farmhouse."

I laid flat on my back with my .45 caliber pistol in my hand on my stomach. I didn't think anyone would shoot me without waking me up, and I would be ready. Berta made sure I had a cup of water near my bed, pulled the shutter tight, and disappeared from the room.

I woke up and the morning sun was passing through the cracks in the shutters. I saw civilian clothes on a small, wooden chair next to my bed. Berta entered the room with a biscuit and a hot cup of coffee. "My husband was your size; you should put them on after I bandage your leg. If someone comes to door, I will say you were hurt in the war fighting for the Fatherland and can't be disturbed."

"What about my parachute?"

"I got it down from the tree and hid it in the barn."

"We need to bury it. How did you get it down?"

"I tied a rope around a piece of pipe, threw it through the straps and pulled it down."

"That was very smart. We need to bury it soon. Some German soldiers upriver killed my crew when we tried to surrender. Call for me if you see anyone coming toward the farmhouse. They can't be trusted. "

"The ground will be frozen and covered in snow soon; nobody will be able to find it or dig up your parachute."

Berta left the room and returned with bandages and bowl of warm water. "I will change your bandages and give you a bath."

She helped me remove my pants, jacket, and shirt. I left my underwear on as she washed me and bandaged my leg. My leg was cut, discolored and swollen. My knee was shattered and locked in place. Her washing felt good and refreshing. While she washed me, I took the time to study her good looks. Her clothes were simple, but flattering. Her large breasts were rounded and firm, her hair blond and wavy, her skin smooth and fair; she was the German girl American men dream about. The war probably didn't let her smile often. She gave me a quick smile, and it was the prettiest sight I have ever seen.

One week passed. The swelling in my leg went down; there was no sign of infection. Her husband's handmade crutch was standing in the corner just out of my reach. The crutch was very unique, with carvings of deer on the handle. From that point forward the crutch was part of my life. I would never feel sorry for myself or complain; so many of my friends never made it back home. I constantly thought about my crew and going home.

Berta entered the room wearing a pair of pants and a thick, wool sweater. The thick sweater could not hide her figure.

"Can you hand me the crutch? I would like to try to walk."

She helped me sit up. I was stiff and sore. She handed me the crutch and I pulled myself up.

"Can you help me walk around the house?"

"*Ja.*"

We slowly made our way through the door, out into the open living area. The fireplace was burning and popping sparks. The room reminded me of a country lodge. I saw vegetables on the table, a shot gun and rifle in the corner, a large pot on a wood burning stove, and knitting needles and a ball of wool.

"Willie, do you think you're strong enough to go outside?" She asked with the exotic German accent.

"I would like to try."

She put a blanket over our shoulders and we stepped through the door. The air was still but damp and cold. You could tell the snow would be coming soon, you could feel winter in the air. The trees along the river had lost most of their leaves. The trees in the forest to the south were thin and still. The sky was a snow sky, white with no definition.

The damp air carried sound and you could hear faint sound of artillery shells in the distance. We walked one hundred feet to the dirt road and back.

"Can I sit at the dinner table until I get tired?"

"*Ja*, you can talk to me while I knit a sweater."

"Do you like American music?"

"Very much. I want to go to America after the war. I studied English in school and learned about your country."

I reached down for my pack of cigarettes that were in the pocket of her husband's gray plaid robe.

"Would you like a cigarette? I have only two left."

"*Ja.*"

We had dried salt meat or sausage for every meal.

"When I get stronger, I would like to fish or go hunting."

"My husband and father's pole is in the barn."

"What did they catch in the river?"

"Trout."

"I need to get my strength back before the river freezes over. Maybe I can catch enough to get us through the winter. We can pack it in the snow. Are there any deer or wild hogs in the forest?"

"*Ja*, many animals."

"I will set a trap; I don't want anyone to hear a gunshot. We can freeze the meat in the snow."

"Tonight I'm going to fix you a rhubarb stew for dessert."

We talked for another hour. She helped me back to my room. She sat on the side of the bed looking at me as I fell asleep holding my .45.

I woke up from my nap and she was sitting on the side of the bed. I sensed she was sitting there watching me sleep.

"I have dinner made. Would you like me to serve in here?" She said with an alluring German accent.

"No, I need to walk and get my strength back soon as possible."

We had hot potato soup.

"The rhubarb is really good. This is the first time I have ever tasted it. I like it."

"They don't have rhubarb in America?"

"I live in the Deep South where the weather is too hot. I trained with a gunner from Michigan and he told me about rhubarb pie."

"I will put more wood on the fire."

"Did you chop all that wood outside?"

"*Ja.*"

"You are very resourceful; I admire that."

I looked over Berta's shoulder through the small, square window frames and noticed flakes of snow slowly falling. I stood by the front door while Berta brought in more wood. The snow was so peaceful and relaxing; the air perfectly still. None of it was sticking to the ground.

XXVIII

"You have been having nightmares and screaming in your sleep," Berta said.

"I know. I keep having the same dream over and over."

"What is it? You hold both hands in the air like you are shooting a gun."

"The fighters are closing at my plane and my guns jam and I can't move. I am cramped and stuck and no matter how hard I try I can't fire back. My crew members are begging me to shoot and I can't. The plane is hit and starts to spin and before we crash I wake up in a cold sweat."

"Were you close to your crew?"

"Yes. Kip was like a brother and we all had plans to get together after the war."

"I am sorry."

"When I get my strength back, I will need to get back to England and join the fight."

"We will be snowed in soon. I'm knitting you a sweater."

"When your grandfather comes to visit, ask him what he knows about the war. Ask about the Russian front. Ask him if any brigades have broken through the German lines. Has the line held?"

"Why do you ask?"

"I heard faint sounds of artillery fire from the east. I'm concerned what they might do to German civilians. We are east of Berlin and they may get here before the Americans."

"I will ask my grandfather what he has heard."

"I may need to move west toward the American front lines when I get my strength back."

"You will need to wait for spring."

"I need to join the fight."

"Don't leave me."

XXIX

Two weeks passed.

No sign of the German deserters. The farmhouse was remote; Berta's grandfather was the only visitor. I hid as he delivered some supplies and checked on her well-being. He told Berta that the Germans were losing the war and the Russian Front was moving toward Germany. He felt the Russians would slow down when the snow arrived.

My left leg was locked straight and I needed a crutch to move with any speed. My hip was damaged more severely than I had realized. My strength was returning and the weather was unseasonably warm with a slight breeze from the south. Berta helped me find her husband and dad's fishing pole. The poles were of a high standard: split bamboo with brass and stainless steel reels. The eyes to the poles were porcelain and tied to the pole by cat gut thread. There was a tin tackle box with home-made wooden lures and flies.

We walked to the river. I was holding the poles and my .45. Berta brought a rifle and the tackle box. I cast downstream and let out a little slack and let the current carry my lure. The trout were biting on the long, thin, brown lure that had a blunt nose painted dark red. The lure had a propeller and one treble hook on the tail. I wasn't concerned that the treble hook would snag. The bottom of the river was pebbles and very small, smooth rocks. I dragged the bait along the bottom against the current.

We were excited to land our first trout. We stopped after catching fourteen trout and one pike. I strung them together and carried them back to the farm house. I used my survival knife to clean the fish with Berta's assistance. My knife was sharpened between every mission to a razor's edge and sliced through the fish with ease.

"Why are you cutting the heads off?"

"What do you mean?"

"We clean the guts from the fish, but cook it with the head on. The head has meat in it and some people eat the eyes."

"Yuk. I am cooking American style."

We both laughed.

"How are you going to cook it?"

"On the half shell; it's a Louisiana trick to cook red fish. We don't have butter or grease so I am going to leave the scales on one side of the fillet and cook it over the fire. You eat the meat off the skin of the trout; I promise you will like it."

"Let's cook four filets and bury the rest in the snowbank next to the house."

"Good idea. I noticed the ice is starting to form along the river bank. We need to fish every day before it freezes over. How bad does the snow get here?"

"We will be snowed in within three weeks. The roads will be impassable. You can only walk in the forest or open fields with snow shoes or skis."

"Let's go in and cook the fish."

"What do you need me to do?"

"Grab your black pan and your thickest knitted pot holder. Fish doesn't take long to cook; I'm going to hold the pan over the fire place fire."

"I have been saving some carrots and mushrooms."

"Great, bring those; I will cook them in the pan with the fish."

Berta brought me the large pan with four trout filets scales down and sliced carrots and mushrooms. Using a steel spatula, I moved and turned over the carrots and mushrooms while keeping the fish scales face down.

"This looks wonderful," Berta said.

"It won't be much longer now; when the fish starts to curl on the edges and gets a flaky look it will be done."

"We will be using dishes my mom left me. I put the last fresh flowers from my garden on the table."

"The fish is ready."

We were both happy to see something different on our plate.

"I wish we had a bottle of wine or a beer."

"That would be nice." We both smiled and laughed.

The dinner was excellent—first class. We forgot the hardships of the war for that evening. I was hurt deeply over the loss of my crew, but kept those feelings below the surface and in check. We added more wood to the fireplace before I retired to my room and my usual routine of falling asleep with my .45 in my right hand.

Three weeks passed. We caught and buried seventy trout and twenty pike in the snow. This would provide us the protein source to survive the winter and keep our strength. Berta gathered blackberries, apples, and hazelnuts to store for the winter to provide vitamin C. We stored four jars of stewed tomatoes and a small jar of pear preserves in the pantry. We froze the berries and apples in the snow and kept the hazelnuts in a small barrel near the fire place. Water would never be an issue.

The temperature dropped below zero many nights. The farmhouse stayed warm near the fireplace and wood-burning stove. My room was remote and in the far corner of the house and would reach forty degrees many nights. Berta gave me a thick wool comforter that helped keep me warm. Berta's room was just past the fire place and her room never dropped below fifty-five degrees. The snow was piling up each day. The roads and forest seemed to protect us from intruders or the murderers who killed Kip. The snow barrier was welcome, but I did not let myself fall into a false sense of security.

I felt trapped in time, in a place far from the war. The only reminders that the war was still ongoing were the formations of B-17s that flew over almost weekly and the sound of artillery in the distance. Other than those reminders and moments of sadness, I tried not to think about the war. We both were trying to make the most out of a bad situation.

XXX

I put a layer of trout at the bottom of a pot covered with stewed tomatoes, and then another layer of fish covered in tomatoes, and let it simmer.

"Do you like the trout couvillion?"

"*Ja*, I like very much."

"It should have cooked with slices of lemon, onions, and other spices and then served on rice, but I must admit this came out pretty good."

"I'm glad that I am not spending the winter alone. You make me happy and I am glad you are here."

"You have done much for me."

"I would like to stay friends after the war; I like our time together."

After dinner we talked for two hours. She gave me a long hug before we headed for our rooms. The hug was warm on a cold night. She pulled me close, and her body felt comforting and warm against mine. I was becoming very fond of Berta.

XXXI

I looked back before entering the trees bordering the river. As usual, Berta was sitting in the window of the farm house looking at me. The frozen river was easy to travel because it cut through the forest. With the trees so thin, the outline of the farmhouse was visible from several points on the river.

Three weeks passed. We had spent hours talking and becoming very close. Three blizzards had passed, but the day was still and gray. No wind or snow, just loud quiet. Other than a deer appearing at the tree line, the outside was perfectly at rest, motionless. Just before dark, Berta quietly came rushing into my room.

"There are four German soldiers walking from the river!"

I ran to the window. They were carrying rifles; the leader of the group had his pistol drawn. They were the deserters that killed Cole, Mark, Sal, and Kip.

"Should I tell them that you are my husband and wounded from the war?"

"No! Don't tell them I'm here. If they ask for shelter for the night, send them to the barn, don't let them in the house. They are deserters and are up to no good. Don't let them in the house. I will be in the pantry looking through the crack in the door."

"Should I answer the door?"

"Yes. If you don't they will break in for shelter."

Berta sat bravely at the table knitting a green wool sweater as they looked through the windows. They looked through all windows before knocking on the door. I was smart to conceal myself in the windowless pantry. I was not discovered and was hidden from view. When I got my chance, they would pay for what they did.

They knocked loudly on the door, four quick, deliberate knocks. Berta calmly opened the door; she stood between them and the opening to the house. The leader who killed Cole questioned her with a forceful tone. I heard Berta say "*nein*" several times. The leader of the four pushed her down and entered the house. He pointed to all the doors, and then the three others began to search the rooms. I saw the youngest of the four approaching the pantry. I held my knife in my right hand and my .45 in my left; my rifle was next to me in the corner. I hid behind the door as he opened it and gazed into the room. He saw nothing. He walked back to join the others, leaving me a view to Berta and the German soldiers.

The unshaven, rough-looking leader of the group stood over Berta yelling and shouting while holding his belt buckle. Berta was crying and pleading *"nein, nein, nein!"* One soldier moved to guard the front door. Two of the others grabbed Berta's arms and picked her up off the floor and violently threw her on the table. The soldier closest to me was holding her left wrist. He was tall and strong. The soldier holding her right wrist had an evil smile on his face. He was holding her wrist tightly with his left hand while he unbuckled his belt with his right hand.

The leader of the group positioned himself at Berta's feet. She held her legs together with her knees up. He strongly grabbed her ankles and separated her legs. He leaned over and ripped her shirt off, exposing her bra and breasts. He pushed her breasts together with both hands and leaned over to give her a kiss on the neck. Berta resisted by turning her chin to cover her neck. He stood back up with a look of anger and yelled some German words, then lifted his right hand and slapped her violently across the face. The one with the evil look laughed while still firmly holding her right wrist.

I would shoot from the front door forward. I could not let the soldier by the door escape. It would be a risk to start from the back, but I could not let anyone get out of this room. The tall, strong soldier holding Berta's left wrist was only ten feet from me. I could not risk a head shot, so I aimed for the chest of the guard holding a rifle at the door.

A few seconds passed. With my pistol now in my right hand, I slowly opened my door to a forty-five degree angle. All eyes were on Berta and the movement of the door went unnoticed. I took quick aim at the soldier guarding the door.

His chest exploded as the heavy, lead bullet hit its mark. The leader was next. He looked up at me with a shocked look on his face as my second bullet entered his forehead. My third bullet hit the ribs of the small, skinny soldier holding Berta's right wrist. He was just beginning to move toward my door. As he was struck, my door swung open against me, slamming me against the wall. The bulky, tall soldier entered the pantry with no weapon. My knife and pistol were knocked to the ground. He swung and missed. The close quarters favored me. I dodged his punch and countered with a left hook to the chin. He looked at me with a startled look, but did not fall. He instantly knew he was overmatched by my speed. He swung again and missed wide of my left ear. I caught him square with a right uppercut to the bottom of his chin and he stumbled four steps backward through the door, out into the open room. I reached down and picked up my pistol. I wanted him to go for his gun or come at me. I could not take him prisoner or let him leave this house. He stood there with his hands in the air, trying to surrender. I made a decision that would haunt me for the rest of my life. As he stood there, motionless next to the table, I fired one accurately placed shot to the heart. It felt like cold-blooded murder. It was cold-blooded murder, but I had no other option.

Berta was crying as we embraced each other. "Berta, calm down, it's going to be all right," I said softly as I stroked her head with my left hand.

"I need you to hold me."

"We need to bury the bodies in the snow before it gets dark."

"I will help."

"We are going to keep all the weapons and ammunition. Keep the one German uniform that would fit me and any identification papers."

"Are you going to leave me? Are you going to try to escape?"

"No! Just in case we both need to travel through Germany."

"Do you want their knives too?"

"Yes, put weapons and uniforms under the loose plank in the floor."

"It will be dark soon."

"We can't wait. Maybe someone heard the gunshots."

We dragged the four bodies across the open field, leaving a red trail of blood on the white snow. The bodies could only be moved one at a time. We picked a location where the ground began to gradually slope toward the river. The sun set early in the middle of winter. The full moon lit the white snow and we dug for two hours. The hole was six feet wide and three feet deep.

"Let's go in the house," Berta said.

"Ok."

"They left you no choice."

"The war changes people."

"That is why I hate this war."

"What did the soldiers say about the war?"

"They were deserters from the Russian front; they said we are losing the war. The Russians will kill civilians when they reach Germany."

"I won't let anything happen to you."

We talked for three hours about our youth and the war.

"Willie, I can't sleep alone tonight. Will you hug me and keep me warm."

"Yes."

We added more wood to the fire and moved to Berta's room. The hugging kept us warm in the cold room. I hugged her from the back then we would turn together staying in the middle of the bed. My pistol was at the corner of the bed just left of my head. The night was not sexual but extremely emotional and filled with affection.

XXXII

I woke up as the sun was passing through the small window and landing on our bed. Berta's head was lying in her folded arms as she stared at me.

"How long have you been awake?" I asked.

"Maybe one hour; the sun woke me. I like the shutters open to feel the morning sun."

"We need to keep the shutters closed, but the sun does feel good."

"It will help warm the house."

She pulled me closer and hugged me firmly as she lightly scratched my back. She gently rubbed her head against mine. I rolled more to my back. She put her leg and arm over me; her forehead rested against the side of my head. We both closed our eyes and fell back to sleep.

I woke up first and added wood to the fireplace. There was some dry blood splattered on the leg of the table and between the cracks of the wood floor. I did not want her to see any blood or reminders of what happened in this room.

The weather outside was clear and cold with no wind. There was a firm, crisp shell covering most of the snow. The surface of the snow was smooth, other than our path to the burial site near the river. I re-walked our path covering many red drops of blood with white snow. I spent twenty minutes at the location of the dead soldiers. I hid blood and exposed glimpses of their uniforms. My leg and hip ached, but I made good time.

Berta passed through her bedroom door into the open room. She stood in front of the fireplace and rubbed her hands together. Her loose, flannel gown could not hide her perfectly shaped figure. The weight of the fabric pulled it over her right shoulder exposing her back and the top of her right breast. The material draped over her breasts and hips in a flattering way. I hugged her from behind and rested my chin on her left shoulder. She turned her head slightly to the left and gently made contact moving her head against mine. Our bodies were in full contact.

Six days passed. The skies stayed shades of gray with no sun. I woke up and saw Berta getting out of bed. I was cold and got out of bed to add fire to the fireplace. The ambers were red hot, and the wood immediately ignited. Looking out the front window, I saw flakes of snow landing in the field. The leafless tree branches in the forest were outlined in snow. The air was still and the snow had a peaceful feel as it floated straight down between the trees.

I returned to the bedroom and was surprised that Berta was back in bed. She was lying on her left side in the cool room. "Willie, come back to bed, hold me, and keep me warm."

I reached out to hold her. I moved up alongside her back and felt her warm silky skin. I loved her and she loved me. I was happy, but nervous to discover she had removed her night gown. I took off my undershirt and boxer shorts. She arched her back slightly in a way that pushed her firm, rounded curves against me. The warmth of her back contrasted with the chill in the air. Then she reached back behind my neck and gently pulled my head toward her. She looked back at me and gave me a little smile and a warm, soft kiss on my cheek. She held my head against hers for a moment. I held her closer; my entire upper body and legs were in contact with her warm skin. She laid in a way that exposed her golden, rounded breast. I moved up a few inches to kiss her cheek and temple. She could feel how aroused I was; her arm moved down and reached behind her to lightly stroke me. She knew this was my first time and was being patient and understanding. I pulled her back against me to feel the warmth of her back. Still behind her, I moved up to gently kiss the side of her head. Our breathing increased as the passion built. I held her close to me and could feel her heart beating. She pulled my right arm over her shoulder and placed my hand on her right breast. I could tell by her soft moans she took pleasure in me caressing her. Her panting increased. She moved to her back as the level of our breathing increased. She was hypersensitive to my touch. I was over her with my weight on my knees and hands. My hands were placed just above each shoulder and my knees were between her legs. I gently kissed her eyes. She moved her hips in a way that asked for me to satisfy her. I unhurriedly entered her; her moans and shivers asked for more. Together we moved our hips toward each other. I stroked her at a pace that brought the most groans of satisfaction. We made love and became closer than ever.

Two months passed. We both became better lovers; our love making was passionate with just the right amount of laughter and experimentation. We were two young adults trying to get the most out of life. The deep drifts of snow isolated us from the rest of the world. We both knew everything had to change in the spring.

XXXIII

The days were longer and warmer. The snow on the roof of the farm house began to melt and drip past my window. The snow in the open field was slushy and wet and felt soft under my feet. The river ice was thinner and becoming clear and wet. The artillery fire to the east increased in intensity, and the Russians were back on the offensive.

"We need to make plans before the Russians get here," I said.

"Can I go with you? Don't leave me."

"How will your grandfather react if we talk to him? We will need his help."

"He should come here tomorrow and we can talk to him."

"What will he think about me?"

"He would never turn you over to the soldiers; he knows what would happen to me for helping you."

The next morning, I looked out over the field and saw a lot of red blood covering the snow.

"Berta, wake up! Look at the blood trails on the snow."

"What is that from? Did you hear any gunshots?"

"Shit, I think some animals dug up the bodies. We need to get dressed and bury them soon as possible. "

We could tell by the prints in the snow that it was wolves. The morning was the warmest that spring. The frozen pieces of blood were melting into the snow. As we dug the holes they would just cave in and fill with water and snow.

"We are going to need to put the body parts in the river. We can't dig a hole."

"My grandfather will be here soon."

"It is hard to cover the blood; it's bleeding back through the snow."

"Willie, do you hear that noise?"

"I hear artillery in the distance. It seems to be getting closer."

"No, that squeaking noise from the forest."

"Oh Shit! I think those are German or Russian tanks coming up the road. Let's get back to the farm house."

Before we walked sixty feet, we saw the first German panzer tank. It cleared the forest and entered the open field. The camouflaged tank with its military insignias was impressive, but intimidating. The German tank commander stood proud as he led the four other tanks and troop carriers onto the open field. He spoke into his headset as the four panzers lined up in front of us. The tank commander raised his arms in a motion that signaled us to halt. It was obvious he was a high-ranking officer by his uniform. He disconnected his intercom and climbed out of his tank. He approached us as his troops jumped from their vehicle. The tank commander had a sidearm on his hip, but it was not drawn. The ten German troops that rallied behind him were holding their rifles across their chests. The tank commander was six foot tall and looked very noble and aristocratic. His uniform was crisp; he had blond hair and blue eyes. He spoke in German and Berta responded. The conversation lasted for ten minutes as she looked at me and pointed at the blood on the snow. The tank commander was very interested in what she had to say. He surprised me when he addressed me in English.

"I am Colonel Klaus Hameister, commander of the Twenty-Ninth Panzer Division."

It was evident that Berta felt comfortable letting the tank commander know I was an American.

"My name is William Abraham, belly gunner in the ninety-fifth bomber group, Eighth Air Force."

"I spent time in America before the war."

"Where?"

"I have relatives living in Detroit, Michigan, and studied two years at the University of Michigan."

"What is going on with the war?"

"The war is lost. We were ordered back to Berlin to protect the city."

"How far east is the Russian front?"

"Only thirty or forty miles, they will be here within a few days."

"What are they doing to the people?"

"They are not allowing any German civilians to relocate or move to the west. The Russians are going to occupy any land they control; civilians will not be allowed to leave. The German soldiers they capture are being sent to the German prisoner of war camps. I am concerned that they will not be released after the war. Do you still have your uniform?"

"Yes."

"Keep it with you at all times. If you don't have any identification that you are an American soldier, you will be sent to the German prisoner of war camps to be never heard from again."

"What is happening to the American soldiers?"

"The Russians are returning them to the American army, based in western Russia."

"Will they let me take Berta with me?"

"No."

"You need to stay here or move to the nearest city. Don't try to move west to the American front, it will be too dangerous."

"Why don't the Germans surrender and stop the war?"

"It is too late for that, the Russians won't agree to surrender, and our leaders are cowards hiding in their bunkers while we die and our country is destroyed."

The tank commander turned to his troops and spoke German with a commanding tone. The troops loaded into their halftrack troop carrier. The commander saluted me, turned briskly, and walked back to his tank. He swiftly climbed onto the tank. He stood proudly and tall through the hatch of his panzer. He spoke into his intercom headset and all the tanks began to roll toward Berlin. The diesel engines were loud and there was the familiar, high-pitched, squeaky noise from their tracks.

The tanks were beautiful in a strange, unexpected way. The large metal tracks moved the heavy tanks with ease through the snow. The background of the forest only made them more striking.

XXXIV

That afternoon, Berta's grandfather arrived at the farmhouse. He walked for five miles to bring her some supplies. He was surprised and worried when he saw the tracks from the tanks. Berta introduced me and followed with a long story in a German. I could tell by her grandfather's facial expression that he was taken aback by my presence and long stay at the farmhouse. He was old and tired looking, and probably worn out and defeated from living through two world wars. His cheeks were sunken and drawn, only to be out done by his sad eyes.

"My grandfather understands and said I did the right thing to help you."

"Does he think we should go back to the village?"

"He is not sure what we should do. He is very worried about what the Russians are going to do with us."

"Tell him I going stay with you until the Russians arrive. I will talk to the Russian officer and make sure you are treated properly. I will not let anything happen to you."

Berta translated my message in German and her grandfather nodded with approval. I knew Berta was scared and nervous, but she only displayed strength and confidence.

"It is late and Grandfather Schuster is going to spend the night," Berta said.

"That is a good idea."

"Willie, do you see the flashes in the sky from the artillery?"

"Yes, they are getting closer, just over the horizon. Do many people travel this road?"

"No, I was surprised to see the tanks."

"I think we should stay here. We have plenty of food. If the Russians find us, I will try to take you with me. If not, I promise to come back for you."

"Come back for me, bring me to America."

"I promise."

That night we only hugged and held each other as we looked out the farmhouse window at the blue and white flashes against the sky. We did not speak, just stared out the window thinking about how much we despised this war.

I could not close my eyes. I just laid there in a trance. I thought about my crew and the friends. I could see and hear Kip with complete clarity. I could see him on the banks of the river in England laughing with Jane. I could see Red being Red busting our balls. I could see Cole being that great, strong, confident leader. I could see Howard trying to make us laugh and break the tension. I spent the entire night watching the flashes of artillery fire and thinking about my crew, the friends I lost.

XXXV

Two days passed.

The noise of the war surrounded us. We could hear small arms fire from all directions. Most of the heavy artillery fire moved just north of our location. East Germany was getting shelled steadily by the Russians. The weather did not slow the fighting. The afternoon was still and foggy; the temperature well above freezing.

My leg was stiff. I grabbed my crutch and limped down to the level area near the embankment of the river. The dampness in the air carried sound for a long distance. I heard noises deep into the dark shady forest. The tree lines zigzagged, blocking any penetrating view. I quickly hobbled back up the path through the open field to the farmhouse.

I noticed several foot soldiers moving through the tree line. Their appearance seemed Russian. Seventy or more infantry soldiers took position behind the trees that bordered the open field. Light artillery was brought into position to fire on the farmhouse.

"The Russian soldiers have arrived. I need to surrender before they fire on the house," I said.

Without hesitation I walked through the front door, holding up a white piece of cloth. Immediately, twenty foot soldiers ran toward me with rifles drawn.

"I'm American, don't fire! I'm American." They circled me and waved to their commander. A Russian officer appeared from behind the trees and walked in my direction. He attempted to speak broken English.

"You American?" the Russian asked.

"Yes, I got shot down over Germany."

"Who inside?"

"A German girl and an old man."

"Tell them step out, hands up."

"Berta, you and your grandfather come out slowly, with your hands up."

They both calmly passed through the door and stood behind me.

"I need to speak to your highest ranking officer."

"I am Colonel Khostikoff, the highest ranking officer."

"Can you take us to an American base in Russia?"

"No! Absolutely not. I have strict orders to only return with American soldiers. It would not be safe for them. If I return with the girl and old man, they will be sent to a prison camp. Where is your uniform?"

"In the house."

"Put it on. I have orders to move American soldiers back to Russia soon as possible."

"I need to take them with me."

"That is impossible."

"Will you see that they are not mistreated?"

"Yes, comrade."

I turned to Berta and said, "This is what we must do. I promise to come back for you." I walked past her into the house to put on my uniform. I reappeared in five minutes wearing my flight suit, and under my flight suit was my green sweater knitted by Berta.

"Comrade, what is wrong with your leg?"

"I was hit by flak and my leg was shattered when I landed."

"Bring your crutch—we must walk a long ways before I can get you to the truck."

I turned and gave Berta a long hug goodbye; I could feel her cry.

"Be strong. I will be back."

I thought it would be best to not drag things out. I joined the Russians and we disappeared into the forest.

XXXVI

After two days of travel we reached an area that had seen an intense tank and artillery battle. The land was stripped and lifeless. The dark stumps of the trees were the only thing taller than the gray, dirty, melting snow. Horses extended their necks to snatch the last blades of grass. There was the smell of death as the light wind came down from the large hill and passed over the valley. The shelling must have been intense. There was a light mist that settled in the low spots and large holes created by the artillery shells. The only colors on the landscape were gray and black. We kept walking as the trucks, troops, and horses splashed in the mud.

The rain was not heavy but steady. The road had turned from mud to a mire of sludge. One of the Russian soldiers offered me a canvas cape and a cigarette. The Russian-issued military cape was functional, and kept me warm and the rain off my back. The Russian cigarette was not very good, but I enjoyed it very much. Our group was heading east back to Russia; we crossed paths with reinforcements heading west toward the front lines. Several artillery guns, trucks, and light-armored vehicles passed in the opposite direction.

Travel was hard, but I was determined to keep pace. My limp was noticeable. I earned the respect of several Russian soldiers and officers by my ability to keep stride with one leg. The temporary rear base was less than a two days walk. General Selznick said there were other American flyers at the base, and we would be transported by truck to our American base.

The march gave me time to think about Mom, Dad and Elaine. They didn't know my fate. They were probably informed that I was missing in action and presumed dead. I wanted them to know I was alive. I hoped they were well. That night, we camped near the south side of the road. Most of us had cold, wet feet.

Some of the Russian soldiers had the proper winter boots, but most suffered from foot rot and frostbite. Mercifully, the rain stopped and allowed us time to get reorganized and try to get dry. As we rested near the road I could hear several foot soldiers, trucks and tanks heading for the front lines. The Russian soldier to my right offered me a cigarette; I smoked it to the last possible puff, flicked it into the mud, and fell asleep.

Two days passed. We finally reached the Russian rear base. I didn't know if I could have walked another mile. My left arm pit was raw and blistered from the crutch. My right foot hurt with every step.

They processed me in a small tent and gave me some dry clothes and a pack of Russian cigarettes. After some questions from an interpreter, a Russian military woman escorted me to a tent where I joined other Americans. There were three Americans in the tent.

"Hello, I'm William Abraham."

"Hello, I'm Colonel Prevot; this is Captain Young and Major Burgess."

"Are you with the Eighth Air Force?" I asked.

"Yes, we got shot down on a bombing run over Brunswick. What about you?" Colonel Prevot asked.

"We got shot down over Berlin."

"Where are you from in the states?

"Louisiana."

"Are you Ox Abraham, the boxer?"

"Yes."

"I saw you fight The Biloxi Kid at Barksdale! That was a hell of a fight."

"Colonel Prevot has talked about that fight several times," Major Burgess said.

"What plan do they have for us?" I asked Colonel Prevot.

"They are going to truck us to a small, American air base in western Russia. The base was set up for B-17 shuttle runs over Germany. We will be flown to Italy and then back to England."

"When?"

"We are leaving the day after tomorrow. What is wrong with your leg?"

"I fractured my leg when I cut myself down from a tree."

"I guess the war is over for you."

"Colonel Prevot, I need you to help with something important."

"What is it?"

"I want to get the German girl that rescued me out of Germany."

"Is she east of Berlin?"

"Yes."

"If she is caught behind Russian lines, no one can help you."

"Why not!"

"Russians are not allowing any German citizens to travel. The war will be over soon. Try after the war."

I felt so helpless. I wanted to protect her, to reach out and hold her.

XXXVII

Four days passed.

We spent twenty hours traveling east by truck. The American air base was nothing more than open fields with grass runways. The meadow was large and outlined on the edges with a forest. To my right were hundreds of barrels of fuel, racks of bombs and ammunition boxes. In front of me were several small tents for housing and operations. To my left were six Russian fighters, eight B-17s, and two P-51 Mustangs.

The Russians had an operation center to offer assistance and air cover if needed. This was where I met my first female fighter pilot. Her name was Olga Trachestco. All the Russians were supportive and engaging.

There was no mail service or personal transmissions allowed. I was no closer to letting my family know my situation. I was disappointed. I loved and missed them, and they loved and missed me.

Five days passed. The crew of *"First Time Luck"* came to our tent and said we had to leave for Italy, immediately. A German scout plane found the base and escaped before it could be shot down. All the American planes were to be relocated soon as possible. The Russian fighters and American ground crews were to stay and protect the base. I became fond of the Russians during our short stay. We drank vodka and smoked cigarettes every night. We couldn't understand most of the conversation but we all had fun and laughed.

Usually the bombers would be assigned a target to strike on the way to Italy. There was no time to load bombs. Five of the eight B-17s were operational and immediately loaded with fuel and .50 caliber ammunition belts.

Only an hour passed before we rolled down the grass runway. Olga was circling high above the base, providing cover. The bombers were light and did not need much runway. We climbed to seven thousand feet and turned south for Italy.

Colonel Prevot spent most of the flight standing in the opening to the cockpit. I wanted to spend time with the belly gunner but his commanding pilot required him to man the turret the entire trip. I spent most of the time with the waist gunners, or just sleeping.

We crossed the mountain ranges north of central Italy. The mountains had a clean edge caped in white ice; the surface was shiny with no snow. The large grooves in the ice had no drift and also shone brightly from the sun. The B-17 crew did not provide their guests with electric flight suits. The temperature was ten below zero and our altitude just under ten thousand feet.

The temperature in the plane became noticeably warmer as we traveled south. The sky was clear with only a few white, puffy clouds. Colonel Prevot notified us that we were approaching the Adriatic Sea and would be landing at Prescara, Italy in less than two hours.

XXXVIII

After we landed, we were told that the German's Luftwaffe had attacked the American base in Russia. We heard the entire base was destroyed, including the three remaining B-17s. We asked several times but got no information on casualties.

The small port city of Prescara was made up of colors of bright green, blue and white. The weather was balmy and the light breeze smelled like the combination of flowers and the sea. All the trees, shrubs, and grass were a healthy green; the sand was white; the Adriatic was blue-green.

My medical building didn't feel or have the look of a military hospital. I thought it was a grand old hotel that the Italians converted to an infirmary or sickbay for the war. My room had perfectly finished, lightly stained, hardwood floors. To my right was a freshly painted white door that was trimmed in thick molding. The molding circled the room against the floor and ceiling. The bright, white moldings contrasted crisply and handsomely with red walls. In front of me was the smaller white door to the bathroom. To my left and near my bed, a large open window was trimmed in white molding, and beyond that was a beautiful view of the blue-green Adriatic Sea.

My nurse's name was Maria Vilineo. She spoke poor English, but had the ability to communicate through hand movements and facial expressions. I told her many times of my sister Elaine. She was young and energetic with a positive demeanor. Her hair was dark and wavy; the weight of her hair flowed over her shoulders. Her skin was olive and smooth, her eyes green and penetrating; and her smile was vivid, revealing the dimples in her cheeks.

Maria washed me and changed my bandages daily. She was caring and dedicated. Every afternoon, she arrived at the same time with a wooden wheelchair and took me for a walk under the vine-covered pathway and through the courtyard. We always stopped near a concrete bench between the roses, fountain and short stonewall. We tried to talk and pick up bits and pieces of each other's thoughts; we had fun and smiled. From there, we walked to the large front porch of the converted hotel and stared out at the sea and enjoyed the breeze.

Maria made me realize how glorious her language was. I loved to hear the Italians speak, especially when they were arguing and laughing. Maria wanted to teach me some words, but I always was too tired. I always felt tired, distant, and vague; my exhilaration was gone. I was grateful to Maria. At a different time I could have become very fond of her; but my thoughts were still with my crew and Berta.

XXXIX

Dr. Otillo was a small, thin man probably in his midfifties with a broad jaw and engaging smile. At five foot five inches tall, he would have made a great belly gunner. His face was always framed with the dark shadow from his cut whiskers. He was small in stature, but has sophisticated look and commanded respect.

"How is your foot today, William?" Dr. Otillo asked.

"Much better. I am getting my feeling back; it doesn't hurt to put pressure on it."

"You will be going America soon."

"When will I be released?"

"Tomorrow. Colonel Robinson is arranging a flight for you back to England."

"He is trying to get some information on my sister's hospital ship, the *USS Mercy*."

"Where was she stationed?"

"She was stationed in the Mediterranean for a short time, then moved to the Pacific. She wrote me several times that the Marines were catching hell."

"Colonel Robinson is trying to get your mail from Horham sent here; maybe you will get a letter from your sister."

"I need to let my family know I am safe."

"What do you think of Maria?"

"She is a beautiful girl. Even though we have trouble with each other's languages, we like to spend time together."

"Did she tell you about her family saving an American airman?

"No, what happened?"

"They hid him in their attic for four months until the Americans liberated Prescara. Maria oldest sister's boyfriend was jealous of the American flyer and threatened to turn him over to the Germans"

"What would have happened?"

"They would have killed the entire family. Maria's father talked the boy out of it. The boy was lucky; the villagers have killed many of the Nazi sympathizers. We all hated those German bastards."

XL

Three days passed.

Colonel Robinson walked into my hospital room with a letter from Elaine.

"I had your mail from Horham forwarded to Italy," Colonel Robinson said.

"Thanks Colonel Robinson."

The one piece of mail was from Elaine. It was emotional just to hold the sealed envelope. I slowly and deliberately opened and unfolded the two thin sheets of stationary.

Dearest William,

Dad and I were informed from the military that you were missing in action and presumed dead. I know you will hold this letter in your hand someday. I have a sense that you're still alive. I love you very much, and look forward to fishing with you soon. If you have been killed, you already know Mom passed away suddenly from a stroke; she will be by your side in heaven. Dad has been saddened by Mom's loss and your situation. I am concerned because Dad lets his pride get in his way- he is holding everything in and is too proud to share his feeling with others. He needs you; there will be great happiness when Dad and I see you again. If the day should come that I find out God did take you, I will keep our promises. I have been preparing myself for bad news, but I know your eyes will read these words.

A few little things- I met a doctor at the hospital and we have become very fond of each other. I love him and he loves me. Dad has been distant, but keeps himself busy at the store since Mom's passing. He has expanded the store to sell watches and low end jewelry and is doing quite well. You are a special brother, we had mutual respect and tolerance for each other, but most important we enjoyed our time together. This will be my last letter for now, it hurts too much. I have confidence we will spend time together on the river bank and share some laughs. The war sent us separate ways, but is almost over. If your eyes are not shut forever, I will see you soon.

Love Always,

Elaine

Colonel Robinson gave me the happy news that Elaine was well and stationed at a navy hospital at Pearl Harbor. Elaine was informed that I was safe in Italy. I wondered if she would recognize me; had the war changed me in a way that my personality might not be familiar to family and friends? The nightmares and bouts with depression were increasing each day. It hurt too much to think about Kip and the rest of my crew; I would never understand why I was the only one to survive.

The crew of the B-17 tried to make small talk, but I was not interested. I just wanted to be left alone to think about the sad twists and turns of life and war, about my crew dead on the Germany countryside and the special girl I left behind at the farmhouse. I almost didn't care what happened to me on this trip back to England. If a German fighter appeared from the clouds, I was just going to sit calmly and quietly, staring at the inside of the plane.

XLI

We landed just before dark at the 401st bomber group airfield at Deenethorpe. Deenethorpe was a large base shared by the 401st Bomber Group of the 94th Combat Bombardment Wing and a fighter group from the RAF. I was very familiar with the 401st because of my training missions to Great Falls, Montana. I spent a lot of time in Montana playing cards and drinking with the 612th Squadron. I became very close to the crews from *Danny's Girl* and *Booby Trap*, especially Derrick and Jarred.

I spent the better part of two days being debriefed about my last mission and what role I would like to take in training new crews. I was housed with officers from the First Divisions mission planning group. They avoided me, more out of courtesy than rudeness. Did they think I resented them or blamed them for our heavy losses? Red was right all along, we should never have attempted to bomb Germany without fighter cover.

None of the crews from the 401st looked familiar. Many seemed green and new to England. Nobody remembered the fate of *Danny's Girl* or *Booby Trap*—hopefully Derrick and Jarred were back in the States or alive in a prison camp in Germany. I could probably have dug harder, but was afraid of what I might have discovered.

Four weeks passed. The local pubs were becoming habit forming. My favorite pub was Jake's, located in the small village of Kettering, nine miles from Deenethorpe. I drank hard while avoiding conversation with the British and American aircrews. If I couldn't hitch a ride to Kettering, I would drink at Kelsey's, a small pub located in the village of Deenethorpe.

Jake Barns was a strong, stocky man who ran his pub with a gapped-tooth smile, always puffing on his handsomely carved pipe. His mahogany bar was long and could seat ten patrons. The walls were stone with seemingly excessive amounts of concrete mortar. The fireplace was made of larger chiseled stone pieces topped with a wooden mantle. The nine dark oak tables in the pub seated a variety of clientele, but the bar stationed the regulars. I grew fond of the locals from Kettering.

Pappy and Chubs had to be the most interesting characters the village of Kettering had to offer. Pappy, in his early fifties, was the happiest drunk in England. He was always engaging and would go out of his way to make me feel like one of the locals. Chubs had a strong look from spending years working on the docks. They were both great joke tellers. Between the shots of scotch and beer were plenty of cigarettes. We had two things in common: the war and boxing. Chubs, Pappy, Jake and I argued over the great fighters from Germany, France, Great Britain, and America. It was closing time at Jake's, so I offered to help clean tables and move some fire wood.

286

Chubs was sitting at the long bar, asleep with his head down on his crossed arms. The second round oak table to the left of the door and near the fireplace was occupied by three loud, drunken, new recruits. Jake cleared their table of empty mugs while I wiped the top of the table between them and the large stone fireplace.

"Hey you, I recognize you from the base!" The loud mouth of the group said. I looked up, but did not answer and just kept wiping the table.

"Did you get to fly any missions over Germany?" the skinny but strong-looking one to the left the loud mouth asked.

I said nothing, just kept wiping my table and hoping they would drop the subject.

"He didn't fly any fucking missions over Germany; he probably washed dishes in the mess hall," The third loud mouth in the group said as they laughed at me.

"Ignore them, Ox," Jake said.

"We are all pissed. The war is over and we didn't get a chance to fight the Germans," the loud mouth of the group said as they all stuck out their chests, not knowing the horrors of war.

"You fucking idiots need to pick up your shit and leave this pub before I kick your asses," I said.

"Aren't the odds a little lopsided, three of us against two?" the big mouth one asked as he stood up.

"You are right, the odds aren't fair. Jake, go behind the bar. I don't need you."

The loud mouth standing directly in front of me reached out and took hold of my collar with both hands. I reached across his left arm and grabbed his right thumb and twisted his palm to face toward the ceiling. I had complete control of him; you could see the pain in his expression. I twisted his wrist harder as I drove him into the stone wall. As he recoiled off the wall, I head butted him between the eyes, breaking the bridge of his nose.

The second attacker snatched me from behind and swung me around opposite the third loud mouth. He got in one good punch to my left cheek. I purposely threw my head backward to hit the face of the second attacker who had seized me from behind my back. He released me as he stumbled backward on his heels. The third attacker made the mistake of swinging widely at my head. I had plenty of time to see the punch coming and move down to the right as his fist passed over my left shoulder. I immediately popped back up and countered with a right upper cut to his chin and down he went. All three loud mouths left the bar with new appreciation for my boxing skills. They would never understand what went on over Germany.

XLII

Colonel Bridges called me to his office to discuss my future with the Air Corps. Due to my permanently damaged left leg, he gave me the option to reenlist or return to civilian life. He complimented my service several times, repeating that I had served my country well and the choice was mine. If I choose to go inactive, Colonel Bridges would arrange that I would disembark at Barksdale Air Base in Shreveport.

"Ox, would you speak with Dr. Scruggs before you make a decision?" Colonel Bridges ask with a concerned tone.

"Why do you ask that? Why do you think I need to see the base shrink?"

"He has met with you four times and interviewed soldiers that you have made contact with. He has concluded that you suffer from severe depression and your attempts to mask it with isolation or alcohol are obvious."

"I can work it out with time."

"Sit down with Dr. Scruggs before you make your decision."

"Why do you take special interest in me?

"A high-level general told me to look out for you, but I take a special interest in everyone under my command. I have made an appointment for you to see Dr. Scruggs in the morning."

"I will see him in the morning."

Dr. Scruggs was a highly respected psychiatrist from Boston. He was a tall skinny man with a long neck and protruding Adam's apple. His hair was black and greasy, combed across his bald head with some type of oily tonic. He always wore a long white lab coat. The backs of his hands were hairy and his fingers were long and narrow with big knuckles. His office was cold and impersonal. As usual, he was seated at a metal desk located in the middle of the room; I was seated on a white metal chair directly in front of his desk. All walls were white to match the floor. The room was unoccupied other than his desk and my chair.

"William, are you OK?"

"Call me Ox."

"Colonel Bridges said your boxing matches were legendary."

"Let's stop the bullshit. Look, I don't want to be here, so let's make this quick."

"Ox, you have been here less than five minutes and you have already smoked three cigarettes. Hold out your left hand. Did it shake like that before the war? You could hardly light your cigarette."

"So, you fucking know all about me in five minutes. Yeah, you're right, I am having a lot of anxiety about the war. Isn't that normal? What the fuck do you know about war?"

"Were you this hostile before the war? Is it true you threatened a British officer last week for accidently sitting in your chair in the mess hall? What about the three new recruits you beat up in Kettering?"

"They deserved what they got."

"Are you having more frequent nightmares and moments of depression?"

"What in the fuck do you know about war? You sit behind your desk with your fucked up hair and your stupid lab jacket and pass judgment on me. Who in the fuck do you think you are?"

"Calm down and answer this question honestly! Are your anger and depression increasing as time passes? Did you have these anxiety issues in Italy or Germany?"

"No, it is worse now. Ever since I landed in England, my depression and nightmares have increased."

"You took comfort from your peers who were also struggling to survive and had shared experiences. Does it bother you to know most people you make contact with now don't truly understand your experiences?"

"Yes! The war in Europe is over and these new fuckers on this base will never understand what Commander Cole, Kip, and the rest of us went through."

"You know it will be even worse in the States. Most the people you meet will not be able to relate to your experiences. Someday, you may get married and have kids and they will not truly understand what you have been through and seen in war."

"I can't help how I feel! Do you think I want to feel like this?"

"Why do you spend so much time drinking off base?"

"I can forget the war sometimes. The beer and whiskey do help."

"Here, do you want a smoke?"

"Thanks."

"The war in Europe is over; I'm going to recommend to Colonel Bridges that you return to civilian life. You have already won the Distinguished Flying Cross for bravery and a Purple Heart. You owe your country nothing. You should go home and begin to recover emotionally and start a new life. Ox, the first step to recovery is recognizing you have a problem. Always remember you have the power to choose. Choose to be happy and productive."

XLIII

At quarter to six the troop train arrived at London's Waterloo Station. The loading platform for the passengers was elevated two feet above the perfectly spaced ties. The long loading dock was crowded with soldiers.

The thin lieutenant to my right made eye contact and asked about my destination. To my left were two soldiers from the army that could pass for brothers, both with dark hair and medium builds, each stood just an inch taller than me. The soldier second to my left noticed me looking at the quarter-empty bottle of scotch protruding from his green duffel bag. He reached down and pulled the bottle from the bag with his left hand, then awkwardly passed it to me. It was obvious his right arm was damaged from the war. I took a hit from the bottle and offered him a cigarette before I lit up and took a long drag. The thin lieutenant to my right bumped my shoulder and asked for a hit from the bottle. The owner of the scotch was glad to share.

The train stopped but seemed to go on forever. The view of the long train disappeared past all the heads and shoulders of the thousands of soldiers waiting to go home. The passenger cars had large windows; I looked in and saw people standing to exit and the stained wood panels on the wall. The train unloaded civilians and military personnel.

Twenty minutes passed and the whistle blew for us to board the train. I walked up two steps at the rear of my car and turned left through the opening to the sitting area. To my left and right were sitting areas for groups of six. The handsomely stained wooden benches were facing each other stationed next to large windows. Between the benches was a low small mahogany table, just large enough to hold a drink, ashtray, and small dinner setting. I walked to the front of the car and sat in the first grouping for six. The two army soldiers sat across the table from me, and moments later the thin lieutenant asked to join our group. The car began to fill up when an army chaplain and an intelligence officer asked if we had room.

We all exchanged names before starting our long trip to Scotland. In front of me, sharing the window, was Bill Glass from Patton's Third Army; to his right was Richie Blake from the same army; to Richie's right was Father McDoyle from Chicago; to my left, Lieutenant Dale Canning from the 101st Airborne; to his left, Major Clarke, a military lawyer and intelligence officer.

"Bill, can I have another hit from your scotch?" I asked.

"Sure, pass it around."

All six of us took a hit. I lit up a Chesterfield.

"If we can get our hands on small glasses, I have a bottle of cognac," the priest offered.

"I will find some glasses," Major Clark said as he stood up and began his search.

Major Clark was in his late thirties and struck me as being very resourceful. In our brief introduction he impressed me with his openness and was very engaging. He was the tallest of our group with an athletic build. His hair was brown with a tint of red and wavy, but neatly cut. His looks reminded me of Errol Flynn, and he seemed to have that swash-buckler personality to match.

"I found two shot glasses!" Major Clark said as he returned with a smile.

"Good, one for each side of the table," Father McDoyle compromised.

"Father, pour me a shot!" Richie Blake said as he slammed the shot glass down on the table next to the bottle of cognac.

Father McDoyle filled the small glass to the top.

"What do you think of that?" Father McDoyle asked as Richie slammed the empty shot glass down.

"That will warm you up on a cold night. That was really good," Richie said.

"Let me have the next shot; I found the glasses," Major Clark said.

The priest filled the shot glass to the top and took the next drink

"Don't be angry, Major Clark, but I brought the cognac."

We all started laughing. Father McDoyle poured Major Clark a full glass. The Major picked up the shot glass, and with one swift motion returned it empty to the table. We all took turns until the bottle was clear.

The train rolled out of the large station ten minutes after seven. We cleared the low roof covering the tracks and passed the tall buildings near the station. The setting sun passed through the window to my left and across our shoulders. I lit up a cigarette as we crossed the bridge that spanned the Thames. Looking down through metal framing, I could see the slow-moving river. Beyond the embankment of the river I saw several soldiers walking toward the train station and behind that several busy shops and outside cafes. The city was coming back to life. The world was not at war any more.

We reached the open fields and marsh land just north of London. To the west and beyond the row of distant trees was the setting sun. The shadows stretched long from the train and over the grassy areas along the tracks. In the fields of green grass were cattle, horses, flowers, and English farmhouses.

Our route was going to take us north, through Birmingham, Stafford, Manchester, and then up the west coast of England into Scotland. Our final destination would be the port city of Gourock, Scotland and the Queen Mary.

"Father, where were you stationed in the war?" Major Clark asked.

"I was with the Twenty-First Army Group at Omaha Beach on D-Day and spent most of my time on the front lines. What about you?"

"I worked with counter intelligence and spent some time behind the front lines working with the resistance."

"What type of counter intelligence?"

"I was with the group that broke the codes to the German Enigma machine."

"What else?"

"I worked with the resistance to stop the Germans from developing the atomic bomb."

"Were they close to developing the bomb?"

"Yes."

"Father, do you have a moral problem with us dropping the bomb on Japan?"

"I have mixed emotions; I wish they would have surrendered."

"Do you think it is morally or legally right for the American government to order the death of an American citizen without due process?"

"That is a funny question," Bill Glass said with a curious look.

"Major Clark, why did you ask that question?" Father Doyle asked.

"There was an American scientist who was helping the Germans develop an Atomic bomb. We had a team trying to kill him."

"I think it was the right thing to do," Lieutenant Canning said.

"I will drink to that!" Richie said as he poured himself a shot of scotch.

"What did this scientist look like?" I asked, wondering if he was our secret passenger.

"I didn't see his photo. What if he would have been assassinated on American soil without due process?" Major Clark asked.

"I think it would have been justified," Bill answered.

"I think we may be going down a dangerous road. I may write a legal paper on this subject."

"It is a very interesting question," Father Doyle acknowledged.

"Are you going to practice law when you get back to New York?" Bill asked Major Clark.

"Yes, I will either work at my uncle's firm or start a practice with a classmate of mine from Yale."

"William, what do you want to do after the war?" Father Doyle asked.

"I am not sure. Maybe work at Dad's store."

"If you need to talk about the war, let me know."

Father Doyle was very intuitive and understood my problem. The loss of my crew and leaving Berta were causing me to drift into a state of constant depression.

"Bill, did you say you were in Patton's Third Army?" I asked.

"Yes."

"Did you ever meet a boxer named "The Biloxi Kid"?

"Yes, everyone knew The Biloxi Kid. He was the best fighter in the army. He said he only lost one fight."

"Did he tell you his name?"

"Some kid from Louisiana. I think he said his name was Ox. He said his right was like a sledge hammer. He said he would never forget how hard he hit. You're from Louisiana. Did you ever hear of a boxer named Ox?"

"I knew him a long time ago. I don't know him anymore. Do you know if The Biloxi Kid made it back home?"

"I heard his M5 Stuart Tank was destroyed when we tried to recapture St.Vith during the Battle of the Bulge. He was severely injured and moved to a military hospital in Paris."

"Major Clark, let me out; I need some air."

I stood up and squeezed by the Lieutenant and the Major and turned left and made my way to the rear of the train car. My leg was stiff, and I walked with a limp. I opened the door between the two cars and walked outside; I leaned over the small railing and gathered my thoughts.

The war was defining who I was; my frame of mind, recent bad temper and sadness. I look at the world differently; the war had changed the way I related to people, the way I communicated, even my step. I knew I needed to be strong.

I cupped my hands over my lighter and lit my cigarette. I took a deep drag and looked out over the English countryside. The moon and stars were clear and bright. The moon was straight overhead; must have been around midnight. The moonlight reflected on the tree tops created a thin, silver line.

"Come back inside, William. We are going to pour another round," Major Clark requested.

Everyone seemed concerned for me and my state of mind. Maybe I had one of my nightmares when I dozed off for a moment, or maybe they knew what hell the B-17 airmen experienced.

Bill tapped the shot glass on the table.

"Another round, boys!" Bill said.

"We drank until both bottles were empty. The scotch was better than the cognac. We talked more, and then fell asleep to the rocking motion of the train.

Morning came. The scotch and cognac helped soften the hardness of the wooden benches. I was the first to wake as the morning sun found my window. The porter offered me a cup of coffee.

"Where are we?" I asked.

"We passed through Manchester and Carlisle. We should reach Glasgow by early afternoon"

"How much longer to Gourock?"

"We should arrive just before sunset."

Our conversation woke the others. I needed some space and walked outside, between the train cars. The outside was different, cool and fresh. The train was turning west, away from the morning sun and toward Glasgow and the port city of Gourock.

I looked across the green, dew-covered plain and saw hills with grooves of dark green and brown. On the tall hill above the thin row of trees, I saw a castle. The sun was shining on the face of the hill, making the view bright and clear. I cupped my hands and lit my cigarette while thinking about how much I missed Berta. What I promised her seemed impossible.

"William, do you want come inside? The porter brought food," Major Clark said.

"Come have a smoke with me before we go in."

"It's chilling out here."

"Cup your hands around the cigarette and I will light it for you."

"Major Clark, is there any way I can get a friend out of Russian-occupied Germany?"

"No, forget it. Maybe in a few years when things settle down. East Germany is going to stay under Russian control."

"Let's go back inside."

I didn't say a word as we ate; a feeling of hopelessness and depression came over me.

The weather turned misty and damp as the train moved toward the coast. We could see glimpses of Gourock Bay as we approached the docks. As the train cleared the last group of trees, we finally got a clear view of the bay. I was the first to spot the Queen Mary docked across the bay. She looked like a ghost with her drab war paint. The mist on the bay and her four tall funnels only added to that look. For a moment or two she would fade away in a blur and then reappear.

The train stopped within walking distance and we saw crowds of soldiers walking toward the majestic ship. Major Clark stated there would be over nine thousand military on the ship.

We walked up the long, narrow walkway to be processed before boarding. In spite of the long lines, spirits were high. The soldiers were glad to go home. I was not cheerful; I was heartbroken and distressed about leaving.

The great ship slowly left the dock and turned west from Gourock Bay to West Bay, just south of Loch Lomond. We turned north and entered the North Channel. Ireland was to the south and the North Atlantic was just ahead.

The war was over. We had no escorts, and there was not a military ship in view. As we reached the North Atlantic, the Queen Mary gained speed and turned for America.

XLIV

The DC-3 approached Shreveport from the west. Off the left wing tip I could see the south shore of Cross Lake; to the right of the lake I could see the Red River turning south through the city. We crossed the river and I smiled for the first time in weeks, thinking of all the fun I had fishing with my friends and Elaine. I looked forward to that so much.

We touched down at Barksdale midafternoon on a cool, sunny fall day. As the plane taxied, I could see Dad standing against the fence, waving. Dad had his Sunday best on. Mom was sadly missing. I was in my dress uniform, showing all my medals proudly. The press was in full force.

The press asked me if I felt lucky to make it home. They went on to inform me that five thousand B-17s were shot down and over fifty thousand airmen were lost. The question caught me off guard and stung. I didn't understand why I was the unlucky bastard that survived. I put on my smile for the press and Dad, but that stupid fucking question hit a nerve.

Dad showed me his new used Buick that he bought Mom for church.

"It's great to have you home, son," Dad said.

"When is Elaine coming home?"

"She is moving from Pearl Harbor to San Diego; she met a doctor from San Diego and they both were hired at the county hospital."

"She's not coming home to visit?"

"No, the hospital is shorthanded."

"Have you heard from Roy?"

"He reenlisted in the army; he is in the accounting and administrative group. His dad said he will be stationed in Washington, DC."

"How are Bert's parents doing?"

"Not good. Bert's dad is drinking too much."

"Have you heard from Charley or any of my friends from school?"

"No."

"Dad, I want to start at the store soon as possible."

"You can start tomorrow. You can help me unload a shipment of pumpkins."

Six months passed. I missed both my past lives. Friends from high school and my sister seemed so far away. Friday and Saturday nights were spent at home alone on the front steps or standing on the porch smoking. Thinking of my past relationships and war occupied my time and imagination. Fishing with Kip, time in Boston with Commander Cole, shooting pool in Marshall with Mike, my trip with Elaine to Sal's family farm in Paris, Texas. Those were dreams that haunted me. Most of all, though, was my constant need to be with Berta.

Dad was concerned for my mental health and wanted me to be content and jovial. The war had left scars that could not be covered or masked by a fake smile. I mundanely went through the daily routine of assisting my dad at the store. The thoughts and experiences of the war were not created, but seemed to pass through me and could not be stopped. "Be aware of your depression and you have the power to choose." That is what Dr. Scruggs would say.

I was standing still and the world was passing me by; people my age were moving on with their lives by taking on the world. The return to post-war civilian life was more difficult than sitting in my turret thirty thousand feet above Germany. I was in a dark place and needed to find a way to stop the pain.

XLV

Sunday morning was like the last six days; cool, damp, and gray. The weather conditions matched my emotions. With no other option, I decided to walk to my favorite location on the banks of the Red River. I thought it would be appropriate to wear my uniform; the uniform would comfort me, but could not protect me from today. I wanted to be found this way so people understood I was proud that I served my country.

With only my crutch from Berta, uniform, medals, and my military issued .45, I began a slow walk to the river. I passed my high school on the right; to my left, the football field. I could see Charley shouting signals before the play. Bert and Roy looked over at me with curious expressions. Elaine turned and looked over her left shoulder and gave me a goodbye smile. I looked up as I heard the roar of their great engines; through the limbs and small branches of the trees I saw my squadron of B-17s stacked to each side and above the other squadrons from my bomber group, trailing Red Wright's bomber group. German fighters must have been waiting just beyond the horizon. I walked past the empty field and turned left down the alley behind my church and crossed under the leafless vine-covered wires. The trees were bare and the floor of the alley was covered in colored leaves. I stopped and looked back over my right shoulder; I could see the church steeple over the tops of the trees. I paused for a moment for a short prayer; my journey would soon be over.

I turned right down a narrow path outlined with fig trees and shrubs. I paused and noticed Elaine and me as kids picking figs from the trees; we were laughing, carrying our fishing poles. I continued down the path past the small, old barn covered in loose shingles, broken branches, and leaves. I turned to my right and walked the last sixty yards down the wooden sidewalk that the city put in to accommodate the fishermen.

Even though the river was high, the sand bar on the inner turn of the river was exposed. I walked out on the red sand and stared at the fast-moving river. The river was carrying several large tree trunks that it had picked up from the banks. I looked up the river where the water flowed in from the lake and ponds to the north.

German soldiers were leaning low in the trees and shrubs to my left. I heard a noise from the highway passing through the woods. Then I jumped in fear. I started to shiver and broke into a cold sweat. Something in the river was moving up and down with the small waves as it approached. I saw the brown from his bomber jacket and began to cry. I could only see Kip's lifeless body. My nightmares and moments of severe sadness would not let the war go away. For me, the war could only end one way. Kip's lifeless body floated down river. Where the river turned left and met the bayou that flowed to the marsh, Kip vanished from my view.

Ox, this is Captain Cole; back to your turret. Fighters three o'clock low! Three more B-17s going down!

This is Red; you will never make it home.

It was time. I couldn't go on. I secured Berta's crutch under my left shoulder. I stood, gazing at the passing river. I cried and wished I was stronger. I had one option to stop the pain and be with my crew. I would be at peace soon. I lifted my .45 and put it against my right temple.

"Stop! Stop! Let me talk to you!" she shouted.

Epilogue

I

Forty years passed.

My wife was the one who yelled "Stop!" forty years ago and saved me from myself. I could not save her from cancer, and she passed away three years ago, in 1982. I would always love her.

Cancer was like the German fighters and attacked from all directions. Elaine was struck by cancer 3 years before my wife. I didn't feel helpless against the German fighters like I did cancer. The German fighters attacked from a distance. Cancer struck from within, insidious by nature. Some Germans had a heart and soul, cancer had neither. Cancer was no different than a hyena biting at the legs of its living prey, a hyena biting off a piece of flesh from the thigh, or a lion pulling a villager from their tent by their throat. Elaine lost her breast to cancer, but won her war. She was declared cured and was raising three beautiful children. She was my cancer fighting super hero.

Elaine visited every Thanksgiving. She and her husband had a busy schedule at their hospital, but always found time to visit me from California. We tried to call or write once every two weeks. We both missed our mother. She had proven she was much stronger than me. To her, everything on earth was a miracle. She was like the tallest tree in the forest during a blizzard. She stood tall even with the weight of the heavy snow. I was the weak branch that was bending and trying not to break.

My daughter and son were the biggest part of my life. I would always be grateful to my wife for helping me cope with my depression from the war. After she died my depression returned, and was more frequent and severe. My son was concerned with my state of mind and recent heavy drinking. There was a void in my life. The void was being filled with haunting thoughts of the war. Red was right that night forty years ago at the Red Feather Club. *War enters your soul and changes the person you are.*

My loving son spent time with me, hoping to help. "Dad, Mom died three years ago, and you're only 59. Why don't you try to find someone with whom you can share the rest of your life?" Kip asked.

"Now that you've moved out, I do get lonely."

"Mom would want you to be happy."

"Do you remember we always told you we met at the river?"

"Yes."

"She saved my life that day."

"Mom said she met you at the river when she was taking a walk."

"That's right. I was in a bad place, and my spirits were low. Your mom saved me from myself. I miss your mom; she was a great person."

"Dad, she loved you and would not want to see you this sad."

"I miss the way she made me laugh."

"Dad, do you ever think about the German girl that gave you the crutch?"

"Yes, more lately."

"Have you been watching the news about the Berlin wall coming down?"

"They are going to unify Germany to allow access to East Germany."

"Do you think a trip to Germany would heal some old wounds and improve your spirits?"

"I thought about it."

"I want to go. Let's stop in England and visit your old Air Force base. Then we can go to Germany, land in Frankfurt, rent a car, and drive to Berlin."

"That would be expensive."

"Dad, you have plenty of money and the trip would be good father-son time."

"You have my interest, let me think about it."

"Let's talk about it on our hunting trip."

II

The plains of northwest Texas and west Kansas seemed endless. Shreveport and Dallas were far behind; Montana and our elk hunting trip were to the North. I was glad to be spending this special time with my son. This was our first hunting trip since cancer stole his mother. The fall made the grassy plains one color: light brown. Now and then we could see a barn or farmhouse in the distance, but mostly open fields covered with long shadows. We hoped to make Rapid City, South Dakota, just after midnight. When we woke up in the morning we would see the far mountains.

At twenty minutes to one, the lights from Rapid City were just in view.

"Kip, let's fill up before we check into a motel."

"I think there's a truck stop ahead on the right. I'll pull in."

Kip turned off to the right and our green Jeep Wagoner bottomed out from the slope of the steep ramp. We were fully loaded with camping gear and our shocks were old and tired. Kip circled and found a position between the Texaco truck and other travelers filling up with gas.

"Kip, I'm hungry. Let's grab a late breakfast."

Kip knew one of my favorite things was to have breakfast for dinner or a late night breakfast.

"Yes, Dad. Go on in and get out of the cold."

"No, I'll clean the windshield."

"Go in and get out of the cold. I'll clean the windshield after I pump the gas."

"OK, I'll be in the gift shop."

I loved to browse in the gift area of a truck stop. There was always something interesting to find. I picked out a large, brown, leather trucker's wallet with a chain that attached to my belt. The artwork etched in the leather was of an Indian tepee and a turquoise eagle. Kip stood in line behind me to pay for the gas.

We walked into the diner and I had to pause for a long moment when I saw the artwork on the wall. Rapid City was an Air Force town and to my left was a large painting of a formation of B-17 bombers dropping their bombs while under attack. The painting was not accurate. No bombers were falling, none were burning, and no crews were dying.

"Dad, let's sit down."

The paintings surprised me and changed my mood. I saw my crew in those planes.

"Kip, can we visit Ellsworth Air Force before we leave town?"

"Sure, Dad."

"We stopped there on many training missions. We would fly over the mountains from Washington, spend the night, and fly back. We also stopped there on our way to Europe."

"Let's get up early, and we'll tour the base on our way out of town."

I had trouble sleeping and woke up before Kip. I put on my khaki pants and hunting jacket and stepped out for a cigarette. The motel was a brick, two-story building with each door painted light blue-green. The motel manager was near my age and was brewing a fresh pot of coffee. He talked about how big the elk are on Mount Grizzly. I informed him that our camp site would be near the summit of the mountain at eight thousand feet. He said that was the best place to hunt, but getting the elk off the mountain was difficult.

"Kip, the motel manager gave me the directions to Ellsworth."

"Give me a second to get dressed and we will head out."

We stopped at a local doughnut shop for coffee and pastries and then proceeded to the gates of the base. We approached the two guards at the entrance and asked permission to tour the base. They took Kip's driver's license and allowed us to park at the Air and Space Museum. There were several planes on display. Kip explained my role during the war to the museum curator. He was younger, but understood the odds we faced over Germany.

"We have a B-17 on display. I can let you through the ropes that circle the plane if you would like to show your son the inside of the bomber," the curator offered out of respect.

"We don't have time," I quickly replied.

"Dad, I have never seen the inside of a B-17. Show me around."

My heart sank. I couldn't say no, but was afraid of the emotions it would bring.

"OK, son. I'll tour the bomber with you."

To our right, we walked past the blue Corsair with its large propeller and its wings proudly angled up. Then we passed the B-25 Mitchell, famous for its bombing of Tokyo. Then the B-29 bomber, known for the first pressurized cabin and dropping of the atom bomb. I could see it come into view as we passed the shrubs that separated the planes.

Next in line was the greatest bomber ever built, the B-17. No plane at the museum could match its look or history. It sat proud, with its nose in the air. The ball turret guns were facing aft toward the low tail wheel. I saw more than one plane. I saw all the planes from my squadron, and my bomber group. That plane represented them all. The planes that survived and the thousands that fell from the sky. There was no life in this plane, just the empty shell. The hollow remains of a sad time that had passed. The museum curator started his prepared repetitive speech.

"Over five thousand B-17s were lost in World War II, and over fifty thousand Airmen died."

"Cut your bullshit! I don't need to hear that!"

"Dad, calm down."

I startled the curator, but he had hit a nerve. He should have been more sensitive to my past.

"Let's look in the plane," I calmly requested.

The curator dropped the ropes surrounding the plane and stood to the side. My son walked with apprehension toward the low-slung ball turret. All conversation stopped as he crouched between the two .50 caliber machine barrels and gazed into the round Plexiglas window. I touched the side of the ball turret and thought about my crew. My son shook his head as he attempted in vain to understand the horrors we faced thirty thousand feet over Germany. I was glad he didn't know; nobody should have to know. He knew I wanted to be the one to open the back door.

I slowly walked to the oval door, took a deep breath, and turned the handle. The door swung open like it had many times in the past. I thought about the way it swung open that day over Germany.

The plane was cold and open to the weather; just like forty years ago. We were the last crews to fly at thirty thousand feet in unpressurized cabins. We would never be followed. No future crews would ever understand the cold and lack of oxygen we experienced.

Time was backing up as I took a step into the plane. Joel and Kip were the first to say hello. Mike was by Joel's side, ready to man his waist gun. I walked under Howard as he turned and looked down and smiled from his turret. Sal, standing with his sexton in hand, looked out at the stars to log our position. The North Star must have been high above. Greg was searching for our homing beacon with his radio gear. Mark was busy arming the bombs. Cole and JJ were leaning forward, searching for German fighters. I was moved and could feel their welcoming spirit. My state of mind circled back to that day on the river. I didn't want my emotions to sink any further, so I asked to leave and we headed back to the rear door. We thanked the curator, shook hands, and departed.

"Dad, were you feeling OK in the plane?"

"I'm OK. Let's get on the road."

As we headed west, we could see the large mountains beyond the foothills of the Eastern Rockies. Straight ahead was the ten thousand foot peak of Mount Grizzly. We crossed the border into Montana and the sky began to clear as the trailing edge of the cold front passed to the east.

After three more hours of driving, we reached the base of the mountain. The mountain had many flat, grassy open areas near the top; perfect for elk hunting. We zigzagged back and forth across the face of the mountain until we reached our base camp at nine thousand feet.

Our hunting guide greeted us as we began to unload our gear. He had the mountain man look, strong with a thick beard and chest. He showed us to our cabin and told us to get a good night's sleep; we would be leaving for our hunt at sunrise. The cabin was small, with a wood burning heater. The guide had our fire started, so all we had to do is add wood during the night. The small stack of bundled wood was on the floor next to the door of the heater.

"Dad, try to get a good night's sleep. I will add the wood during the night."

"Let me know if you need any help."

We both lay down for bed.

"Dad, I'm worried about you, and I think a trip to Germany would help lift your spirits."

"I will think it over. Let's talk tomorrow.

We woke up at 5:30 a.m. and began to dress for the severe cold. Our coats and pants were thick and covered three other layers of clothing. Our boots were proven hunting boots from the best outdoor catalog.

Our hunting guide invited us into his cabin for coffee and ham and biscuits. We went over rules of the hunt. We were to climb up the open eastern side of the peak. The slope was not steep, but the hike would be over three miles. We'd set up camp, hunt the high plateau for two days, and return to our base camp. We were instructed to stay hydrated to help avoid altitude sickness. I was in pretty good shape, but nervous about the hike. I didn't want to be a burden or ruin the trip.

We started out with the sun to our backs as we slowly ascended the eastern side of the peak. Other than the high, thin clouds in the stratosphere formed by fine particles of ice, the sky was perfectly clear. Our guide informed us that the temperature was going to drop significantly when the sun passed to the other side of the mountain.

The guide pointed out hoofprints from a recent elk. The camp was far below as we reached the highest open area of the peak. We moved in several different directions looking for more signs of elk, but had no luck.

We decided to make our camp site before the sun was completely lost behind the mountain. The guide had us rest while he gathered fire wood. There were no clouds or atmosphere to hold any of the warmth from the sun. The temperature dropped, and the thin, cold air was hard to breathe. My son could tell I was having problems finding oxygen and asked me to sit down. He sat down beside me and we looked up at the beautiful sky. We rested while I caught my breath.

"Kip, this is the coldest I've been since our missions. The cold is bringing back memories."

"How could you survive hours of this?"

"It was much colder than this."

"It must have been unbearable."

"Your body was cold everywhere. It would never let up. Your sense of touch was overwhelmed. You shivered to keep warm as you sucked oxygen through your mask. Many times the temperature in the plane stayed below negative sixty degrees for hours."

"Dad, look at the high cirrus clouds turning red as the sun sets."

"That is a picturesque sight. Kip, do you see the contrails from the two jets crossing below the thin clouds? Imagine five hundred bombers followed by contrails from each of their four engines. We would fly over these mountains on our training missions."

"I can't imagine how striking that must have looked."

"Kip, look down into the valley at the Canada snow geese flying south."

"Dad, they are in perfect formation."

"Do you see the lead bird?"

"Yes."

"He will move back in the formation to rest while another bird takes his place. The last bird on the right side of the wing is tail end Charlie. He is the last plane in the formation."

"Dad, have you thought anymore about our trip to Germany?"

"I'll make a decision soon. I promise."

"I think the trip would do you good. You've been drinking too much and seem to be in a bad place."

"I'm having trouble coping with the void your mom left. I miss her company and get lonely. She would love this view; I wish she was here to share it with us.

"I miss mom, too."

I paused for a moment as the corner of my eye pooled with a tear from the thoughts of my wife. The warm tear overflowed and slowly streaked down the side of my cold face.

"Son, you need to be happy and live your life and not worry about me. I've already lived my life; tomorrow doesn't mean that much to me."

"You will make me happy if you go on this trip. I want to see your base in England and travel across Germany. Please dad, go for me."

"I will go."

III

Six months passed.

We boarded a DC-10 in Miami for a non-stop trip to England. The plane took off at 6:00 pm on a sunny, September day.

"Dad, this is a lot different from your last flight across the ocean."

"We were always cold and fighting to breathe."

I dozed off and could hear the piston engines of the B-17. *German fighter three o'clock low! Howard, Me 109 above twelve o'clock high! Ox, two fighters two o'clock low. My guns jammed, I'm jammed, I'm jammed, I can't fire! Ox! Fighters are closing at six o'clock low! I can't move! I saw the fighters! I can't shoot, my gun will not fire!*

"Dad, wake up! Dad, wake up, you're having one of your nightmares. Dad, are you all right?"

"I had a bad dream."

"You're sweating; I'll have the waitress bring you a cold drink."

"That would be good."

"Are you OK now?"

"Yes."

"Dad, I know you don't like to talk about the war, but tell me more about Kip."

"Kip was like a brother, we had each other's back. We talked about fishing and girls every day. We dreamed about fishing offshore in Florida after the war. We would drink beer and smoke cigarettes and forget about the war. Kip would have liked you and been proud you were his namesake. Kip and Howard were the comedians on my crew. We had some good times together. They were a special crew; sometimes I laugh when I think about them, other times I cry. After the war I needed someone from my crew. I couldn't talk about the war with anyone else. I felt empty and alone when I returned home."

"Are thoughts of the war still as painful?"

"The past will never pass for me. We were a generation that inherited a war. I can still clearly see the German fighters and bombers falling from the sky. They were too young to die like that. We knew we had no chance against the German fighters but never turned back. We were all so scared, but faced death bravely and proud."

"Tell me more about Berta."

"I loved two women in my life, Berta and your mom. They both saved my life. Berta protected me in Germany and your mom saved me that day at the river. Berta was living alone in farmhouse east of Berlin. When she found me cold and dying, I could barely breathe. She wasn't prudent or cautious; just loving, caring, and supportive. The Germans would have killed her for helping me. We were snowed in for months in that little farmhouse. We spent a lot of time talking and became very close. We made the most of a bad situation. Your mom and Berta made me think positive thoughts. They were special in that way. I miss them."

"We are scheduled to land in London 7:00am local time. You can rest at the hotel before we drive to Horham."

"I would like to take a short nap when we land."

"Dad, I noticed you packed your uniform and distinguished flying cross."

"I want to wear it when we visit the memorial. That is my way to honor all the airmen who didn't make it back home."

IV

I stood at attention, gazing into the mirror. Shining like new were my US insignia on my right lapel and my wings with the propeller on my left lapel. Medals and patches were displayed proudly on my chest and shoulders. My neck tie, shirt, and pants were pressed crisp to perfection. My shoes were spit shined, ready for the most particular inspection from any drill sergeant or general. I stood motionless, looking deep into the mirror with thoughts and images of the war.

"Dad, are you ready to go?" Kip asked from the hotel bedroom.

"Give me a minute to gather my thoughts."

"Dad, are you all right?"

"Yes," I said as I wiped tears from my eye before leaving the bathroom.

"Dad, you look handsome in your uniform. Your medals are impressive, how come you never showed them to anyone?"

"It's not about the medals; it's about the man."

"What do you mean?"

"My medals mean nothing to me; my crew was everything. They didn't live to receive and wear their medals; that is why I decided to proudly wear them. I am wearing my medals for them. These are their medals."

"I'm ready to do this, let's head for Horham."

We entered the abandoned air field from the same country road that I traveled during the war. The wooden control tower was still standing. I was silent as Kip drove toward the center of the base. We parked to the west side of the tower. It was quiet, other than the cool, dry breeze blowing across the long grass and through holes of the old wooden tower. My son could tell I was becoming extremely emotional and gave me some space to be alone. I slowly walked up the steps to the balcony that circled the control tower.

I stood facing the unmaintained runways; still visible after all those years. I put my hands on the railings and gazed out over the horizon. I could hear the thunder from the B-17 lining up for takeoff.

Colonel Klein, B-17s approaching from the north east. I count nine. Flares are being dropped from the lead plane. A second squadron is approaching from the east. Several planes damaged, engine two's on fire.

"Dad? Dad, are you all right?"

"I need to sit down."

"I'll come up and help you down."

I didn't want my son to see my cry, but I could not control the effect of my deep sorrow and sadness. My son wrapped his arms around me as I sat in the grass weeping. He could feel me cry.

"Dad, are you sure you are up for visiting the monument at the Red Feather Club?"

"Yes, I owe it to my crew and all the crews that died."

We drove north past the large B- 17 parking circles that were adjacent to the unkempt runways. Behind me was the control tower; to my right, the concrete runways with long straws of grass waving in the wind; to my left, broken-down hangars still painted in a dark green camouflage; in front of me, the arched roof of the Red Feather Club.

As we approached I noticed the solitude; no tour guide, and no other visitors.

I stood in front of the door and watched as Kip, Cole, and Howard waved me in for a drink. Glenn Miller was playing in the back ground. Jane and Sally were leaning against the door smoking a cigarette and holding a drink. Red and his crew were doing shots of whisky between beers; Mark and Sal asked me where I had been all those years.

"Dad, sit down." My son knew where I was. He put his arm around me as I sat down—he saw the tears pool in my eyes, overflow, and streak down my face.

"I loved my crew. I miss them so much."

V

We landed in Frankfurt, rented a light green BMW 720i, and began our three day trip traveling the German countryside. We headed south east along the Main River passing through the cities of Aschaffenburg, Wurzburg, and Nuremburg before heading north for Berlin.

The city of Nuremburg was bombed heavily during the war, but showed little damage after thirty years. We stopped and visited many of the majestic churches and castles.

We woke up early the next morning and started north toward Berlin via Dresden and Magdeburg. The Germans have a great tradition of midafternoon pastries and coffee. Kip and I decided to stop at a quaint, roadside café just south of Dresden. Located in front of the white store front was a colorful garden with six tables. The low, white, stucco fence that circled the perimeter of the garden gave the feel of a courtyard. The weather was cool and damp, but comfortable.

"Dad, would you like to sit outside?"

"Yes, the coffee will take the chill out of the air."

The pretty, blond German girl who was waiting on the two tables to our right stopped to take our order.

"I'll have a cup of coffee and a piece of Black Forest cake," I said.

"Coffee and stollen for me," Kip added.

"Dad, I contacted Berta, and she wants to see you."

"I don't think that is a good idea. I am sure she has a family."

"No, she lives in the same farmhouse thirty miles east of Berlin."

"What did she say?"

"She knew you would come back someday."

"Your mom and Berta were the two loves of my life."

"You need to give her crutch back," Kip said, and we both started laughing.

"I'm nervous just thinking about it. There is so much time between us."

"Dad, she is having the same thoughts and apprehensions. This may be your last chance to see her again."

"I wanted to find the farmhouse, but didn't think I could ever find her again. I wasn't sure she was still alive."

"You can't come all this way and not stop and say hello. She knows you are here and would be disappointed if you went all the way back to America without saying hello. Didn't you tell her you would come back for her someday?"

"Kip, you really know how to twist my arm. I will go."

VI

We left Berlin with a map in hand. The morning was cool and clear, much like the afternoon of our bombing run. We passed through the small village of Berta's great uncle.

"Dad, just seven more miles to the farmhouse."

"Are you sure you are going the right way?"

"Yes we just passed the church the hotel manager told us about. He grew up in the village."

"How do I look?"

"Great, Dad. I'm glad you decided to wear your uniform."

"Kip, take a right before we reach the river. I would like to find a bend in the river about a mile upriver from the farm house." I asked.

"Ok Dad."

"Kip, see the fork in the road; turn there. Let's try to find the river."

"If we keep heading east we should find it."

We made three turns that were probably taking us up river, but we were still heading east.

"Dad, I saw a glimpse of the river. We must be close."

"Take that left. The road should run into the river."

We stopped at the incline that sloped gradually to the flowing water. I got out of the car and walked apprehensively to the pebbled river bank. I knew I had been here before. The same large rocks, the same bend in the river, the same sad feelings. This was where my crew died. That moment from years ago wounded me, altered my view on living, and stole my spirit. I saw it all over again. I tried to block it from my mind, but after all those years what happened that day was still visible. As I stood there, my crew died again. Their struggle silhouetted against the back drop of the far shoreline.

"Kip, I need to go."

"Ok, Dad."

I hoped Berta might help heal my old injuries, including the lacerations of my soul. Kip knew I wasn't winning my battle against depression. He secretly found out the status of Berta and hoped we both could fill a private void. Our struggle together, and that time making love had kept us attached by the heart. We were separated by an ocean but still connected by a common concern for the happiness and wellbeing of each other. My son knew this encounter was what Berta and I both needed to move forward.

We turned left down a country road to an area that began to look familiar. My anxiety and emotions reached a lifetime high. My collar was wet and I was feeling the effects of an upcoming panic attack. As we drove down the wooded country road, I saw an approaching field on the left. As we cleared the last row of trees, the farmhouse came in view. Nothing had changed in forty years. The farmhouse was painted in all the same colors and the gardens were in the same location. It was like she was waiting for me to come home. I told Kip to stop at the grassy area one hundred feet from the front door.

I needed the space to gather myself. Emotions were deepening my breathing and accelerating the beating of my heart. I reached for my crutch and stood next to the car. I stared up at the blue sky and found the spot where three hundred majestic B-17s in perfect box formation were passing over Germany. I could see with perfect clarity the white contrails behind each engine.

I started slowly walking toward the farmhouse. As I got closer, I noticed a silhouette of a striking woman peering through curtains of lace. The curtains moved back in place as the door swung open. I was fifty feet from the door. Behind me a war and forty years, in front of me the German girl that saved my life. I recognized her immediately. She focused on my face and slowly began to walk toward me. As she got closer, she started to smile and walk faster, and then she ran into my arms. She hugged me firmly and I pulled her even closer. That moment we embraced the forty years of separation were wiped away.

THE END

Goodbye from a B-17

We take off for the heavens
Only to find hell
Three hundred of us strong
Three thousand airmen aboard
Cabin far below zero
Air is thin and impossible to breathe
Sun high above tells me its near noon
Time to beware
The North Sea is far behind
Berlin is straight ahead
Twelve o'clock low is shouted
Fighters low on the horizon
The German fighters are too swift
Zigzag past as they fire at will
Many propellers will be stopped
For several the battle with gravity is over
Bombs will fall from those that remain
We fly over bombed cities and plains
Scorched dark gray from the war
Leaving only broken tree trunks
Horses extend their necks
To snatch at the last blades of grass

From above the battle goes on
My crew fights with bravery
I shake as my machine guns fire
Only to be struck from beneath
Mortally wounded and I cannot survive
Please find a way out before I start to spin
Jump from me now
It may already be too late
I cannot hold on much longer
I slowly roll to my right then on my back
Ball turret aiming at the sky
Now pointed to the ground
Faster and faster toward my end
Jump before you are pressed helplessly against me
Against my body they all reach for the door
One by one they pull themselves free
I look back to see my crew floating down
There is no defying gravity's last pull
I was created from the elements of earth
To protect ten brave men
We fought together fearless and courageous
Traveled next to the stars and moon
Our time together is over
The ground is now here
Do not look down at me with sadness
When the war is over stories of us will be told
Live a long life
My end has come
My world is not at war any more

Poem by Forrest Fegert

Second Lieutenant Bob Wilson, co-pilot, (second from left, top row) was very instrumental, offered valuable insight and inspiration during the writing of "Belly of the Beast".

Second Lieutenant Bob Wilson in his flight suit.

Francis W. Hoffpauir (second from right, first row), belly gunner in the B-24 Liberator in the 415th bomb squadron, was a family friend from Louisiana. He earned a Distinguished Flying Cross and Purple Heart.

Ward Rose, B-17 co-pilot in the 342nd bomb squadron – 97th bomb group, was the father of a family friend from church.

Printed in Great Britain
by Amazon.co.uk, Ltd.,
Marston Gate.